Wilma had to admit she didn't like it herself, but it was time to face the truth. Ghosts existed—however improbable that sounded. And it was now quite clear. The only hope for all of them—including Mr. Goodman (imagine his embarrassment if it was found out he'd gotten it all wrong)—was her. Someone had to do something to stop the spooks taking over at the Hoo. However scary it might be. "Nothing and nobody stops Wilma Tenderfoot," she whispered determinedly to Pickle. Besides, Victor would help her—hadn't he been trying to do so all along? HE believed in ghosts! Yes, apprentice detective she was, ghost hunter she would become. Because sometimes, if you want something done properly, you have to do it yourself.

A Fatal Phantom on the loose. Mr. Goodman gone crazy. Wilma up against it on her own. Surely this can't get any worse? Surely?

Other Books You May Enjoy

Wilma Tenderfoot

The Case of the Fatal Phantom

by Emma Kennedy

PUFFIN BOOKS
An Imprint of Penguin Group (USA) Inc.

PUFFIN BOOKS
An imprint of Penguin Young Readers Group
Published by the Penguin Group
Penguin Group (USA) Inc.
375 Hudson Street
New York, New York 10014, U.S.A.

USA / Canada / UK / Ireland / Australia / New Zealand / India / South Africa / China
Penguin Books Ltd, Registered Offices: 80 Strand, London WC2R 0RL, England

For more information about the Penguin Group visit www.penguin.com

Published in the United Kingdom by Macmillan Children's Books UK, 2010
First published in the United States of America by Dial Books for Young Readers, 2012
Published by Puffin Books, an imprint of Penguin Young Readers Group, 2013

THE LIBRARY OF CONGRESS HAS CATALOGED THE DIAL BOOKS EDITION AS FOLLOWS:
Kennedy, Emma.
Wilma Tenderfoot and the case of the fatal phantom / by Emma Kennedy. p. cm.
Summary: When Wilma Tenderfoot, the feisty and determined assistant to the world's greatest living detective,
and her beagle, Pickle, find a mummified body buried on the grounds of the gothic mansion Blackheart Hoo,
they seek to identify the body and solve the mysteries of a key, some buried treasure, and a kidnapping.
ISBN 978-0-8037-3542-2 (hardcover)
[1. Mystery and detective stories. 2. Orphans—Fiction. 3. England—Fiction.] I. Title.
PZ7.K3776Wh 2012
[Fic]—dc22   2011009375

Puffin Books ISBN 978-0-14-242609-8

Designed by Jennifer Kelly
Printed in the United States of America

1 3 5 7 9 10 8 6 4 2

For William Chalmers,
a very fine young gentleman

Know this. I am NOTHING without my amazing editor Ruth Alltimes, who is SO incredible she deserves all nations to bow before her. Similarly her assistant, the phenomenal Samantha Swinnerton, should have statues celebrating her forthwith. And heartfelt thanks go to the sensational Camilla Hornby, who served me well for many a year. She has galloped off to explore pastures new, where I hope she has adventures aplenty. A million thank-yous to you all.

Something ominous was on the wind. Wilma looked up, wayward braids billowing, and pulled her scarf tighter. The sky had turned a menacing yellow and had rolled over Cooper Island's one small hill like a heavy pie crust so that everything felt hemmed in and swallowed up.

"Mrs. Speckle says there'll be snow, Pickle," said Wilma. "And lots of it." Pickle, Wilma's pet beagle and best friend, tried to look up, but Mrs. Speckle, the ever-stubborn and wool-obsessed housekeeper at Clarissa Cottage, had pulled an old tea cozy over his head to keep him warm, which was all very well but meant he couldn't see. He did his best to peer through the end of the narrow woolen spout, though. It was far from ideal.

"Now then," said Wilma, making her way to the bottom of the garden. "We've got to get parsnip heads and sprout tops for Brackle Day. And the only place we're going to find them is in the compost heap. And Pickle," she added, turning and shooting her dog a serious stare, "you have to help me *find* them. Not *eat* them." Pickle snorted. He loved compost. It was practically his favorite dinner. Maybe he could secretly snap up one parsnip head. Or maybe two. Or even *seven*.

The compost was contained in a series of large wooden crates at the rear of the garden. "Ooh pooh!" said Wilma, pinching her nose as they approached. "Compost stinks!" Pickle cocked his tatty ear, lifted his snout skyward, and sniffed the tangy stench. Yes, it did. Lovely! The crates were tall and raised off the ground on a platform of short stilts so that Wilma, who was small but determined for a ten-year-old, needed to work out how she could peer into them. She pursed her lips in thought and reached for the apprentice detective's notebook in her pinafore pocket.

Pickle scratched his ear. The tea cozy he was wearing was *really* itchy. "Hmm," said Wilma, looking at a glued-in picture of one of the old cases of her mentor, Detective Goodman. "In the Case of the Battered Cod, Mr. Goodman had to use a pulley system to move a heavy object over a vat of frying oil. That's it!"

Wilma tucked her notebook back into her pocket and looked around the garden. "There!" She pointed. "The clothesline! If we tie it in a loop, we can fix one end to the top of the fence post and attach the other end to the branch of the cherry tree. Then we can fix the ladder to the bottom line with garden twine, use two large spools to create the pulley, and it might just work!" She grinned down at Pickle. His tongue was sticking out of the end of the tea cozy.

After running back indoors to fetch two of

Mrs. Speckle's large spools, Wilma had her make-shift winching system rigged up in no time. The idea was that she would balance on the ladder while Pickle tugged the extra length of clothes-line. His pulling would cause the looped cord to rotate around the spools, which, in turn, would move Wilma and the ladder into position above the compost. From there, she could work out where the parsnip heads and sprout tops were, pick them out, and be winched back to safety. It was devilishly simple.

"Right, then, Pickle," said Wilma as she hopped onto the bottom rung of the ladder swinging from the lower part of the clothesline. "Take that slack piece of cord in your mouth and pull it till I tell you to stop."

Pickle, ears full of tea cozy, followed Wilma's pointing finger to the loose end of clothesline. Taking the cord in his mouth, he stared as she gabbled further instructions. He couldn't hear a word she was saying, of course, because of the wool, but from her gestures he thought he got the gist. So off he went. The cord he was carrying became taut and as Pickle took up the tension, the looped clothesline gave a little jerk. "That's it, Pickle!" shouted Wilma as she inched toward the compost. "Keep pulling!"

Pickle looked back over his shoulder and saw Wilma waving enthusiastically. She must want him to go a bit faster. Biting down on the cord, Pickle broke into a run, but the sudden wrench on the looped clothesline caused it to disconnect from the spools. Wilma, feeling the ladder lurch violently, looked up to see one of the makeshift pulleys ping upward into the air. "No, Pickle!" she yelled. "Stop! Oh no! STOP!" But Pickle couldn't hear her and instead ran a bit faster. The clothesline snapped away from the fence post, flinging Wilma and the ladder downward toward the compost. Clutching the ladder, she ricocheted against the front edge of the central compost crate but was then pitched backward so that she hit the container to her right. As she slowly slid downward into the heap of stinking and rotting matter, there was a deep groan from beneath her. The force of the impact had buckled the stilts below, and with a shuddering moan, the whole platform collapsed, sending the three compost crates and Wilma tumbling to the ground. Pickle stopped and turned around. Before him was a sea of compost, and sitting in the middle of it was Wilma.

"Well," she said, spitting out a mouthful of old potato peels, "this is some mess. Oh, wait. There's a parsnip head," she added, pulling one out from the front of her pinafore. "Pickle! Pass me the basket! Mr. Goodman says you some-times have to get your hands dirty to get a job done. Well, I'm dirty all over, so that must mean the job will get done even quicker. Nothing and nobody stops Wilma Tenderfoot!" And with that, she flicked a piece of moldy bacon from her knee and began gathering up the vegetable bits she needed. Pickle looked on jealously. He'd *love* to be that filthy.

Wilma Tenderfoot, apprentice detective to Theodore P. Goodman, Cooper Island's most famous and serious detective, had plenty of enthusiasm and always did her best, but things never quite went according to plan. Despite all her efforts, she often seemed to find herself in a scrape or a muddle, especially ever since her hero, the mind-bogglingly brilliant detective Mr. Goodman, had taken her in, and accepted her as his apprentice. Abandoned at the gates of the Lowside Institute for Woeful Children when she was a baby, Wilma hadn't the least idea who she really was or where she had come from. For years she had dreamed of growing up to detect and deduct her own story, and there was no one she wanted to emulate more in doing so than the great Theodore P. Goodman. She'd been cutting out newspaper articles about him and studying all his cases since she was old enough to read. And now she lived with him at Clarissa Cottage and worked for him! It had been a month since their last case, a tricky assignment involving some putrid poison at a vaudeville the-atre and (another) near death-experience for Wilma, but Mr. Goodman had rescued her in the nick of time. Wilma was pleased that since then Cooper's Criminal Elements seemed to have been behaving themselves. But at the same time she found herself itching once more to advance her detecting skills and prove that she COULD get things right.

Cooper, an island somewhere between England and France and shaped like a bow tie, has never been discovered. There was once a close encounter with the great explorer Scott of the Antarctic, who almost landed there on his way to the North Pole, but as he had only packed winter clothes, he decided against it, reasoning that it looked "a bit warm." Since then, nobody from the outside world had ever come close to visiting and no one from Cooper had ever left. There were rumors that a slightly deranged man had once been found washed up on the rocks at Filthy Cove burbling in a language nobody could understand but Inspector Lemone, Theodore's right-hand man and Cooper's only policeman, always dismissed this as a "bag of nonsense" and said that it was "probably a large seal or hairy fish." And that was that.

Like all odd places, Cooper had its own traditions: There was the monthly Egg Nudge and the thrice-yearly Cow Stare, but the greatest day of all was Brackle Day, the once-a-year celebration of island life in which the great separation of the island into the Lowside (the woebegone part of the island) and the Farside (the well-to-do bit) was commemorated. Presents were hidden, Brackling Plays were performed across the island, and mighty feasts were enjoyed. As with all big days, preparations were required, and Wilma and Pickle had been tasked with the greatest responsibility of all—gathering up the decorations.

The Brackle Bush was a large, unwieldy, thickety thing with long poisonous thorns and stinging leaves. As plants go it was a menace, but because it had played an intrinsic part in the original separation of the island, every Cooperan was required to acquire one and put it in their parlor for the duration of Brackle Week. Tradition dictated that the Brackle Bush had to lean at a forty-five-degree angle, be covered in parsnip heads and sprout tops, and crowned with a magnificent giant corn-crumble biscuit, which, in fancy houses, was often decorated too. Sometimes the biscuits would be adorned with intricate marzipan paintings of Cooper landmarks like the one small hill or the broken plow at Wimpers Farm, but most people liked to decorate them with short motivational phrases like "Bend at the knees NOT the hips" or "If it's brown, flush it down." At Clarissa Cottage Mrs. Speckle, who was in charge of the icing, always decorated her corn crumble with the same two words—"Try harder"—because, as she said every year, "We can all do that. And I have a very small icing bag. Take it or leave it."

"You have some eggshell in your hair," said Mrs. Speckle, peering into the basket of vegetable tops Wilma and Pickle had brought back to Clarissa Cottage, "and a slug on your shoulder. But I can't be bothering with that now! I've got giant biscuits to make. And get Pickle into the Brackle Apron. That bush isn't going to decorate itself!"

Dogs, of course, are not normally called upon to perform decorating duties, but Cooper custom dictated that the Brackle Bush had to be prepared by the youngest member of the household, which in this case meant Pickle. He didn't have a clue about fancy arranging, draping, or dangling. Still, he'd have to do his best. The entire household was depending on him. And there was always a chance he could quietly sneak the odd sprout top when no one was looking.

Hounds have to put up with all manner of indignities. In his short time as Wilma's loyal dog, Pickle had been dressed as a plumber and forced to wear a tutu. Surely things couldn't get any worse? But as Wilma pulled the heavy Brackle Apron onto him, Pickle realized, with a sigh, that they could. The Brackle Apron was a bit like a large beach ball made of an impenetrable material that had to be blown up so that the Brackler, once inside it, was completely protected from the inevitable thorn pricks and leaf stings. As Wilma pumped with her foot, the apron inflated, and when she was finished, all that could be seen of the beagle was the end of his snout. "Good," she said with a nod. "Now you can get on with it. The basket of parsnip heads and sprout tops is there. Just pick them out with your mouth and put them on the bush. And I'd stop rolling onto your back if I were you. You'll never get anything done if you're upside down."

"Ah, Wilma," said a syrupy voice. It was Theodore P. Goodman, the most serious and famous detective that ever lived. He was tremendous to look at, with a mighty shock of golden hair, a chiseled jaw, and a mustache with caramel-colored tips—the very definition of swoony. "A parcel has arrived. Addressed to you." The great man stopped and sniffed the air, his magnificent mustache twitching in the firelight. "What's that *awful* smell?"

Wilma fidgeted and scraped at an unpleasant-looking stain on the front of her pinafore. "Probably the sprout tops," she said, thinking quickly.

"Hmm," replied Theodore. "It is a great shame we can't decorate our Brackle Bushes with things that are pleasantly fragrant. Still, tradition is tradition, however ridiculous it is." He stared at the inflated hound in front of him. "I see Pickle is this year's Brackler. Might get it done quicker if he can roll in the direction of the Brackle Bush. I think he's stuck under my bureau. You probably want to dislodge him, Wilma."

"Hang on. A parcel?" asked Wilma brightly, giving the bouncing Brackle Apron a small shove. "Is it a Brackle Day present? I'll have to give it to Mrs. Speckle to hide if it is."

Hiding presents seems a perfectly reasonable custom. In England presents are often hidden, sometimes beneath a bed or in a cupboard under some stairs. The hiding is merely a stopgap until such time as the present can be brought out and given to the person it's intended for. On Cooper, however, people *really* hide presents. They get buried, stuffed into cracks and crannies in perilous places, and sometimes even fed to sharks or crocodiles, because a person would have to be crazy to try to get back a soap-on-a-rope from a ten-foot reptile. And that's the point! On Cooper, the joy is in the hiding. And if the present is retrieved, well, the day has been ruined. Thankfully, Wilma's parcel was not a present. It came from her headmistress, Kite Lambard.

As an apprentice, Wilma had been enrolled at the Academy of Detection and Espionage, a venerable if slightly bizarre institution where she was the only pupil and her headmistress, Kite Lambard, the only teacher. The headmistress, however, had recently gone off on an adventure, leaving Wilma to her own devices. Many children might leap for joy at the prospect of going to a school with no teachers or lessons, but not Wilma. Not only did she want to learn the mysteries of detection, she also had some mysteries of her own, namely her family origins, to come to grips with, and without Kite's help she might as well be stuck in glue.

She had already unearthed some crucial evidence, and with a little guidance from her mentor, Theodore P. Goodman, had made a Clue Board for what she was calling the Case of the Missing

Relative. A Clue Board, Wilma had learned, was a vital tool for any detective: It was a quick visual summary of every piece of evidence gathered so far—a bit like a fridge door, but only covered in very serious things.

On her Clue Board Wilma had pinned the following:

1. The small tag that had been tied around her neck when she was left at the Institute, with the words "Because they gone" scrawled on it.
2. A scrap of muslin with a crest of crossed lamb chops on it that had been wrapped around her baby body. Penbert, the island's assistant forensic scientist, had also identified a stain on the material as being pig's blood.
3. One of the many notes given to Wilma by the revolting matron of the Institute for Woeful Children, Madam Skratch, listing monthly payments for Wilma's upkeep and referring to her as "Child 427." Now Wilma knew there was still someone alive who was either related to her or felt responsible for her, but WHO?

And why had they let her remain at the dreadful Institute for so long?

4. A page from an anonymous handwritten note to Madam Skratch asking about an abandoned baby, and

5. Wilma's most exciting clue—a note by Kite Lambard that appeared to be in the same handwriting as the anonymous note to Madam Skratch.

These were the beacons in the fog, the clues that would help Wilma piece together her past, discover who her parents were, and at last give her the sense of belonging that she had always longed for. However, until she saw her headmistress and asked her about that mysterious letter, she would be none the wiser. Wilma would have to be patient.

"There's a card stuck on the parcel, Mr. Goodman," said Wilma, blinking with excitement. "Look at the handwriting. It's definitely the same as that letter I found. Do you think Miss Lambard could be my missing relative?"

Theodore turned and reached for his pipe on

the mantelpiece. Slowly packing it with rosemary tobacco from the leather pouch in his waistcoat pocket, he frowned a little and pondered. "Remember, a good detective doesn't jump to conclusions, Wilma. Until you have spoken to Miss Lambard, there is no point in speculating."

"Does speckle-eating mean feeling fizzy in your tummy? Like when you've drunk too many Sugarcane Swizzles?" asked Wilma, twiddling the hem of her pinafore. "So that you can't concentrate and you think you might be a bit sick?"

"Not really," answered Theodore, sitting at his desk. "It means to guess or make your mind up about something when you don't have the full facts before you. Speculating is the very last thing an apprentice detective should do. It can cause a lot of bother."

"I see." Wilma nodded wisely, steering Pickle from behind the armchair. "Though it's quite hard not to." Having established that the parcel was not a Brackle Day present, Wilma ripped it open. "Oh," she said, eyes widening. "It's a study sheet. For detecting and spinach."

"Espionage," corrected Theodore, lighting his pipe.

"Yes, that." Wilma nodded again. "I expect Miss Lambard wanted to make sure I'm keeping up with my studies while she's away. And there's a piece of paper too," she added, unfolding it. " 'Dear Wilma, just to let you know I will be returning on Brackle Day for the traditional Academy Play. I am enclosing the cast list.' Oh, Mr. Goodman! Miss Lambard's coming back! I'll be able to ask her about that letter. But why has she sent me a cast list?"

"It's an Academy tradition, Wilma," replied Theodore, puffing out a plume of rosemary smoke. "Every pupil has to perform the Brackling Play. Consider it a rite of pass—"

"Ooooh!" Wilma interrupted. "I've been cast as Melingerra Maffling! I always wanted to be her when I was at the Institute! And I'm Old Jackquis. And Stavier Cranktop. And the Porpoise. Actually, I'm everyone. Except the Brackle Bush. That's you, Pickle! What do you think about that?"

But Pickle couldn't respond. He was rolling slowly but surely toward an old clue from Mr. Goodman's Case of the Krazy Knockout. It was an oversized boxing glove attached to the end of a very temperamental spring. Suddenly realizing what was about to happen, Theodore stood up. "Not there, Pickle! Quick, Wilma, grab him!" Wilma leaped forward but slid on a banana peel that had fallen from her shoulder and collided with Pickle, sending the inflated Brackle Apron careering even faster into the sprung boxing glove. With a deep *thwack* the glove exploded outward, punching Pickle across the room as fast as lightning.

"Oh no!" yelled Wilma as Pickle smashed into the untethered Brackle Bush, which, shuddering from the impact, quietly keeled over and fell into the open fireplace, where it burned to a crisp in an instant.

"Goodness," said Theodore, surveying the charred mess. "Well. We shall need a new Brackle Bush, Wilma, or there will be no celebrations for us."

Wilma stared at the small scene of devastation that she had had a part in causing yet again. One day, she thought to herself as she let the air out of an indignant Pickle's Brackle Apron, she would get something entirely right. She really would.

Being new to her detective apprenticeship, Wilma still had plenty to learn. During their last two cases, she had tried to follow Mr. Goodman's detective top tips as best she could and to live by the apprentice detective's Golden Rules but, according to the Academy textbook she'd been given on being enrolled, there were still plenty of basics to come to grips with: things like hunches and suspicions. Wilma couldn't wait to find out about those. If only they had a new case where she could put these techniques into practice! But until then, she had an important errand to be getting on with.

"Still snowing slightly," muttered Mrs. Speckle, opening the back door for Wilma and staring out of it. "Getting late too. I wonder if you should wait till tomorrow."

"No, it's all right, Mrs. Speckle. I'd rather go now," replied Wilma, grabbing her scarf. "I made everything wonky, so I need to fix things."

"Well, all right then." The grumpy housekeeper shrugged. "But make sure you're wrapped up. Now then, do you know where the Brackle Bush farm is?"

Wilma shook her head.

"You'll need to go past the pig poke, across the fields, straight on after Blackheart Hoo, and it's the other side of Hare Forest. And put these on. They're duffel coats. One for you and the smaller one's for Pickle. I made them."

Mrs. Speckle pulled out a pair of heavy knitted garments with large hoods and held them up. Wilma, who was a scrap of a thing with a tendency to look crumpled, stared at the enormous bundle of wool in front of her. The hood was yellow, the left arm was blue, the right was red, and the main body was green melting into an indiscriminate striped pattern. The smaller one, intended for Pickle, was even more colorful. She blinked and said nothing. Sometimes, if you have no immediate talent for fashion, it's hard to know whether something is cutting-edge or ludicrous. Wilma, who only ever wore her pinafore and baggy socks, wasn't entirely sure. But if she was to take a first stab at having a hunch, she thought it was probably the latter.

"I used up all my old wool," explained Mrs. Speckle with a sniff, bending down to help Pickle into his coat. "Hood's a bit big on this one," she added, trying to plump the beagle's hat into some sort of useful shape. "Hang on." Opening a drawer, the housekeeper pulled out two large wooden clothespins. "There we go," she said, pinning the hood to Pickle's ears. "Much better."

That was a matter of opinion, thought Pickle.

"And there's mittens on string that runs through the sleeves," continued the housekeeper. "Two for you, Wilma, and four for Pickle. He can put them on his feet. Right, then. That's that. Off you go. And get a good one!"

Though it had nearly stopped now, the snow

had been falling heavily for an hour and had started to settle. As Wilma and Pickle made their way across the main square, children all around them were having snowball fights and building snow-sheep and snow-chickens. On Cooper, children are only allowed to make snow-animals, as it is illegal to make snowmen. This is because hundreds of years ago a very pale, rotund gentleman called Roland Dennob, who lived in Arewenearlythereyet, took the matter to the Cooper Court of Spurious Lawsuits, complaining that snowmen were an affront to very pale, rotund gentlemen everywhere. He won. His case was clearly helped by the fact that he liked to smoke a pipe and suffered from a strange cold-like ailment that meant he also had a pointy orange nose.

As the woolen pair left the main town of Coop and headed out into the countryside, the sky suddenly darkened, the wind picked up, and the snow began to fall harder again in fat, swollen flakes. At first Wilma and Pickle trudged onward, their tracks instantly covered behind them. But eventually, Wilma stopped and looked up. "I'm not sure where we are anymore, Pickle," she yelled anxiously over the wind. "Everything is covered. I think we're on the road to Hare Forest, but it's very hard to tell. I'd say let's turn back, but I'm not even sure what way *back* is."

With dusk drawing in and no light other than the strange sickly glow from the sky, Wilma found herself quite disoriented. Landmarks and signposts had been turned to unidentifiable white lumps. It was all a bit eerie, not helped by the strange howls of the wind.

Wilma lifted her heavy woolen hood and tried to spot anything that might look familiar. Pickle, always ready to be of use, sniffed the ground for memorable smells, but with the snow now up to the top of his legs, all he succeeded in doing was sniffing icy crystals into his nostrils until a large frozen snowball formed at the end of his muzzle.

"I don't know what to do," admitted Wilma as she knocked the ice off Pickle's snout with her mitten. "I don't think this situation arises in any of the knotty problems in my Academy hand-book or Mr. Goodman's previous cases. Although there are always the apprentice detective's Golden Rules. Number four might be useful—if in doubt, stand very still and do nothing. Let's try that. An opportunity may present itself."

With the blizzard raging about them, Wilma and Pickle stood motionless in the hope that something, somewhere, would help them work out what to do next. However, Pickle, who was only a small hound, soon realized with a twinge of concern that by standing stock-still he was in grave danger of being snowed over. He quietly hoped he wasn't about to be buried alive. Imagine the embarrassment of having to be dug up by the emergency services while he was wearing Mrs. Speckle's home-knitted duffel coat! And the clothespins. Don't forget the clothespins. Oh, he'd never live it down.

Wilma, whose face was scrunched up against the biting cold, put her mittens to her forehead to shield her eyes from the onslaught of snow. Through the thick swirl of flakes she thought she saw something . . . moving. Ahead and to the left, on a raised mound, she could just make out what appeared to be the silhouette of a small boy. Phew! "Hello!" she called. "Is someone there?"

There was no reply, but a dim orb of lantern light flickered through the gloom. Wilma scooped Pickle up and made her way toward it. She was more certain now that there was someone ahead of them on the mound. She could definitely see a boy, hair blowing in the wind, gesturing for them to clamber up the slope. Slipping on a patch of ice, Wilma fell forward, her mittens plunging into deep snow and her hood flopping over her face. Pickle plopped down beside her and in desperation they both crawled wetly up the small hill. At the summit, Wilma straightened and the silhouette before her vanished into a blaze of bright light as a lantern swung toward her face.

"Who are you?" asked a gruff voice below her that didn't sound like a boy.

"I'm Wilma Tenderfoot," Wilma answered, trying to make out who she was talking to. "I'm an apprentice detective. This is my dog, Pickle. He doesn't normally look like that," she added, acknowledging the wooden pegs on Pickle's ears, "but he can't see without them. We've been sent to get a Brackle Bush. Ours got burned. And we're a bit lost, what with the snow and everything. But I saw the lamplight and the boy and——"

"There are no Brackle Bushes here," interrupted the voice gruffly. "You're in Blackheart Hoo. This is private land. You're not allowed here. And what's more, you're damaging my excavation trench."

"Ex-ca-whatsit?" asked Wilma, scrunching her nose up.

"Excavation trench," replied the man, clambering up beside her and lowering the lantern in his hand. "I'm Dr. Irascimus Flatelly. I'm an archaeologist. I am conducting a dig on the Blackheart estate perimeters and you're standing on the edge of my excavation trench."

"Oh," said Wilma, stepping sideways. "Although with all this snow, it's quite difficult to see what I'm standing in."

Dr. Irascimus Flatelly was a small, wiry man with a scrappy beard and round spectacles worn over droopy-looking eyes. He had an intense way about him, as if he might recite a poem at any moment or crush walnuts with his bare hands. He was dressed in a leaf-green tweed suit with his trousers tucked into long socks and was wearing a battered trilby hat that was slightly too small for his head. Wilma looked around her. She could just make out the edges of what appeared to be a rectangular pit. There was a spade stuck into the ground and a sizable mound of earth behind it, both partly snow-covered. A large wheelbarrow with an empty sack in it stood at one end of the site and Irascimus, lantern held close to his face, looked anxious. Wilma had never met an archaeologist before and wasn't entirely sure what one was or what they did. Perhaps they always looked worried, she thought. Because some grown-ups do.

"If you're looking for the Brackle Bush farm," continued Dr. Flatelly, "then you will need to go back down this bank and bear left. I think it's about a mile in that direction." He waved off into the distance. "Actually, I have a map in my pocket. I can show you if you like."

"Yes, please," replied Wilma, smiling. "My Academy textbook says looking at maps is generally to be encouraged. I am a pupil at the Academy of Detection and Espionage. I'm an apprentice detective."

"Yes, you said," mumbled the archaeologist, fumbling in a pocket.

"I work for Theodore P. Goodman," continued Wilma, trying to look official. "I have a badge."

"Theodore P. Goodman?" said Dr. Flatelly, looking up suddenly. "Is he with you?" He raised his lantern and looked over Wilma's shoulder.

"No. It's just me and Pickle."

Wilma stepped closer to Dr. Flatelly. Pickle gave himself a little shake and tried to follow her, but as he did so, he lost his footing and slid sideways into the excavation trench. Falling into a rather deeper drift than he was expecting, he was momentarily flummoxed. Above him he could hear Wilma taking directions from Dr. Flatelly and below him he could smell the deep, rich scent of just-turned soil. But there was something more. No hound worth his salt would pass up a smell as fertile as that. It was the sort of ancient buried bouquet that could send dogs into rhap-sodic trances. Pickle began tentatively to paw at the ground beneath him. Feeling something hard and round under his claws, he dug deeper and gave the small uncovered protuberance a little lick. It tasted rusty and metallic, but there was something else . . .

Giving a little whirrup, Pickle scrabbled far-ther into the trench and began to dig frantically. Snow and soil flew upward behind him. "What the . . . !" yelled Dr. Flatelly as icy mud splattered his tweed suit. "This is an important historical site! Your dog is destroying it!"

"No, Pickle!" yelled Wilma, jumping into the excavation trench. But she was too late. Pickle was already tugging something from the earth. Dr. Flatelly, spluttering and spitting snow, saw what the determined dog was doing and let out an anxious wail as Pickle, his jaws clamped tightly about his prize, lowered his shoulders and yanked one last time. The ground beneath his quarry cracked open and with a mighty jerk, Pickle fell backward, pulling whatever it was he had with him. "Oh my goodness," whispered Wilma, her eyes popping.

There before her, sticking up from the snow-covered ground, was a large, ancient-looking key. And clutched around it was a dried and life-less human hand.

"There's someone d-d-dead in my excavation trench," stuttered Dr. Flatelly, pointing at the mummified hand.

"But who is it?" whispered Wilma, scrabbling backward. "And why are they holding a key?"

Who and why indeed. Get ready for the long haul. This could be another case for Theodore P. Goodman (and his apprentice, Wilma Tender-foot).

"A sort of hand, you say?" shouted Inspector Lemone over his shoulder the following morning. "Like a claw? Of some sort of unidentifiable monster?"

"It was a bit like a claw," yelled Wilma as she bounced along in the trailer at the back of Theodore's tandem. "But I've looked up the chapter in my Academy textbook on Things That Clutch, and it was definitely a hand. One that looked like it had been pickled, then roasted, but left in the oven too long."

The Inspector gulped. He didn't like the sound of this. It was bad enough having to pedal anywhere on the tandem, but pedaling toward something ghoulish seemed positively reckless. Inspector Lemone was Cooper Island's only police officer. It had happened by accident. On leaving school, all children on Cooper are required to fill in a form saying what job they would like to do. Lemone, hoping for an easy life, had declared that he would like to be a "polite officer," a straightforward job that required the occasional pleasantry. But the Minister in Charge of Island Jobs had forgotten his reading glasses that day and misread Lemone's request. And so Lemone, a rotund fellow with a deep love of biscuits, had found himself in charge of all manner of laws and orders. Which was quite a shock. "That claw sounds awful," he panted, reaching up to wipe the sweat from his forehead.

"Actually, it sounds mummified," said Theodore, indicating left as they rode in through the gates of Blackheart Hoo. "Which means whoever it is may have died a very long time ago."

"That's what the ark-ologist said," added Wilma, making a few scribbles in her apprentice detective notebook. "Dr. Flatelly said it looked ever so old and that he was going to get the Blackheart butler to help dig it up. He said that was why it wasn't urgent you saw it either. I couldn't stay, of course, because Pickle and I had to get the Brackle Bush, so I didn't see the rest of it. But I expect it's HORRIBLE."

"Ah! Titus!" called out the great detective with a wave. "Glad you've made it."

Wilma looked over her shoulder. Coming up the driveway behind them was a rickshaw in which sat the island's forensic scientist, Dr. Kooks. He was a large fellow with a jolly demeanor who liked to spend his spare time singing songs about body parts in the hope that one day he would be in an opera. Pulling him along, with consider-able effort, was his long-suffering assistant, Pen-bert. Kooks was wrapped in a large blanket and singing a song about elbows. "Ah-ha!" he boomed with a broad beam upon seeing Mr. Goodman and his friends. "Isn't it cold! Absolutely frozen! Still, not as frozen as the poor chap they found last night, I'll wager! HA!"

Penbert rolled her eyes. It was quite against every rule in the book to make jokes about dead bodies in front of non-medical personnel. Most improper. She would have to enter this in her incident book.

The morning was crisp and sharp. The snow-storm had left the island feeling fresh as the flick of clean sheets. Horse-drawn snowplows had been hard at work since dawn's first light to clear the roads, and the fields were full of snow-animals hastily built by children on their way to school. Theodore and Inspector Lemone traveled everywhere on the island by tandem with Wilma and Pickle sitting in a two-wheeled trailer attached to the back. With the icy conditions, however, the journey had been a little more treacherous than usual. At one point, swerving to avoid an out-of-control donkey spinning toward them on a patch of black ice, they had ridden headfirst into a snow-filled ditch and had to be pulled out by a passing funeral procession, which in anyone's book is nothing short of awkward.

The main house at Blackheart Hoo rose into view behind a long line of oak trees. The manor was vast, the sort of place where you could sit in a different room every day of the year without ever getting back to where you started. Dark brickwork gave the place a sense of unwelcoming menace, spiny turrets clambered toward the sky as if trying to escape, and Wilma was a little taken aback by the gargoyles of pigs that snarled down from every corner of the building. "Legend has it," explained Inspector Lemone, following her gaze, "that the Blackhearts actually invented pigs. True story." Theodore rolled his eyes and pulled off his bicycle clips.

Even Mr. Goodman had never been inside Blackheart Hoo before. The Blackheart family were notoriously secretive and very little was known about them even though their estate was the largest on the island. Some families like to keep themselves to themselves—usually because someone has done something unspeakable, like making a birthday cake out of cow dung for a visiting dignitary—so they avoid contact with the rest of the world out of embarrassment. Wilma had consulted her Academy textbook on this very matter. There was a chapter on Dastardly Deeds on Big Estates that explained, very clearly, that the bigger the house, the greater the host of Likely Suspects. "This could be quite tricky," she explained to Pickle as she tucked her book away. "When it comes to murder, there's wayward sons, desperate daughters, rotten cooks, bad butlers, and malicious maids. We might have our work cut out on this one, Pickle!"

"Don't go jumping to conclusions yet, Wilma," advised Theodore, popping his bicycle clips into his top waistcoat pocket. "There's no evidence that there has been a murder. And remember, even if there has, it was probably a very long time ago. This might turn out to be a case that cannot be investigated. Or no case at all, for that matter."

Wilma screwed her mouth sideways. She hoped it was a case. She hoped that more than anything. Jumping out of the trailer, she helped Pickle down from his seat. He was in something of a grump and had a large bandage on the end of his nose after the unfortunate Brackling incident from the previous evening. The bandage was pink and sparkly and had a picture of a cat on it. Pickle just hoped none of the big dogs from Coop would see it.

Standing waiting for them at the top of the front flight of stone steps was a tall man with hunched shoulders in a black morning suit. His jaw looked far too long for his face, and his eyes drooped at the corners. "That must be the butler," whispered Wilma, giving Pickle a nudge with her foot. "My textbook says butlers are generally not to be trusted. Apparently they've always got secrets." Pickle sniffed.

"Mr. Goodman?" said the man, with a small bow, as Theodore strode up the steps. "Master has been expecting you. No doubt you have heard of the unfortunate discovery in the bottom field? We would have had the body taken to the island laboratory in normal circumstances, but with the snow, I felt it best to keep it in the library. It's been quite an inconvenience. I'd been hoping to plant my award-winning peas. As well as being the butler, I'm also in charge of the Hoo vegetable patch. But that's by the by. If you would like to follow me, I can take you to the body immediately."

"Thank you," replied Theodore, giving the magnifying glass hanging on a chain from his waistcoat pocket a twiddle. "Perhaps you could ask all the family to meet me there. And household staff too, please. I may have some questions."

The butler's dark-ringed eyes stared at the great detective without responding. Wilma gave Pickle another nudge. "Classic suspish," she whispered again. "Not reacting instantly to basic requests. My book calls that a 'physical tell.' It's when your body accidentally gives away secrets that reveal what you're *really* thinking. It's quite technical and a bit advanced for me. I'm not supposed to read that chapter till next year."

"Wilma," said Theodore, "you may think you are whispering, but I can hear every word you are saying. What did I tell you about pointless speculating?"

Wilma gulped.

"Precisely. Now then, shall we have a look at this mysterious body?"

"Yes, Mr. Goodman," answered the butler, before glancing at Wilma. "Quick enough for you?"

Wilma mustered a weak smile and cleared her throat. This wasn't quite the impressive start to the new case she'd been hoping for.

Despite the early hour, the interior of the house was dark and filled with shadows. The library was on the first floor, to the left of the main staircase at the end of a long, narrow corridor. The walls in the hallway were covered with dusty paintings of large and impressive pigs. "Told you so," noted Inspector Lemone, pointing. "Actually *invented* the pig. Remarkable, don't you think?"

As Wilma walked, she couldn't help but be impressed by the grandeur of the place, but she also noticed how shabby everything looked. The rugs were a little threadbare, the statues a little chipped and grubby. Even the butler's morning suit, she realized, had frayed trouser ends and cuffs.

"The body is in here," murmured the butler, his hand resting on a dull brass doorknob set in a large oak door. "I should warn you, it is rather alarmingly illuminated. One of our gas lamps is burning a little bright."

He twisted the knob and with a groan, the heavy door into the library opened. "Ooooh!" cried Inspector Lemone. Wilma, who couldn't quite see from behind the inspector's bulk, pushed around him. Her eyes widened and her mouth fell open as she saw what sat before her. Leaning against a high-backed velvet chair, its strange angles and shrunkenness exaggerated by a bright beam of gaslight, was the desiccated body. Its legs were twisted across each other and one arm was wrapped about its torso while the other was extended upward, the large, rusty key still in its grasp. But it was the face that was most disturbing. Black sockets seemed even deeper in the lamplight, the mouth agape as if in mid-scream. It was the single most frightening thing Wilma had ever seen.

"Interesting," Penbert muttered, pulling on her official white coat and getting to work immediately. Within seconds she had placed small red cones around the body and taped off the area. "The body looks ancient but perfectly preserved, as if it's been in some sort of embalming fluid. But that's impossible."

"Fascinating," agreed Theodore, stepping between Wilma and the body and giving her a reassuring pat as he did so. He approached the near-skeleton to take a quick look at it through his magnifying glass. "It's as if all the moisture has been sucked out of it."

"It's a phenomenon that's not as uncommon as you might imagine," said a voice from behind the chair, making Wilma jump. "Dr. Irascimus Flatelly," the archaeologist added, emerging from the room's shadows and extending a hand. "I found the body."

"Pickle found it, actually," chipped in Wilma, flicking to a page in her notebook. "I wrote that bit down."

"Thank you, Wilma. Now, remember your top tips and Golden Rules. Observe and contemplate for the time being," said the detective seriously as he reached for the archaeologist's hand and shook it. "Theodore P. Goodman," he added, introducing himself. "I don't believe we have ever met, though you do look familiar. I am aware of your work, of course. I read a paper you wrote on early Cooperan correctional devices. Fascinating stuff. Of course—that's why I've seen you before. There was a picture of you holding a large wrist-slapper, though you had on your rather big-brimmed archaeologist's hat at the time, so you looked a bit different."

"Indeed." Dr. Flatelly removed his glasses and began to polish them with a small strip of cotton taken from his pocket. "But as I was saying, preserved bodies are not unusual finds in this part of the island," he went on, looking down. "Something in the soil seems to prevent the bodies from decomposing. It may be the salt, but there is also a significant presence of acetic acid."

"The stuff found in vinegar!" declared Dr. Kooks, lifting a finger in the air.

"So the body," mused Penbert, getting out a large pair of magnified glasses and putting them on, "has, in effect, been pickled."

Pickle's ears pricked and sensing his moment had come, he stepped over the tape around the body and gave it a quick lick. He clacked his lips together. It was like a preserved onion. A very old preserved onion.

"Please don't lick the evidence," retorted Penbert, bustling Pickle back out of the taped area. "And don't breach the perimeter. Very irregular." Penbert returned to examining the body. "Hmmm," she continued. "There seems to be an unusual build-up of something in patches on the skin . . ." Reaching into her pocket, she pulled out a small pair of tweezers and a scalpel. Taking the blade, she scraped off a sticky black mass, tweezered it onto a strip of glass, and slipped it under her field microscope. "Well, I never," she muttered with a sniff. "Fascinating." She made a quick scribble in her notebook.

Wilma, who liked to think she was the same level as Penbert, what with them both being assistants, stood on her tiptoes and tried to read Penbert's notes. "No looking at the official records until they're completed, thank you," said

Penbert, shielding what she'd written with her arm. "I still have working out to do."

Wilma scrunched her nose up. She hated waiting for the good bits.

"I must say," chipped in Dr. Flatelly, stepping forward, "this is a particularly fine specimen. And what do you make of the body's expression of abject terror? I take it you have all noticed that? Quite disconcerting." And even as he said it, the room seemed to darken and grow cold. In the distance, a dog howled.

"Don't worry," Wilma explained, holding a hand up. "That's Pickle. I sent him outside. To stop him licking the evidence."

Abject terror? Are things about to turn positively PETRIFYING? Let's hope not, eh?

4

A chilling scream rang out behind them.

Wilma spun around and saw a young but plain woman in a pale cream lace dress falling backward into the arms of a raffish-looking fellow in a bright red blazer. "Sorry!" he shouted at them in a jolly fashion. "It's my sister, Belinda. She screams and swoons at the slightest thing."

"That must be Tarquin Blackheart," muttered Wilma under her breath. "Young sons can also be trouble, according to my textbook. Best keep an eye on him. And Belinda Blackheart. She's the daughter. She may be desperate. I'd better write them in my Likely Suspects list."

"I can still hear you, Wilma," hissed Theodore. "Ah. Lord Blackheart," he added as an elderly gentleman in a hunting jacket strode into the room. He had a napkin stuffed into his collar and was carrying a fork with a large fish on the end of it.

"Middle of breakfast!" Aloysius Blackheart bellowed. "Chap dug up at the bottom of the estate by all accounts! Portious—take this fish. Now then. Where is the nuisance? By golly," he added, bending to look closer at the body. "Looks like a smoked eel." Spinning around, he snatched the fish back from the butler Portious and took a bite out of it. Chewing, he stepped toward Theodore and had a good look at him too. "You the detective? Fine mustache. Never trust a man with no facial hair. That's my tip. Oh. This fellow with you is quite clean-shaven. Hmph! Well, we shan't be giving *you* anything important to do. And who's this?" he added, glancing down at Wilma. "Far too short for a police officer. What are you? The mascot?"

"I'm Wilma Tenderfoot," Wilma replied, bewildered. "I'm Mr. Goodman's apprentice."

She stuck her thumb behind the silver apprentice badge she wore on her pinafore and pushed it upward.

"Please excuse my husband," came a smooth, serene voice from the doorway. "He's impossible until he's had his breakfast. How do you do?" The woman who'd spoken glided into the room. She had a slight frame, a pinched nose, and hair arranged in a high and intricate heap. As she wafted past, the gentle scent of roses filled the air and Wilma saw that the shawl wrapped about the lady's shoulders had a few holes in it and looked a bit moth-eaten. The woman extended a soft lily-white hand toward Theodore. "I'm Lady Blackheart. Oh dear," she added, noticing the body. "Is this the ghastliness Portious was telling us about? Tarquin, do fan your sister, please. You know how she has a tendency to drift."

"Mr. Goodman," interrupted the butler gloomily, gesturing toward a small group of people who were gathering behind the family, "here are the rest of the house staff, as you asked: Mrs. Moggins the cook, and Molly and Polly the housemaids."

Wilma leaned sideways so that she could see them all. Mrs. Moggins was a short, red-faced woman who looked like a steamed pudding, and Molly and Polly were slightly disheveled-looking things wearing headbands that pulled the hair back from their faces. Molly, the pudgier of the two, was blinking a lot, while Polly, who was as skinny as a bone, was chewing her bottom lip and sniffing.

"Likely Suspects . . ." Wilma muttered to herself. "'Cooks often harbor terrible grudges,'" she recited, "'probably because they eat too much salt. And maids can be flibbertigibbets.' I have no idea what that is, but it sounds painful."

Wilma looked back at the group of servants and pursed her lips. Given the size of the house, there seemed to be precious few staff. Her textbook listed lots of possible servants. Where, for instance, was the pruner or the gamekeeper? Perhaps this family wasn't as rich as they appeared. And besides that, there was definitely someone missing. There was no sign of that boy she had seen helping Dr. Flatelly the day before. Where was he?

"Now then," bellowed Lord Blackheart, wiping his mouth with his napkin and turning to Theodore. "My son tells me you're the great and very serious fellow to call on Cooper when something like this happens. Dead body uncovered and all that. Thought you could sort it out."

"You are correct," said Theodore, taking the reins. "The question for us all is who is it and how did he come to be dead and buried here with a key in his hand? A cursory examination, however, leads us to believe that this person—murdered or no—has been dead for over a century."

"Which means come what may, no one here's a suspect," chipped in Lemone, trying to be useful. "Unless anyone here's about a hundred and fifty years old," he added, scanning the room quickly, just to be sure.

"If he's been dead for years, how can you possibly work out who it is?" rasped Lord Blackheart, taking another bite out of his fish.

"I might be able to help with that," piped up Dr. Flatelly. "As you know, I have been investigating the Blackheart family for my next paper on

Cooper history. I wrote to you some time ago seeking permission to visit and you kindly said I could conduct a small exploratory dig toward the very edge of the estate. When Mr. Goodman's apprentice found me I was trying to preserve the site, given the onset of the freezing weather. Little did I know it would uncover such a thing as this. Anyway, if you look carefully at the body, there are two things of interest. One of the front teeth is missing. And here," he added, reaching for the hand wrapped across the corpse's chest, "on the right hand, there is a ring with the Blackheart crest barely visible."

"Good grief," gasped Lady Blackheart. "So there is!"

Belinda, who had been out cold and slumped over a heap of books, woke just in time to see the archaeologist holding up the shrunken hand in the lamplight. Staring at it with horror, she let out another short gasp and swooned again. Tarquin began fanning her distractedly once more while listening, rapt, to everything Dr. Flatelly had to say.

"Now let me show you something else," said the archaeologist, reaching into his jacket pocket. "Here I have a book of portraits of the Blackheart dynasty stretching back for generations." He opened it to a marked page. "In this portrait, the same tooth is missing. And there, on the right hand, the same ring on the same finger."

"Is anyone else finding this a bit frightening?" Inspector Lemone gulped, looking around him. Nobody replied. One and all were hanging on the archaeologist's every word.

"Well, who is it, man?" barked Lord Blackheart, spitting bits of fish.

"Bludsten Blackheart," declared Irascimus. "I believe this body is that of Bludsten Blackheart, your great-great-great-grandfather!"

"Well, that's the quickest case we've ever solved," said Inspector Lemone, rubbing his hands together and moving toward the door. "Come on then, Goodman. Job done!"

"We don't know how he was killed yet, Inspector Lemone," whispered Wilma, pointing to the relevant page in her textbook. "Thank goodness

I'm here to point that out. Don't worry, though. That's why I'm the apprentice and you're not. Happy to help."

"Bludsten Blackheart?" said Theodore, tapping his chin with the end of his pipe. "Am I right in thinking that there is an old legend about him?"

Lord Blackheart nodded. "He's supposed to have buried an artifact of unbelievable wealth on the estate for some reason—a golden claw, they say. He then disappeared, presumed dead, without telling anyone where it was. Don't know much about it. I don't think anyone paid much notice, perhaps because he was a bit crazy. He might have made the whole treasure thing up."

"I say," said Tarquin, eyes brightening. "You don't think the legend is true, do you? And that the golden claw is still on the estate? And that key has something to do with it?"

Everybody in the room turned and stared at the large key in the mummy's hand.

"Because according to Cooper's Finders Keepers rule, whoever finds it gets to keep it," Tarquin added.

The room bristled with tension. Sometimes,

when an enormous fortune is up for grabs, people, even honest ones, realize that if they keep their ideas to themselves, they might end up finding it and becoming very rich. During the silence, everyone shuffled on their feet and looked a bit shifty—something that didn't go unnoticed by Wilma.

"Stop everything," said Penbert, picking out the piece of blackened skin from under her microscope and holding it up. "I have something to announce. This is carbonized adrenaline. That means solidified fear. I think I have the 'How was he killed?' bit solved. Bludsten Blackheart was *frightened* to death!"

A gasp rippled through the room.

"But by who or by what?" whispered Wilma, clutching the hem of her pinafore.

"Maybe I can answer that too," offered Iras-cimus Flatelly, holding his book of notes aloft. "Something Lord Blackheart said rang a bell, so I have been going back through my notes. And yes, it seems Bludsten Blackheart did find gold some-where on the island. He excavated a mine, the location of which he kept secret. A mighty and magnificent claw was made from the gold, but his obsession with keeping it for himself drove Bludsten to the point of paranoia and madness. Folklore suggests that in his delusional state he hid it and tried to summon up an evil spirit to guard the gold trophy forever. A Fatal Phantom, if you will. But from the moment he enacted the ceremony, his madness worsened. It was as if the Phantom haunted . . . HIM!"

"You mean . . . it scared him to DEATH?" Wilma whispered, eyes wide. "It jumped out at him or something and he dropped down dead on the spot and his body was never discovered until now?"

"Nonsense, surely!" wailed Lady Blackheart, her face white with terror.

"Madame, I am sure it is," Mr. Goodman began.

"Maybe, but maybe not," whispered Dr. Flatelly, gesturing toward Penbert's tweezers. "Solidified FEAR. Let the evidence speak for itself."

"And this Fatal Phantom is guarding the thing forever?" whimpered Inspector Lemone, gripping the edge of a bookcase.

"So the legend is true . . ." whispered Belinda, opening one eye. "There is a treasure . . ."

"But where is it?" warbled Lady Blackheart, licking her lips. "What does the key fit?"

"That I do not know," said Dr. Flatelly, "but I do know this: Finding it may be more dangerous than any of us can possibly imagine."

"Don't like the sound of this," said Lord Blackheart, frowning. "Perhaps you should set up shop here at the Hoo, Dr. Flatelly. Carry on your research. There's an old hut in the grounds— you can work there if you like. That way you can do some more poking around without getting under my feet. Help get to the bottom of this business. Maybe track down the treasure," he added hopefully.

"Of course, Lord Blackheart," replied the archaeologist. "To find it for you would be of immense historical interest to me, and would help round off my paper nicely."

"Well, now we know who the body is, and as there are no apparent signs of foul play, we'll help Kooks and Penbert pack it up for further confirmation tests back at the lab and be on our way." Mr. Goodman began to usher Wilma toward the forensics gear to help gather it up.

Wilma's eyes widened. No signs of foul play—no signs of human foul play maybe, but what about all this spooky stuff? Surely there was a case somewhere in this for them? Reaching for her notebook, she turned to her latest scribbles. "The thing is," she pointed out frantically to Mr. Goodman, "according to my Academy textbook chapter on dug-up bodies, any attached curses are reawakened as soon as the body is uncovered, so that Fatal Phantom is probably about to start another *enormous* haunting."

And as she spoke these fateful words, out in the garden Pickle threw back his head and howled.

"I really wish he'd stop doing that," Inspector Lemone said in a strangled tone.

A treasure AND a spooky curse? Well. Didn't things just get interesting!

5

When horrible things are afoot on one side of an island, there are invariably horrible things afoot on the other. On small islands it is very important to achieve balance, as one end could tip up at any moment, resulting in sinking and multiple deaths. And no one wants that. So mirroring events at Blackheart Hoo were the hideous happenings at the Lowside Institute for Woeful Children, the revolting establishment where Wilma had spent most of her life and where the island's most notorious villain was now stuck good and proper.

"I am FURIOUS!" yelled Barbu D'Anvers,

slamming his fist down on the chopping board in front of him. "FURIOUS! How have I, Barbu D'Anvers, criminal mastermind BEYOND COMPARE, ended up in a stinking kitchen cutting up onions for woeful children? Woeful children, I might add, who seem to have permanent plugs of snot hanging from their nostrils and an ignorance of basic hygiene. They don't just smell, they've got MOLD growing on them! HOW? How has this happened?"

"The Health and Safety Officer came to that theatre where you were the manager and made you pay a fine for all the actors who died, and then she seized your property and—" began Tully, Barbu's stupid henchman.

"Yes," hissed Barbu, throwing a potato at him. "I know *that*. I don't need reminding, thank you! What I mean is how am I *still* here? It's been a month! That's FOUR weeks!" He slumped forward onto the workbench in front of him, his once magnificent pompadour flat and dull. "I fear," he mumbled, "that I may be . . . *depressed*."

Barbu D'Anvers, wrong'un of the highest

order, was living at the Institute for Woeful Children under duress. His own home, Rascal Rock, was currently under a confiscation order until Barbu could pay the hefty fine he had been given following the unfortunate events a month previously at the Valiant Vaudeville Theatre, where Goodman's last case, that of the Putrid Poison, had unfolded. No two people disliked each other more than Theodore P. Goodman and Barbu D'Anvers. The detective had spent most of his working life chasing around after the diminutive villain, but Barbu had always managed to elude capture by shifting blame and just being plain, old-fashioned sneaky. Until now.

Squeezed into a tiny room with a triple bunk for him, his apprentice Janty, and his sidekick Tully, Barbu was seething. He had been forced to do menial chores like defrosting the frozen underpants from the clothesline and shaving the Institute matron Madam Skratch's bunion, but worst of all, especially for a gent so dedicated to fashion, he had to wear the Institute uniform— dingy gray overalls with a flat cloth cap.

Criminal Elements, you must understand, are never happy unless they are hatching evil, spreading misery, and accumulating fortunes by any means necessary. "I am rankled BEYOND BELIEF!" yelled Barbu. "To think it would ever come to this! Barbu D'Anvers *working to pay off a debt*! Oh, the humiliation! I have striven all my life never to do an honest day's work and here I am, being *paid* to peel onions. This is all Goody-Goody Goodman's fault! And that revolting child that works for him! Outwitted by a girl! Oh . . . oh, help me . . . I think I may be . . ."

Barbu's eyes rolled back into his head and the tiny villain toppled sideways. Janty and Tully dropped their peeling knives and ran to their master's side. "Should I slap him?" asked Tully, staring down at Barbu's crumpled body. "Throw water in his face?"

"Don't you *dare*," snarled Barbu, opening one eye. He lifted a limp arm in Janty's direction. "You there, help me up," he growled. "My brilliance may be diminished, but it's not extinguished yet."

Janty had been taken on as Barbu's apprentice a few months previously. His father had been a prominent forger but had come to a sticky demise during one of Goodman's cases, leaving the boy an orphan. Rather than have the boy fall into his enemy's hands, Barbu had plucked Janty from under Goodman's charitable nose, pumped him for information, then ended up taking him on as his own. Like many boys, Janty had been lured by the promise of fast living and crazy horseplay, but had found himself a novice in the ways of menace and misdeeds. Though he was doing his best to learn fast. Young boys sometimes think that being terribly naughty is a sharp thrill, but they are wrong. And all girls would do well to remember that, however handsome those boys might turn out to be.

"That's the spirit, master," said the curly-haired young man now, grabbing hold of the villain's wrist and heaving him upward. "If it helps, I conned two five-year-olds out of their monthly apple ration last week, I've stolen some blankets from the baby dorm, and I've set up a protection racket in the boiler room. I've made quite a few groggles already. It doesn't matter where we are, we can always be bad."

Barbu sniffed. "Protection racket, you say? And I suppose we *could* do a little scamming. Children, woeful or not, are *terribly* gullible. The problem, of course," continued the tiny terror, "is that woeful children don't have much to lose. Yes, we can take their apples, grab a few groggles, but if we're going to get out of here, we need to think bigger."

"You there!" shouted a voice through the kitchen window. It was Madam Skratch, her bony nose quivering with disdain. "Small boy with the beard!" she yelled, pointing at Barbu. "No slacking! I want those onions for a dessert!" And with that, she marched off.

"Oh no," mumbled Tully, "not again . . ."

If there was one thing guaranteed to send Barbu D'Anvers spinning into a blind rage it was any reference to his size. Short men are painfully aware that they are squat, and any reminder of their slight stature is guaranteed to cause a psychotic episode. History, for example, teaches us that tiny men are much given to rampaging, marauding, and invading countries. Consult any history book you please and you will discover that every single dictator and bad sort was on the stunted side. Napoleon, an infamous tiny Frenchman, invaded Russia simply because a passing Cossack asked him if he needed a hand up some steps. Short men are VERY sensitive. Be warned. And Barbu, being an exceptionally short man, was no different. He glared in the direction of the now empty window. His left eye twitched, he squeezed his hands into tight fists. "Small boy with the beard?" he whispered through gritted teeth. "SMALL BOY WITH THE BEARD?"

"Stand back," warned Tully, pressing Janty behind him.

Barbu, face blood-red with fury, picked up the large peeling knife in front of him and, with a yell, threw it hard. It rotated fast across the kitchen, cut a turnip in half, and embedded itself in a large hanging hare. Next, he took up a rolling pin and began to bash all the boxes of eggs, one by one, until yellow yolk splattered every surface. Then, in one last fit of ferocity, he grabbed a large potato and battered it until it was mashed to mulch.

"Small boy with the beard???" he screamed, raising his rolling pin aloft once more. "I need to KILL something!"

"You killed that potato, Mr. Barbu," proffered Tully, poking his head up from behind the barrel where he had ducked with Janty moments before.

"Yes, Tully," panted Barbu D'Anvers, calming slightly. "I *did* kill the potato, and let that be A LESSON TO THEM ALL!" he added, throwing the rolling pin to one side. "I have had just about enough of being down in the dumps and told what to do by a woman with a BEAK for a nose. That's not what being the greatest villain that ever lived is all about. Go and find our old clothes and those stolen groggles you mentioned. We're hitting the Plumbus Club."

"The Plumbus Club, master?" asked his young apprentice.

"A gaming establishment for young men with more money than sense. We are going to divest them of their inheritances. Gambling, young Janty, has been many a promising fellow's ruin."

"You're going to play them at cards?" asked the boy.

"Oh, not just play, Janty. Win. By which I mean cheat, obviously."

"Obviously." Tully nodded. "It's good to see you back to your old self, Mr. Barbu."

"Don't ever let me get depressed again," declared the villain, throwing his gray cap into a bowl of greasy washing-up water. "The time has come. Barbu D'Anvers is BACK!"

Yes. You're right. It is a cause for worry. Let all the people quake.

Wilma was still in the library waiting for Mr. Goodman, with Pickle back at her side. The mummified body of Bludsten Blackheart had been carried carefully to the kitchen, where Theodore and Lemone were helping the scientists wrap it in wet bandages to protect it before being taken to the lab. The key that had been clutched in its hand had been carefully removed and given to Dr. Flatelly for further analysis in the hope that, if there was a treasure to be found, he might be able to uncover something in his papers that would match the key to the treasure's location.

Wilma had given herself an apprenticely job to do to pass the time while waiting: She was scanning the Blackhearts' books for any further information on Bludsten or anything about ghouls, spooks, and other paranormal hoo-ha. But where to start?

Wilma looked around her. The library was shrouded in gloom. Dark mahogany shelves ran from floor to ceiling, packed with old books and dusty manuscripts. Ladders on rollers stood resting against the pillars at intervals between each set of shelves. Behind the velvet chair where the mummy had sat, there was a large globe in a wooden frame. Wilma gave it a spin. It was entirely blue apart from one tiny bow-shaped island three-quarters of the way up one side. Wilma stopped the globe with her hand and pointed toward the tiny land mass. "Look," she said to Pickle, smiling. "Cooper Island."

"That globe was made specially for the Blackhearts," said a small voice just over Wilma's shoulder. She spun around, momentarily startled. Standing before her was a very thin boy, his cheeks and eye sockets slightly hollowed. He was wearing a pair of knee-length shorts tied about his waist with a belt made of string and both his shirt and jacket, Wilma noticed, were tatty and threadbare. In short, he had the look of someone not quite looked after. All the same, his eyes were kind and he was smiling. "I saw you yesterday," he said quietly, "at the excavation site. My name is Victor. I'm the Blackhearts' stable lad."

"The boy I saw in the snow!" Wilma exclaimed, beaming. "I wondered where you had got to! Stable lad? So what were you doing at the excavation site that evening—just keeping an eye on things for the Blackhearts?"

Victor nodded. "I often like to visit the library at night," he added. "I never went to school, so I come here to read and teach myself. I can help you if you like. I know my way around the shelves."

"Thank you." Wilma smiled. "There are so many books, it would take forever to check every single one of them. How rude! I haven't told you my name! I'm Wilma Tenderfoot, apprentice detective. And this is my dog, Pickle," she added, looking down. "Oh. Where is he?" Pickle was hiding underneath the velvet chair, shaking slightly. "It's all right," she said, beckoning to her quivering hound. "They've taken the mummy away! He'll be fine in a moment. I think he's a bit spooked. Anyway!" Stepping forward, she grabbed Victor by the hand and shook it vigorously. "I work for Theodore P. Goodman," she said. "He's a very serious and famous detective. Here's my badge." Wilma stuck her thumb behind the shiny silver badge on her pinafore and thrust it forward for Victor to see. "I was hoping to find out stuff about Bludsten Blackheart. But I think I should also be reading up on ghosts and other weird hoo-ha, because if there *is* a haunting, then it's best to be prepared."

Victor smiled and wandered over to one of the tall stacks of books. "Well, there's this," he said, climbing the nearest stack ladder and pulling out a large blue book. "This is *Mummies and What to Do if You Find One*. It's got some excellent illustrations." He climbed back down to

Wilma's side. "Look. It's a mummy strangling a hot-chestnut seller. And look at that one. He's bitten that lady's head off."

"Dear me," mumbled Wilma, shaking her head a little as she took the book. "That's terribly bad manners. Oh crumbs," she added, having flicked to the front. "'Chapter One: Whatever you do, don't dig up a mummy unless you absolutely have to. Not unless you want to endure a painful and dreadful death.' Hmm. Well, that's mistake number one. Although the mummy in the book is all covered in bandages. Bludsten was turned mummy by the vinegary soil. I wonder if that makes him even MORE evil."

"Perhaps you could just bury him again," suggested Victor, his eyes twinkling in the candlelight. "That might reverse the curse or something."

"I'm not sure," said Wilma, frowning as she read on. "Oh no! This could get even worse. There's a bit further on about how mummies hang out with zombies and vampires. Blimey! Better keep our eyes peeled. They might turn up and be all rotten and blood-suckery."

Victor had no reply to this. Instead, he touched Wilma lightly on the arm and said, "There's a book I think you should see. It's tucked away. I'm sure it'll be useful."

At the other end of the library, Victor led Wilma to an alcove where there was a small, decrepit bookcase with a wire mesh door. On the shelves were hundreds of leather-bound notepads. There was a lot of dust and the paper inside the pads was fragile and crumbling. "Here." Victor gestured, pulling out one of the most ancient-looking notebooks. It was a dark red and the leather was torn and weathered. He handed it to Wilma.

"What is it?" she asked, afraid to open it in case it fell apart in her hands.

"The diary of Bludsten Blackheart," whispered Victor, his soft blue eyes blazing.

Wilma's mouth fell open with a small gasp. "Oh my," she declared. "Well! I'll certainly find out plenty about Bludsten from that!"

Taking the notebook to a round reading table to her left, Wilma sat down and opened it. On the inside cover, there was a picture of a raised claw made of gold. "Look at that." Wilma trembled. "Do you think it's the treasure that Bludsten hid?"

"It might be," whispered Victor, peering over her shoulder.

"This diary is amazing, Victor," enthused Wilma, wide-eyed. "Look at all the pictures. This looks like a series of designs for the claw thing. It says it's made from ten thousand gold nuggets. That must make it very valuable. And what's this," she said, turning the pages. "It looks like sketches of some funny rocks . . ."

Before they could look any further, a piercing scream rang through the house. Pickle, still under the velvet chair, barked a few times and then ran out toward the library door. Wilma, carefully placing the diary into her pinafore pocket, jumped up to run after him. "Come on, Victor," she called over her shoulder. "Something's happened! We'd better go and check it out!"

"I can't," he said, retreating into the shadows. "I'm not supposed to be in the house. I'll get into trouble."

"I'll have to go," Wilma explained, still backing toward the library door. "My textbook says that when in the vicinity of screams, apprentice detectives need to get their skates on." She raised a hand as Victor disappeared into the gloom of the library. There must be another exit straight into the grounds back there, Wilma thought to herself as she dashed after Pickle. She had read about how Big Houses are filled with secret doors and passageways.

How nice it was though, to have made a friend her own age. And in many ways, Victor seemed to have had a similar start in life to her. Only, Mr. Goodman had found her. Perhaps she could introduce him to Mr. Goodman. Victor seemed to like cases and conundrums, and he was good at finding things. Perhaps he could be Inspector Lemone's apprentice. Yes, that was a good idea. But first things first. There were screams to deal with.

Wilma and Pickle scampered into the hallway. Ahead of them they could see a small group gathered. Inspector Lemone was bending down, tending to Polly, one of the housemaids, who had clearly suffered some sort of collapse.

"What is it?" Wilma panted as she ran toward Mr. Goodman. "What's happened?" But her mentor said nothing. Wilma followed his gaze toward the wall before them. Scrawled on it, in what looked like fresh blood, was a large raised claw and beneath it the dripping words "So it begins." Wilma took a sharp breath. Pickle didn't like this, not one bit. And so he whimpered a little, just to register his feelings on the matter.

Absolutely terrifying.

7

Tarquin Blackheart had heard enough. The house had been thrown into something of an uproar since the news that a ghoul might have been unleashed on it and, not wanting to be stuck fanning his constantly fainting sister, he had sneaked out and taken a carriage into the center of Coop, the island's main town, despite the snow. Young men from well-to-do families can go one of two ways: They can devote themselves to a life of charitable works saving donkeys or, as in Tarquin's case, they can laze about being of no use to anybody. But despite the fact that he was a Blackheart, Tarquin had very little money. In fact, the Blackheart fortune, once impressive and considerable, had been frittered away over the years to virtually nothing. If Tarquin was going to continue to live in the manner to which the Blackhearts had been accustomed, he was certainly not going to be able to rely on his inheritance.

The other setback for Tarquin was that he was profoundly stupid. You will often hear it said that fancy people talk "as if they've got marbles in their mouth." This is because they often *have* got marbles in their mouth. They can't help it. Some of them are just foolish. Tarquin was especially so.

Dressed in a purple velvet tailcoat, long silk scarf, and top hat set at a jaunty angle, Tarquin leaped from his carriage. "You there! Valet!" he shouted, tossing the carriage reins to a pimply youth. "Park my carriage, would you? And don't scratch it, there's a good fellow." He had driven to the Plumbus Club, a gaming establishment for young men with more money than sense, and given that Tarquin had very little money, this was even more senseless.

The Plumbus Club was a grand affair. A set of deep red heavy curtains acted as a doorway into a round entrance hall where a string quartet played in front of a huge fountain in the shape of tumbling dice. The air was filled with musky cigar smoke that wafted out from the gaming rooms. As Tarquin entered he was approached by a well-dressed man with greased-back hair. "Master Blackheart," he began, extending a hand. "So good to see you again. May I take your hat?"

"Thank you, Carter," replied Tarquin, tossing the man his top hat and scarf. "What tables are fun tonight? I want to see some action. Everything is so gloomy at the Hoo. I demand froth and bubbles!"

"The Lantha room is rather quiet this evening," replied Carter, the club's manager, referring to Cooper's national board game. "And there's not much happening in the Jickjack arena. But there is a rather enticing game of Descendo Supter unfolding in the games room to your left, sir. There's a gentleman doing very well, I believe."

"Is that so?" Tarquin grinned, loosening his tie a little. "Then perhaps it's time for me to reverse his fortunes. Bring me a hundred grogs' worth of counters and a decanter of Squifty Juice. Oh, and Carter . . ."

"Yes, sir?"

"If my father sends Portious looking for me . . ."

"I haven't seen you, sir," replied Carter with a discreet bow.

Supter, for those of you who have never played, is a card game of cunning and bluff. Players have three cards and must play each individually, starting with their highest and ending with their lowest. The trick is to make your opponent believe that you have a lower card than they do, and then bet accordingly until you either bluff your opponent into folding or win with the lowest hand. Normal packs of cards are made up of four suits—hearts, diamonds, spades, and clubs, but on Cooper, packs of cards are completely different. Instead of numbers the cards are animal-based, with suits comprising birds, mammals, fish, and insects. In Supter, the smaller the creature on the card, the lower the value, so a good card would be the gnat of insects or, best of all, the plankton of fish, whereas the elephant of mammals or the eagle of birds would be the very worst cards to be dealt. Most games of Supter are played with Descendo Rules—playing highest to lowest with one given suit—but a more dangerous and more thrilling version is Chance Supter, where any card from any suit can be played at any time.

The Supter gaming room was octagonal in shape with black walls and low, brooding lighting. In the center of the room stood a traditional Supter table, triangular and covered in blue baize. At one corner sat an anxious, sweaty-looking young man with a very small pile of counters before him and opposite, at the table's far end, was a small but well-dressed dark-eyed gentleman flanked by a larger, thuggish-looking man. Between them was the dealer, a very boyish-looking man with curly hair and a rather fake-seeming mustache. The more anxious of the two players was taking a look at his last card. His hands were shaking. "Twenty counters!" he exclaimed desperately, pushing all he had into the center of the table.

The well-dressed fellow pursed his lips and let his head fall to one side. "I think you're bluffing," he sneered. "No one with the gnat would let their shaking hands give them away. I call." He tossed a matching number of counters into the pot. The young man's head fell into his chest.

"You have read me again," he sighed, turning over his last card. "But I do have the stag beetle," he added hopefully.

The smartly dressed man smirked and turned his own card over. "The ant. I win once more."

The young man pushed back his chair and stood up shakily. "I . . . I have lost everything."

"In that case, go away," snapped the diminutive gambler, gathering up his counters. "And don't come back until you've got more to lose. Right. How much is that now?"

"Two thousand groggles, Mr. D'Anvers," answered the curly-haired dealer, taking the cards and giving them another shuffle.

"Not enough," growled the man. "Who's next? We've got an empty seat at the table."

"Tarquin Blackheart! Mind if I sit down?" said the young nobleman swaggering toward the table.

"One hundred counters . . ." said the black-eyed player, glancing at Tarquin's stack as he placed it on the table in front of him. "Not much . . . but it'll do. So you're a Blackheart, eh? Live in that estate to the south of Coop? The BIG estate?"

"That's right," boasted Tarquin. "The biggest estate on the island. And you are . . . ?"

"Barbu D'Anvers. You may have heard of me . . ."

Tarquin's grin froze. He had indeed heard of Barbu D'Anvers. There weren't many people on the island who hadn't. As a general rule it displays a level of basic stupidity to gamble at all, but to gamble against a known villain requires an advanced sort of stupidity that only absolute idiots possess. Tarquin's grin came back to life and broadened. "Barbu D'Anvers!" he guffawed. "Imagine that! Well! Let us play!" See? S.T.U.P.I.D.

Barbu watched as a decanter of Squifty Juice was placed on a small side table next to his opponent. A cunning grin settled on his lips. Gesturing toward Tully he mumbled, "Order another flagon of Squifty Juice for our friend. And make it a big one."

"Are you trying to get him drunk, Master Barbu?" Tully grinned evilly.

"Roaringly so," muttered the villain. "We shall get more out of him than his hundred counters, mark my words. Watch and learn." And he winked at the boyish dealer.

For the next half hour Barbu allowed Tarquin to beat him time and time again. As the young Blackheart's counter stack grew, so did his confidence and swagger . . . and his appetite for drink. "Looks like I've stolen all your luck, D'Anvers!" he cheered as he took what seemed to be Barbu's last counters. "More Squifty Juice! Ha-ha!"

Barbu's head was bowed in pretend defeat. "I do seem to be financially compromised," he said, gesturing to the empty space in front of him, "but I've never been a man to walk away from a Supter table until I absolutely have to. Let us have one more wager. One hand of *Chance* Supter and winner takes Double-Double. If I lose I shall, of course, honor my debt with an IOU."

"Double-Double?" guffawed Tarquin, taking a swig from his refilled glass. "Are you crazy? That's about ten thousand grogs!"

"Well, let's make it interesting. Any card from any suit. The lowest card wins it all. Janty—I mean, dealer—shuffle the deck. Tully, another glass of Squifty for our friend."

Puffing a wayward curl out from his eyes and almost blowing his mustache off in the process, the "dealer" picked up the Supter cards. As he did so, he masked them with one hand and, while Tarquin was distracted by Tully's clumsy efforts to serve drinks, he slipped the existing deck up one sleeve and let an identical-looking pack slide down the other. Barbu's jaw twitched a little. "One card please."

The boy dealt a card to each player. Tarquin leaned forward with a wide smirk on his face and took a look at his. Throwing his head back, he roared with laughter. "You shall regret this, D'Anvers," he crowed. "I say, let's make it Double-Double-Double-Double!"

Like a shark that knows it has its prey in its sights, Barbu allowed a small glint of triumph to dance briefly in his eyes before blinking slowly and blackly. "That's a very large wager, Master Blackheart," he hissed. "I accept."

Taking his Squifty glass in one hand, Tarquin raised it. "Gentlemen!" he bellowed. "I have the lowest card in the deck! The plankton of fish! Ha-ha! I have you beaten, D'Anvers!"

Barbu, still seated, fingered the corner of his own card. "The lowest card in the pack?" he replied, a dangerously quizzical expression creeping across his face. "In normal Supter, yes. But we are playing *Chance* Supter, Master Blackheart. Where the lowest card is . . ." He turned his card over with a flourish. ". . . the joker!"

Tarquin, glass at his lips, stared in disbelief. "But . . ." he began, in a daze, "I had the plankton . . ."

"Yes," answered Barbu, standing and pulling on his cloak. "You also had all the counters. But now you don't. And not only that, you now owe me a further . . . hmm, let me work this out . . . about twenty thousand grogs."

Tarquin fell back into his chair. "B-b-but I don't have twenty thousand grogs."

"Well, you'll have to get them," barked Barbu, banging the floor with his cane. "Just open up your family vaults or something."

"We don't have anything in our family vaults," mumbled Tarquin, despair and embarrassment raging across his face. "Everything has gone . . ." He stopped, his mind racing with fear. "Although . . . hang on . . . they found this mummy on the estate yesterday. It's got a key in its hand. A key to all that's left of the immense Blackheart fortune, they say . . ."

Barbu's face lit up. "A key to a fortune?" he whispered, bending close to a sweating Tarquin. "Interesting." His black eyes narrowed and he turned to his apprentice, who was already peeling off his dealer disguise. "This could be what we've been waiting for. Never look a gift horse in the mouth, Janty. If we find this fortune, then we're back in business. Rascal Rock will be regained and we can teach my rotten critics the lesson they deserve. This island *shall* be mine! My mind is made up. A plan is sprung. You and Tully go and fetch our things from the Institute. We are NEVER going back."

"Yes, master." Janty nodded.

"And as for you, Tarquin Blackheart," Barbu added, crunching the end of his cane into the young man's chest, "you can expect me at the Hoo in the morning. Tully, take his counters. We shall collect the rest of what we are owed tomorrow!"

The tiny villain swept from the room and Tarquin, who really had been a very silly boy, knew he was in a vast amount of trouble. How he was going to get himself out of this scrape was anyone's guess. He owed more money than he could even imagine, and all because he'd been a giddy goat. Listen and learn, children. The lesson here is *never* play cards with a scoundrel. That way you can avoid the crushing nightmare of being saddled with an enormous debt that you have absolutely no chance of paying off. A bit like when men decide they're going to buy a football team and then have to explain to their wives why they can't have a new kitchen.

Oh the horror!

8

The weather was getting worse. The following morning the skies were black, snow squalls were whipping across the Blackheart estate, and drifts were deepening. Tarquin, who was yet to tell anyone of the predicament he was in, was standing at the window of the upstairs sitting room and staring out. Where was he going to find nearly twenty thousand grogs? And how was he going to explain this to his father? Maybe, if he could get his hands on the hidden treasure first, then all his problems would be solved. Barbu D'Anvers had certainly seemed to like that idea. But how could he do that?

"Tarquin," said Belinda, who was resting on a chaise longue by the fire, "please pass me the lemon water. I am experiencing a severe mental strain."

"Get it yourself," he grumbled back at her, "or call Portious."

Belinda sat upright and fixed her brother with a shocked stare. "What's the matter with you this morning? Your mood is frightful."

"None of your business," he snapped back. "I have things on my mind."

"But so do I!" wailed Belinda, throwing herself back on the chaise longue. "What with desiccated fellows being dug up and cursed ghouls and blood on the walls! I mean, what next? I've already been terrified to distraction! And who's going to want to marry me now? We've got a Phantom in the walls!"

"Oh here, take it," relented Tarquin, turning from the window and reaching for the jug of chilled lemon water. "Anything to stop your infernal whining." He crossed the room to her side.

"I say," commented Belinda, sitting up to take

the jug. "Someone is coming along the drive in a barouche. Who would be visiting in this weather?"

Tarquin turned back to the window and looked down. A black horse-drawn buggy was struggling toward the house. Belinda got up and joined him. "Goodness. Look at the storm. We shall all be snowed in by the end of the day." She took a sip from her glass, then added ominously, "There will be no escape for any of us."

The black barouche had slid to a halt before the front entrance. As the carriage door opened and a young boy with curly black hair jumped out, Tarquin gave an involuntary groan. "Oh no," he whimpered. "It's Barbu D'Anvers's boy."

"THE Barbu D'Anvers?" squealed Belinda, peering over her brother's shoulder to get a better look. "The famous villain? How exciting. What's he doing here?"

"Never mind," rattled Tarquin, turning and walking toward the door. "I have to stop him before he speaks to Father."

"You KNOW Barbu D'Anvers?" cried Belinda, eyes widening. "Oh well, I'm coming with you," she trilled, running after her brother. "I've ALWAYS wanted to meet him!"

Barbu D'Anvers stepped down from the barouche and stared upward from under the brim of his top hat at Blackheart Hoo, spread out before him like a smorgasbord of evil opportunity. It is a general truth that people commencing devilish plots tend to feel a little smug. That's because they know what they're up to, while no one else has the slightest idea that they are about to be taken for every penny under the sun. With a sly smirk, Barbu tossed his cloak over one shoulder, turned to Janty, and said, "Let the real games begin. Sound the bell. Tully, unload the bags."

Janty leaped up the heavy stone steps to the Hoo's double doors and reached for the rusty bell pull, but just as he was about to yank it, the door opened. It was Tarquin, with Belinda close behind him.

"Mr. D'Anvers," Tarquin blustered, running down the steps toward the undersized crook, "there really is no need for you to call. I shall honor my debt toward you. I just need a bit more time . . ."

Barbu held up a hand to stop him. "Janty! Tell the man!"

The tousle-haired boy pulled out a small notebook from his jacket pocket. "I have made a brief calculation," he began. "And according to my IOU conversion table, in lieu of the cold, hard cash you owe Mr. D'Anvers, you have to provide board and lodging here at the Hoo for at least fifteen days." He looked up with an insolent smile.

"Maybe longer," added Barbu, leaning in threateningly. "In short, we're staying for as long as we like."

"B-b-but," stammered Tarquin helplessly as the villain marched past him, "I don't know how I can explain this to my father . . ."

"Well, think of something fast," snapped Barbu, striding up the steps.

"Tarquin!" yelled Belinda, throwing herself in Barbu's path as he reached the front door. "Introduce us, won't you?" She held out her hand for it to be kissed. "Never mind him. I'm Belinda Blackheart. Charmed, I'm sure."

Barbu froze and stared in disbelief. "You want me to kiss your hand? Don't be ridiculous. I have absolutely no idea where that has been."

"On the end of my arm?" proffered Belinda, still smiling hopefully.

Barbu's eyes narrowed. "Wait a minute," he growled, "you're a Blackheart. What's this one's status, Janty?"

" 'Belinda Blackheart,' " Janty read, " ' younger child. Second in line to inherit. No debts. No criminal record. Can do impressions of owls.' "

"Yes." Belinda nodded enthusiastically. "I can! Tweeeee-itttt, twoooo!"

Barbu curled his lip. "When you say second in line, that means she gets everything if Tarquin is nowhere to be found, yes?"

"Yes, master, unless she's married and has signed everything over to her husband."

"You're not married, are you?" asked Barbu quickly.

"Gosh, no!" giggled Belinda, twirling her hair

around one finger. "I haven't even got a boy-friend." Her eyes widened and she batted her eyelashes a little.

Barbu grimaced and gave her a quick look up and down. "Not surprised. But if she was married, then her husband would get everything? Good, Janty. Good. Now, you there!" he bellowed, on seeing Portious the butler. "Man with the half-collapsed face! Take us to our rooms. We shall be here for the foreseeable future."

"Isn't he dreamy?" whispered Belinda as she and her brother watched the terrible trio and an impressive number of bags marching up the central staircase. "Do you think he liked me?"

"I think you'll be quite comfortable here, sir," said Portious, showing Barbu into the guest suite. Compared to the garret room the villainous gang had been stuck in at the Institute, the Hoo's guest room was positively palatial. There was a large four-poster bed with a bedspread decorated with pigs, as well as various bureaus and reading tables, a huge sumptuous sofa, and a fireplace with a roaring fire. "Quarters for your servants are through the side door. Will there be anything else?" asked the butler morosely, opening a drinks cabinet and pulling out a tray of tiny bottles.

"Yes," replied Barbu, snapping off his gloves and tossing them onto the bed. "I would like a map of the grounds, information pertaining to any secret vaults, and a footstool placed next to the bed."

"Yes, that bed is unusually high off the ground. It can be a struggle for people who aren't quite tall enough . . ."

"Ooooooh!" interjected Tully, grabbing Portious and bundling him to the door. "Mr. Barbu will ring if he needs anything else!"

Barbu cast an eye around the room. "That sofa's seen better days," he observed, noticing its threadbare corners. "Looks like Tarquin was telling the truth—they are down on their luck. Probably why the family has been so reclusive and secretive in recent years—the shame. All the better for us. That means they're vulnerable to an aggressive takeover." He grinned. "Part one of my evil plot is complete. We're in. As soon as we get the plans, let's start thinking about potential locations for this missing treasure—wells, dungeons, odd-looking cupboards, that sort of thing."

"It might be inside a pumpkin, Mr. Barbu," proffered Tully, slamming the bedroom door shut. "Or disguised to look like a cat."

"I'll do the thinking, Tully, thank you. Obviously we should steal anything remotely valuable we see lying around—you know, to generate revenue to keep ourselves afloat—and if we can't find the treasure, then we can use that daughter thing as a backup plan. Janty's idea is an excellent one. I can do what anyone who regards skullduggery as a vocation does," he explained, settling himself into a large armchair. "I can MARRY into money."

"You? Get married?" asked Tully, momentarily flummoxed.

"Only if we can't find the treasure, obviously," sneered Barbu. "I mean, we'll have to bump off the parents and the son, but that's no bother.

And then I can lose her. At the bottom of a lake, preferably. This place may be shabby, but it'll still fetch a tidy sum. Actually, that's an idea—I could find the treasure AND marry Belinda. That way I get *everything*. Hmmm. I have no idea how to go about getting married, so go and find me something I can read on the subject. A book on wooing or anything revoltingly similar."

"Yes, Master Barbu," answered Janty, heading for the door.

"And then we can get down to our real business," cackled Barbu, leaning back and grinning. "Finding that treasure . . ."

What a ghastly little man.

The return trip to the Hoo that morning had not been a great success. With the snow worsening by the minute, Mr. Goodman and his team had struggled along on the tandem as best they could, but a sharp incline had gotten the better of them and, after sliding back down it for the fifth time, sense had prevailed and they had abandoned the bicycle, choosing instead to make the last of the way on foot.

"I hope we're going to be able to get back to Clarissa Cottage later," muttered Inspector Lemone as he trudged behind Theodore toward the Hoo. "This snow is setting in. Are you sure we shouldn't just turn back now?"

"Lord Blackheart has asked to see us, Inspector," said the great detective seriously. "Apparently there has been another incident."

"Spooky incident?" asked Lemone, startled. "You didn't mention that before . . . You know, the more I think about it, the more I believe it's verging on irresponsible to be out in this weather. Let's just go back to Clarissa Cottage. I expect Mrs. Speckle, fine, fine woman that she is"—Wilma raised her eyebrows in Pickle's direction. Inspector Lemone's shy fondness for Mr. Goodman's brusque housekeeper was the worst-kept secret on Cooper—"has made some sort of pie, and it'd be rude not to eat it . . . so . . ."

"Do you think it's the Fatal Phantom, Mr. Goodman?" wondered Wilma, running to catch up with her mentor. "Still guarding the treasure after all this time? And that uncovering the body of Bludsten Blackheart with the key to the treasure has summoned it? According to *Mummies and What to Do if You Find One,* a long-dead body can be an awful bother. Either way, it's a rather soup unnatural if you ask me."

"Supernatural, Wilma," corrected Theodore. "But I don't believe in hocus-pocus. There is always a sensible answer, even to the most strange goings-on, if you just take the time to look for it."

"And the sensible answer in this situation," added Inspector Lemone under his breath, "is to go home and eat some biscuits."

"And by that, Wilma, I mean," Theodore went on with purpose, "there are no more ghosts at the Hoo than there are dancing cakes in Mrs. Speckle's kitchen. Any suggestion of such is merely someone's conjuring tricks and shenanigans."

"I see," Wilma answered, frowning a little. "I know this isn't like one of your normal cases, but I've drawn a Clue Page in my notebook all the same. There's a mummy and a treasure with a phantomly curse and ghostly scrawls on the wall. If this were a proper case, that would be four clues right there."

"Yet I have seen not one shred of evidence that the dead are walking among us, Wilma. Remember that *proof* is what a detective requires, not speculation. Only that can lead us to the truth."

Wilma screwed her lips sideways. She was no expert on spooks, but there was certainly something mysterious going on. Still, if Mr. Goodman said there were no such things as ghosts, then there were no such things as ghosts. Pickle poked his head out of the top of Wilma's backpack, where he was traveling after an unfortunate incident with a hidden pothole and a deep drift of snow, and gave a small, almost imperceptible yowl. Most dogs, when presented with evil criminal elements, can be very brave. But spooks were another matter. What everyone is forgetting, thought Pickle, is that dogs can *see* ghosts. Quite clearly. He'd just have to keep his eyes shut. Yes, he'd do that.

Theodore had reached the flight of heavy stone steps up to the Hoo's front entrance and was tapping his boots against them to knock the snow off. As Wilma approached, she caught sight of Victor peering out from behind one of the large stone pigs that flanked the entrance. He raised a bony finger to his lips as she reached him. "I should be in the stables," he whispered. "Please don't tell anyone I'm here."

Wilma nodded. Victor was her friend, and she wasn't about to get him into trouble. That would never do. Bending down to pretend she was doing up her shoelace, she whispered in his direction, "Last night they found a claw scrawled in blood on the wall with a message from the Fatal Phantom. Did you know?"

Victor looked shocked and pulled his threadbare scarf a little tighter about him. "No!"

"Wilma," called her detective mentor from the steps. "What are you doing?"

"Er . . . nothing . . . I'm coming now."

Victor gave her a grateful smile.

"Mr. Goodman says it must be someone playing tricks for some reason, though, because we don't believe in ghosts," she whispered again.

"I do," said Victor softly with a small, sad smile. "I believe in ghosts."

Pickle gave a whimper from the backpack. "It's all this talk of ghosts. It's making him nervous," Wilma explained. "I'd better go. If you find anything out, let me know!" And with that, she scampered back to Mr. Goodman.

The Blackhearts were in a state of some distress.

Another scrawled claw had been discovered, this time on the dining table, when they came down in the morning, with the words "You shall not take what is mine" written beneath it. Red streaks dripped down the walls and off furniture all around the room. The effect was terrifying. Even Wilma gulped when she entered. "Blood again," gasped the Inspector, peering over Theodore's shoulder.

"Doesn't seem to have the consistency of blood," commented the great detective. He took a small tube from his waistcoat and scooped some of the thick red matter into it. "I'll get Penbert to have a look at that," he added.

"Is it ghost blood?" suggested Wilma. "Perhaps that's why it's different. Although," she added quickly, seeing her mentor's glance, "that can't be, because there's no such thing as ghosts. Like you said."

"Ghastly business," grumbled Lord Blackheart, shaking his head. He was the only member of his family not white-faced and trembling. "Not only is this disturbing everyone at the Hoo, now it's delaying mealtimes. I want you to get to the bottom of it, Goodman, before this gets out of hand."

"The thing is, Lord Blackheart," began the serious and famous detective, with a troubled expression, "I'm not entirely sure that a crime has been committed. Bludsten may or may not have been killed, but either way it was over a century ago. And all of this," he added, gesturing toward the table, "could simply be someone playing pranks. I don't believe in ghosts and I am positive that this house is not being haunted."

"I believe in ghosts," piped up Inspector Lemone, wiping his forehead with a handkerchief and glancing about the room nervously.

"Having said that," the great detective continued, with a despairing glance at Lemone, "it is clear that *something* is afoot. And I suspect it has everything to do with the legend of the missing treasure."

Lord Blackheart paced toward the window, hands clasped behind his back, and stared out of it. "Yes, the missing treasure," he mumbled. "Look here, Goodman," he continued, spinning back around suddenly. "If anyone is going to unravel this mess, it's you. Find the treasure and find the ghost or whoever the culprit responsible for all this nonsense might be. Will you take on the case? I shall employ you in a private capacity, of course. Think the people of Cooper can spare you?"

Wilma's eyes lit up. Another case! She crossed her fingers behind her back. Oh please, let Mr. Goodman take the job! Inspector Lemone, she noticed, also had his fingers crossed. She grinned at him. He didn't grin back, but then, he was wishing for the exact opposite.

Theodore reached for the pipe in his waistcoat pocket, packed it with some rosemary tobacco, and stood deep in thought. This was not his usual kind of commission, but there was something fishy about these goings-on that was piquing his curiosity. He turned and held out his hand. "I will take the case, Lord Blackheart," he said, and they shook on the deal. "But I shall say it again: I am firmly of the belief that there is no haunting here."

At this moment Lady Blackheart, looking drawn and exasperated, burst into the room and fixed Theodore with a steely glare. "That may be your opinion, Mr. Goodman, but I'm not taking any chances. I have seen enough to convince me that something unnatural is afoot. And for that reason," she announced, pulling herself up to her full height, "I have taken the necessary precautions."

Theodore looked a little puzzled. "By which you mean . . . ?"

"I have also employed someone to help," she declared defiantly. "I have engaged someone who can commune with the spirits and perhaps," she added, looking a little coy, "help find the treasure . . . It's Cooper's most talented psychic . . . Fenomina Daise! Her card was left in my room yesterday. And what is more, she is on her way!"

Wilma didn't know what to do. Theodore looked livid, Lemone looked petrified, and Pickle was sitting with his eyes clamped shut. "Would it help if I made a *wooooooooooooh* noise?" she asked, looking around the room. "You know, to get us in the mood?" The stern stare she received from her mentor told her it might not have been the best suggestion she'd made that day.

Onward and upward.

There will always be people in this world who feel the need to make a grand entrance. The fuss that follows a little pomp and circumstance provides a sense of fizz in an otherwise dull existence. Fenomina Daise was one such lady. Not for her a discreet slipping in through a back door. Oh no. She had been delivered to the front of the Hoo in a purple sleigh adorned with bones, skulls, and black dripping candles and pulled by wolves. Wrapped in a heavy fur coat that had a bear's head for a hood and a pair of hefty earmuffs made from dead hedgehogs, she stepped out of her carriage and swept up the stone steps into the pig-laden mansion. With a diamond-studded patch over one eye, she pierced the gloom of the hallway with the other. "I am arrived to confound the supernatural!" she bellowed, holding her arms aloft. "Bring in my equipment!"

Wilma, who had run down to the entrance hall as the sleigh pulled up, was agog. Servants scurried to and from the carriage carrying what seemed to be a never-ending array of peculiar paraphernalia: There was a small round séance table, an ornate marble Ouija board, various prosthetic limbs, an oversized moth net, a map of the constellations, a voluminous clothes trunk, a range of scientific measuring equipment, a large wheel of cheese, and, last of all, one opaque crystal ball.

"Miss Daise," gushed Lady Blackheart, rushing down the staircase with her arms out. "I am so grateful that you've come."

Fenomina closed her one good eye, lifted her face to the ceiling, and breathed in deeply. "I am already sensing the infernal vibrations of a spectral disturbance. You there," she snapped, opening her eye and pointing toward Molly the parlor maid, who was carrying in a large stuffed alligator. "You are worried about money. A man wearing glasses is telling me that you will find the ring next to the soap. And yes, you will get married."

"Oh, my!" gasped the shocked girl.

"And you!" Fenomina steamed on, turning to gaze at Inspector Lemone. "There is a woman in a hat. Your mother! She is shouting 'Get on with it!' Does that mean anything to you?"

Inspector Lemone, startled at the sudden attention, blushed a bright red and mumbled, "I . . . I . . . Goodness! Mother, you say? Well, I . . ."

But Fenomina was on a roll. She spun around to face Theodore, who was standing across the hall, arms folded and looking more incredibly serious than ever before. "You're a man of deep thought," Fenomina wailed, shielding her eye with one hand while reaching out with the other. "No! Don't tell me! An investigator of some kind . . . Can't quite . . ."

"You're right!" shouted Wilma, who was excited to the point of bursting. "He's a detective! Amazing! Can you tell me something? Something about where I come from? And who my parents are?"

Fenomina peered down at the young girl before her. Clearing her throat and rearranging her prickly earmuffs, she gestured toward the heap of equipment. "Bring me my ball."

Wilma ran to the mountain of equipment and lifted the crystal ball from its peak. It was cold and heavy, and as Wilma stared into it, she could make out nothing except a dense fog. "I can't see any clues in this," she said, offering it up to the psychic. "It just looks like a giant marble."

"That's because you do not possess the gift, child," oozed Fenomina, sweeping a velvet cloth over the ball as she took it. "Live here, do you?"

"No, my name's Wilma Tenderfoot. I'm Mr. Goodman's apprentice. I'm going to be a detective one day. I used to live at the Lowside Institute for Woeful Children. I was left there when I was a baby. And then Madam Skratch, my matron, told me I had a relative still alive. I don't know who it is, but it might be my headmistress, Kite Lambard. She's on an adventure, so I haven't been able to ask her yet. Though she did send me a note saying she was coming back on Brackle Day. So I might find some more out then."

"Yes." Fenomina nodded, adopting a hushed tone. "You didn't need to tell me all that. I knew it already."

Theodore rolled his eyes. "Wilma," he said, beckoning to her.

Wilma looked back at Fenomina, but her one good eye was closed as she circled a hand over her crystal ball. Seeing that she was deeply engaged, Wilma scampered over to her mentor.

When grown-ups feel a serious chat coming on, they often assume a stern aspect and put down the other things they're doing so that they can give being serious their full attention. This is why headmasters clasp their hands together when they are telling pupils off. Headmasters (without exception) spend their days secretly doing crosswords and other puzzles and nothing headmasterly at all, and by clamping their fingers together they are stopping themselves from working out the answer to 5 down or whether the dots really do make the shape of a banana. If they didn't stop themselves from solving puzzles while serious-chatting, then they would run a genuine risk of punching the air whenever they got one right and shouting, "That's what I'm talking about! Yeah!" when they should be saying things like, "We are all very disappointed in you, Matthew." And that, of course, would NEVER do.

As Wilma approached her mentor, she could tell by his stern expression that Mr. Goodman, who was already a very famous and serious detective, was probably about to be a bit more serious than usual. "Now then," he began, knitting his fingers together. "I have noticed that you seem to be dangerously close to being suckered in by this nonsense. Take care, Wilma. Remember what I told you about cheap tricks and shenanigans. I don't want you to get hurt or upset because this woman thinks it is acceptable to make something up about your past in order to pretend she has psychic powers. Don't forget your three top tips, Wilma—contemplate, deduct, and stay sharp. These will get you much further than any of this mumbo-jumbo idiocy." He looked even more serious then.

Wilma nodded solemnly. "And I read my Academy textbook chapter about Hunches and Instincts last night. It said when a detective gets a gut feeling about something, then that can be quite useful. Shall I try working on that too, Mr. Goodman?"

"Good idea, Wilma." The great detective smiled.

"Let me see if the ball wants to reveal your secrets," Fenomina suddenly wailed from behind them. Wilma looked over her shoulder as the psychic pulled back the velvet cloth with a flourish. Wilma gasped despite herself. The ball, which had been dull and lifeless, was now swirling with what appeared to be a bright blue mist.

"Ahhhh," whispered Fenomina, her one eye blazing. "The ball speaks to me. It speaks . . . Answers are coming. You do not have long to

114

wait. I see a woman . . . She is trying to find you . . . There are tears in her eyes . . . She is longing to be reunited with you . . . and there is an overwhelming smell of . . . ham! I can smell ham!"

"Ham?" asked Wilma, blinking. "Gosh, Mr. Goodman, do you think that's because of the muslin I was wrapped in? The one that had the lamb chops on it? Do you think it's a message? From my parents?"

A gong sounded behind them. "Lunch is ready, Lady Blackheart," said Portious with a bow. "Boiled gammon and parsley sauce."

Theodore raised his eyebrows and put a gentle hand on his young apprentice's shoulder. "Tricks and shenanigans, Wilma. The smell of ham is merely lunch."

"Oh. Yes. Of course."

"Well, now you're here, Miss Daise," Lady Blackheart said, putting a guiding hand on the psychic's arm, "I suggest we all retire for lunch and gather our strength. The sooner we can banish these banshees, the better!"

"I think eating is the best idea anyone's had all day," agreed Lemone, pacing toward the dining room. "Haven't even had a corn crumble all morning. It's a wonder I'm still alive."

It is a well-known fact that small and determined little girls are VERY good at giving themselves stern talking-tos. As everyone made their way toward the dining room, Wilma screwed her hands into fists and reminded herself out loud once and for all—"Ghosts don't exist; there's no such thing as a psychic; it's all tricks and shenanigans." She MUST remember this if she was to be any help at all to Mr. Goodman in finding the tricksters or the treasure and prove herself the outstanding detective apprentice she was sure she was capable of being.

"It is clear," Fenomina was opining when Wilma arrived in the dining room with Pickle at her heels, "that the Hoo is in the talons of a terrible aura. I can taste it, I can smell it, and soon, I hope, I shall be able to see it." She extracted what looked like a saltshaker from her billowing sleeve and proceeded to sprinkle a black dust over her plate. "Crushed insects," she explained when she looked up and saw Wilma staring. "It helps with my spiritual connections."

Wilma suppressed a grimace.

"Sorry I'm late," muttered Dr. Flatelly, coming in through the doorway. "I lost track of time. I have been poring over papers all morning."

"Found out what that key fits yet?" asked Tarquin as nonchalantly as he could.

"Not yet, no," replied the archaeologist, sitting down next to Mr. Goodman. "Although there seem to be references to a diary kept by Bludsten Blackheart himself. Sadly, I don't know where it is."

Wilma, whose mouth was full of gammon, choked a little at the mention of the diary. It was sitting quite happily in her pinafore pocket. With all the hoo-ha, she'd plain forgotten about it. She reached to pull it out but stopped. Perhaps she should keep hold of it for the time being— she hadn't even looked at it properly herself. And she was the apprentice detective, not Dr. Flatelly. And when she'd contemplated it thoroughly and drawn some useful deductions, THEN she could take it to Mr. Goodman and impress him.

"I am sensing," Fenomina whispered suddenly, "that someone here is under a most dreadful cloud. I have no wish to alarm, but spirits can sometimes affix themselves to a physical body. A conduit, if you like."

"Is it Pickle?" asked Lemone, wolfing down a spoonful of mashed potato. "He gets up to some pretty devilish mischief, don't you, boy?" Pickle sniffed. That was practically *libel*.

But Fenomina stared wildly about the table and rose slowly as if in a trance. The lights overhead flickered and died momentarily. "Feeling getting stronger," she mumbled. "Someone here is being used as an agent of malevolence. They may not even realize it! It's not you, Lord Blackheart! Nor you, Lady Blackheart!" The psychic's one good eye and glinting eye patch rested momentarily on Inspector Lemone, who had a bread roll stuffed in his cheeks. "Neither is it you, sir!" she continued, moving onward as the Inspector slumped forward with relief. "I am sensing no otherworldly forces in you, Master Blackheart. Your maids are free of spectral torment! Neither is it the butler!" Portious's long face drooped even further at the reprieve. Fenomina's gaze moved toward Goodman. She wavered. "Wait . . . No! It's all right! Our detective friend is perfectly safe!"

"I think this should stop," said Theodore, standing up. "You are making people distressed."

But Fenomina ignored him. One eye glaring, she lifted her arm and began to extend a finger toward . . . "Wilma? No!" Suddenly, spinning on the spot, her accusing finger came to rest on Belinda Blackheart. "It is you!" wailed Fenomina. "The youngest Blackheart! You are possessed by the tortured spirit of the unburied Bludsten Blackheart! And look! As if my testimony wasn't proof enough! Look at her chair! Dripping with ectoplasm!"

Wilma leaped to her feet to see a green gloopy mush surrounding Belinda's seat.

"The physical evidence of a spiritual energy!" Fenomina expounded.

Pickle, extra-sensitive to all manner of ghoulish

commotions, crawled under the table, where he was able to take comfort in a small scrap of discarded gammon. Lemone, equally thin-skinned when it came to spooks, dealt with the onset of this particular crisis by quietly putting a napkin over his face so that he didn't have to see anything. Everyone else jumped up from their chairs and stared.

All eyes were on Belinda. Shocked, the girl looked down at herself, saw the strange greenish slime surrounding her, screamed, and fainted. "Quickly! You, butler man," said Fenomina as she and Lady Blackheart rushed to the girl's side, "you're nearest. Help me get her to a sofa."

As Portious and the psychic carried Belinda from the room, Lord Blackheart threw down his napkin. "Well, I know you seem set in your ideas, Goodman," he yelled, "but by the look of things, this house is in the grip of a haunting!"

"No," mumbled Theodore, his jaw set tight. "It is not. Wilma," he added, gesturing toward his apprentice, "despite my initial reservations, I am now convinced that criminal activity is afoot. It is quite clear to me that the prospect of treasure has turned minds to nefarious deeds."

Wilma scrunched her nose up. "Neffy-what?" she asked.

"Nefarious," explained Theodore. "It means wicked. Quite wicked, in fact. I want you to arrange an operations room and get a Clue Board up and running. I'll let you have first go at it, especially as you seemed quite keen to list suspects when we first arrived. Stick with current Hoo residents—I think the weather rules out anyone else. But I only want to see *facts* when I return—like who might have a motive to pretend to be a spook and why." Mr. Goodman cast a quick glance at his fob watch. "I had hoped to return to Clarissa Cottage by mid-afternoon," he said, "given that the weather is worsening. But we have no choice. There are leads to follow and theorems to formulate. I'll take a sample of this 'ectoplasm' and see if Portious can have it sent over to the lab along with that blood before the snow sets in. I'll use that as an excuse to do some questioning of the staff with Inspector Lemone. Nothing too intrusive, just a gentle sniffing out. Good. I'll see you in an hour, Wilma. I'll have a look at your Clue Board then."

Wilma gave a small nod. Despite being THRILLED to be asked to prepare a Clue Board, she couldn't help but be puzzled. Mr. Goodman was always saying a proper detective needs proper evidence. Well, now there was ecto-plasm and everything! How did you explain that humanly, she wondered.

Baffling, isn't it?

11

Barbu was peering out from behind a statue of a giant saddleback pig, his eyes narrowed to slits. "Is that her again?" he hissed to the companions at his back. "The one with the wet face?"

"Yes. That's Belinda Blackheart. Looks as if she's crying, master," answered Janty, poking his head over Barbu's shoulder. "Which is perfect. This book on wooing a lady says that a gentleman should always offer assistance to a woman in distress."

"Right, then," answered Barbu, pulling down his waistcoat. "I shall intercept her immediately. What am I supposed to say to her again?" he added, clicking his fingers.

Janty flicked through the book in his hand. "You might like to start with a general comment on the weather, then say something nice about her appearance."

"Nice?" moaned Barbu. "Oh, very well. Sooner I get this over with, the better. Once Belinda Blackheart is hooked, we can turn our minds to ridding ourselves of the other Blackhearts. And Janty, I want you to start looking for some building blueprints. There were no obvious hiding places for treasure on the ground plans the butler brought us—I'm not even sure they were for this property! Tully, you stay here in case she tries anything *romantic*."

Belinda had been carried from the dining room to a chaise longue in the rear hall, where she was now in something of a state. Having regained consciousness, she had slumped against a wooden plinth and was sobbing uncontrollably. "Oh, look!" called Barbu as he approached her. "It's . . . general comment about the weather . . . snowing . . ." He wafted a hand vaguely in the direction of the window. Belinda stared at him blankly and sniffed. Barbu stared back. "Sorry, I've dried up. Tully!" he shouted over his shoulder. "What's the next bit?"

"Appearance, master," the henchman called from his hiding place.

"Oh yes." Barbu cleared his throat and examined Belinda once more. Her eyes were red and puffy, her nose was snotty, and she was gulping like a frog. There was a short, awkward silence. "I think I'll skip that bit," he said eventually, with a grimace. "You might want to blow your nose. You're dripping onto your shoes."

Belinda pulled a long handkerchief out from the sleeve of her dress and blew into it loudly. "I'm a conduit for evil!" she wailed.

Barbu blinked. "Really? Oh well, things *are* looking up. Perhaps we can have another chat when you're less . . . damp."

Belinda, still leaking tears, swallowed and nodded with a sniff. Stepping forward she placed her hand on Barbu's forearm. "Thank you for being so nice to me, Mr. D'Anvers."

Barbu knocked her hand away swiftly and

looked toward the pig statue for help. Tully was pointing toward his mouth and grinning exaggeratedly. "Oh heavens," groaned Barbu, "I have to *smile*." Turning back to Belinda, who was staring down at him devotedly, the reluctant villain slowly creaked his mouth into a fixed and painful grin. The rogue was hating every second of it, but when there's a means to an end, a gentleman of no morals will do ANYTHING.

"What on earth . . ." began Theodore as he walked into the upstairs boot room that now had a hand-scrawled note on it reading:

OPERATIONS ROOM. DETECTIVES ONLY (AND APPRENTICES) (AND DOG)

Before him was a host of clutter. Chairs were upside down, boots had been cleared from shelves, and the walls were covered with strange hand-drawn images of the current Blackheart family, while in the center of the room there was a hat stand with a walking stick strapped horizontally across it.

Wilma appeared from behind a large pile of Wellington boots. "I'm going to drape one of the curtains over that," she said, pointing toward the hat stand, "as a visual clue of what the Fatal Phantom might look like if we meet him. Or her."

"Or if it even exists," added Mr. Goodman with a lift of his eyebrows.

"Indeed," agreed Wilma, trying her best to sound like a proper detective. "And Portious has lent me this large wooden tea tray, which I've managed to turn into a Clue Board. Though there is a bit of crusted porridge on it. Which I can't get off."

"Hmmm," pondered Theodore, looking about him. "Well, it's not strictly regular, but . . . not a bad idea, Wilma."

Wilma grinned delightedly.

"Although I'm not sure we'll need all the papier-mâché balloon heads you appear to have made."

"There's a balloon head to represent everyone who works at the Hoo, Mr. Goodman. It's taken ages," explained Wilma, pointing to the one Theodore had picked up. "That's Mrs. Moggins. I found some hair down the back of the sofa, so I made her mustache with it."

The great and serious detective blinked, put the balloon head down, and quietly wiped his hands with a handkerchief. "Now then," he said, regaining his composure, "what have we got to go on? This is a strange case for us. After all, the only body is over a century old and mostly irrelevant, and no real crime seems to have been committed. Yet. Though we may have a treasure to find."

"Well, I know it's a lot more wonky than we're used to, but I reckoned if I thought about it like a normal case, then that might make it less so." Wilma heaved the wooden tea tray Clue Board into view. "We know that a body was discovered at the bottom of the Blackheart Hoo estate. Dr. Flatelly—that's him there in the hat—is pretty certain that it's Bludsten Blackheart." She took a picture of Bludsten that she'd cut from a book and pinned it to the board. "In his hand was a key," she added, sticking up another hand-drawn picture, "that might lead to a lost treasure. Since the discovery of the body and the key, there have been unexplained events . . ." Wilma stopped and looked up, cleared her throat and carried on. "Unexplained events, like the bloody messages, that suggest the Hoo might be being haunted by a Fatal Phantom summoned by Bludsten Blackheart to guard his buried treasure! The same Fatal Phantom that frightened him to death! Not only that, but the ectoplasm at lunch seemed to suggest that Belinda Blackheart was possessed—by the ghost of the unburied Bludsten Blackheart, according to Miss Daise. Here's the picture I drew of Belinda being possessed." Wilma held up her drawing before rushing on. "But since spooks don't exist, which is good because otherwise all that could be considered QUITE scary, that means . . . er . . ."

Theodore nodded encouragingly as he reached for his pipe and began packing it with rosemary tobacco. "Exactly, Wilma. Since ghosts don't exist, all those unexplained events could also suggest that somebody wishes to create the *illusion* of a haunting. Have you thought about that?"

"No, I haven't," chipped in Inspector Lemone

with a small shrug, walking into the room. "Haven't thought about that at all. Ooh," he added, giving the room a sniff. "Smells of cheese. Don't suppose there is any? I'm a bit peckish."

"No. It's not cheese, just loads of stinky tennis shoes," explained Wilma, continuing to point at her Clue Board. "I haven't really thought about it, no, Mr. Goodman. Because it's so unusual, it's sort of hard to know what the case is."

"As far as I am concerned," explained Theodore patiently, "our case is to find out who is causing all this mischief. Somebody is deliberately setting out to scare people, and we need to put a stop to it. Everything to do with this case hinges on *why* these so-called hauntings are taking place. So let's start with the basics, Wilma. Motives."

Wilma screwed her face up in thought. "Well, obviously the main motive is the treasure. And the spookiness is doing quite a good job of making people not want to find it. In case it goes extra-spooky. So perhaps it's someone who wants the treasure all to themselves. And people who want treasure are often people who need money.

And something I have noticed is that even though the Blackhearts have loads of money, they also sort of haven't got any at all. And everything is a bit old-looking and shabby."

Mr. Goodman nodded and lit his pipe. "Well observed, Wilma," he said, taking a deep puff. "I think you might be right. And that means that each and every Hoo resident may be keen to increase their personal funds. What we're looking for is anyone with a greater motive than the others. Perhaps someone has a debt, or plans that require a vast sum of money."

"Oh, wait," said Wilma, picking up some scruffy-looking white canvas sneakers that had faces drawn on the toes. "These are Molly and Polly," she explained. "I ran out of balloons. I'm not sure if they have a debt or big plans, but they did look a bit shifty when Dr. Flatelly was talking about the treasure."

"Everyone did," Lemone blustered.

"Hmm," pondered Mr. Goodman. "When I was asking Portious to send off those samples to Penbert, I did discover that Molly and Polly are hoping to leave the Hoo and open a String Emporium. And not only that, but Portious is looking to retire soon. Both of these things require money." He paused thoughtfully. "Now then, there is one thing missing on your Clue Board, and that's a blueprint of the Hoo. I'll stay here with Lemone and add our new suspects and motives to the board while you go to the map room and see what you can find. Off you go."

As Wilma headed out of the boot room door, there was a sudden strange creak and a scrabbling sound, and she thought she saw a shadow disappearing down the darkened corridor, so she had to remind herself that ghosts just DID. NOT. EXIST! She had to tell herself she believed it too.

The map room was in the west wing of the Hoo on the second floor just past the kite closet. It was a large, dusty room flanked on one side by tall rectangular windows hung with heavy velvet curtains and on the other by shelves, and there was a smell of dampness as if the place needed a good airing. Wilma knew that she was there to find the blueprints of the estate, but this was the first chance she'd had since lunch to sneak a look at Bludsten's diary, and it might prove to be better than a map! She pulled a chair out from one of the room's many long tables and took the diary from her pinafore pocket. The small, battered leather felt almost silky to the touch where the years had softened its once firm surface. Carefully, Wilma opened it. There, at the front, was the hand-drawn claw, then the rock pictures.

"Some of the pages are covered in writing," Wilma whispered to Pickle under the table as she flicked through the front part of the diary, "but it's almost impossible to read. It's like a spider's been dipped in ink and left to run riot." She peered a little closer. "Hang on, what's this?"

Wilma had found a page that was folded over on itself and sealed at both ends, making it a sort of envelope. "There's some scraps of paper in here," she mumbled, sliding them out with a finger. "Just squiggles with village names at the end of them. But why would they be kept specially?"

Wilma popped them back and continued flicking through. "There's blank pages here and there as well. And symbols of some sort. And look at the page at the back. The handwriting's gone all strange . . . 'He haunts me . . . Death . . . Murderer . . . He comes . . .' My goodness! That sounds awful. And a bit cursed, if I'm honest. Even if we don't believe in spooks. Can't see anything obvious about where the treasure might be. But then, I suppose if you buried a treasure, you wouldn't want it to be found easily, would you?"

Then, as she pushed back her chair, she heard a small noise behind her. She stopped and listened. "Victor," she called out quietly, "is that you?" Nothing. The lamp on the reading table flickered. Wilma gulped and reached for Pickle's paw. "There's no such thing as ghosts," she whispered. "There's no such thing as ghosts . . ."

Pickle glanced up to see the petrified look on Wilma's face. He gave a small snort. He hated spooks too, but he was going to have to be brave. The noise came again, this time a little louder, as if something was dragging itself across the floor. Pickle, ears pricked, slowly slunk toward the sound, Wilma tiptoeing behind him. It came from the far end of the map room, where dim recesses hid largely forgotten documents. As he drew close to the darkened alcove, Pickle suddenly gave a deep growl, the hair on his back bristling. Wilma felt her heart thumping in her chest. But she was a detective's apprentice! And in the Case of the Blown Nose, Mr. Goodman did multiple creepings in darkened circumstances! Ghosts or no ghosts, this could be the golden opportunity she'd been waiting for. Perhaps she and Pickle had caught the ghastly ghoul or frightful fake in the act of scrawling threats! Perhaps they could somehow apprehend it. With a small gulp and steeling her nerves, Wilma clamped her eyes shut and gathered every brave bone in her body, then shot quickly around the corner of the alcove, forcing her eyes open as she did so. She gasped. "Janty! What are you doing here?"

The boy scowled at her from under his heavy curls. "None of your business," he snapped, picking up the papers that he had just dropped on the floor.

"I thought you were at the Institute for Woeful Children," continued Wilma, bending down to help him. "You were sent there with Barbu at the end of the Case of the Putrid Poison. I hope it hasn't been too awful. I know what a terrible place it can be. Hang on a minute," she added, realizing what they were gathering up from the floor, "these are maps of Blackheart Hoo! What would you be wanting with these?"

Janty snatched the drawings from her hands. "Like I said," he replied curtly, "keep your nose out. My master and I are here to claim a debt, and we shall be staying until we get it!"

Wilma's eyes widened. "Barbu D'Anvers is here? At Blackheart Hoo? And what debt?" she added, remembering her earlier conversation with Mr. Goodman.

"Tarquin Blackheart's," answered the boy crossly. "My master beat him at cards yesterday and he owes us a lot of money. Not just us, according to the casino. He hasn't got it, of course, so we're taking it by other methods."

"Tarquin gambles and owes lots of money?"

pondered Wilma, blinking. "Goodness. That shoves him right up the Likely Suspects list, what with him being desperate and everything. Hang on!" she gasped, the penny dropping. "Other methods? Barbu's here to find the missing treasure, isn't he? Of course he is! Finders Keepers means whoever gets to it first has sole claim! And if he finds it he'll be able to buy back Rascal Rock and carry on his dastardly deeds! Janty, you must stop helping him! Why don't you give me the plans and help us instead?" She put a warm hand on his arm pleadingly.

Janty paused. For a moment it seemed as if he was about to say something, but then he shook his head vehemently. "You still don't get it, do you?" He pushed her hand away and shoved past her with the maps in his arms. "I LIKE working for Barbu D'Anvers. I LIKE being bad. Like . . . like my dad was. But then, I don't expect you to understand, what with you being a *girl*."

Wilma's eyes narrowed as she followed him. "There is nothing wrong with being a girl, Janty. I can do anything and everything that you can. And

I'll tell you this: I know the difference between right and wrong. The course you're taking is a path to ruin. No good will come of it." Pickle grumbled in agreement.

Janty stared back at her one last time. "At least the path to ruin is never dull," he muttered. "Now leave me alone."

Wilma watched regretfully as the boy stormed from the library. This was a worrying state of affairs. Not only was Barbu D'Anvers somewhere on the estate, but he was now a serious threat to Mr. Goodman's investigations, and even worse, Janty had beaten Wilma to the blueprints. If only she had done what she'd been asked to do instead of concentrating on impressing Mr. Goodman, then she might not be in such a sticky mess. Again. That was two Golden Rules—following orders and NOT mucking things up spectacularly—broken in one! Wilma screwed her face up in thought. "Well, we did get a massive new clue about Tarquin Blackheart and the debt," she said. "And I've got the diary—even if I don't know what to do with it. And it's up to us to warn Mr.

Goodman about Barbu D'Anvers! Maybe those things will make up for the rubbishy bits. Come on, Pickle. We need to get a move on."

"Stuck here?" wailed Inspector Lemone, pacing around the drawing room. "I knew it! We shouldn't have come! And now we're trapped!"

"Hopefully it won't be for long, Inspector," said Theodore with a small sigh. "But there'll be no getting back to Clarissa Cottage tonight. Not in this weather."

"Mr. Goodman!" yelled Wilma, rushing into the room, Pickle on her heels. "Terrible news. Barbu D'Anvers is here with Janty. And guess what? They're after the treasure! They've just arrived, so I don't think THEY'RE the pretend ghosts, but nonetheless . . ."

A deep frown set into the detective's face. "Are you quite sure, Wilma? Nobody has mentioned him being here."

"I just saw Janty in the map room," she panted. "He said they're here to collect a debt. Apparently Tarquin owes him loads of money."

"Is that so?" said Theodore, reaching for his notebook. "How interesting."

"And Janty took the plans of the estate you asked me to fetch," Wilma added quickly. "He beat me to them, Mr. Goodman. I'm very sorry."

Theodore let out a small exasperated groan and rested his hand on the mantelpiece above the fire, staring thoughtfully into the flames. "All right," he said eventually, looking back up. "This changes everything. It is imperative that we find that treasure before Barbu D'Anvers. We can worry about the whos, whys, and wherefores after. The game is on, Wilma. The game is on!"

Indeed it is. But WHO will get to the treasure first?

12

"Yes. The presence of Barbu D'Anvers," repeated Theodore, "has made finding the treasure our top priority. You can write that down in your notebook if you like, Wilma."

Wilma beamed and made a quick scribble. "This is like when you solved the Case of the Dodgy Duck. Do you remember? Barbu turned up then too, didn't he? Disguised as a chicken."

"He did, yes," answered Theodore, twitching his mustache. "But back to this case—without those plans we are at a disadvantage."

Wilma's eyes flashed. "The thing is, Mr. Goodman," she began, reaching into her pocket, "I have this. It's Bludsten Blackheart's diary."

The great detective dashed to her side. "Well done, Wilma. But where did you find it?"

"In the library. Vic . . . I mean, I . . . It's very hard to read . . . it's full of funny symbols and pictures, but I did find these . . ." Opening the diary, Wilma thumbed her way to the page that was folded over and sealed at the top and bottom. Inside the improvised envelope were the three pieces of paper. Wilma hopped down from the sofa and laid them out on the floor. "The lines on the papers just look like random squiggles, but I think what you might call a Hunchy Instinct tells me Bludsten must have made them for something. And look—Cooper village names as well."

Mr. Goodman bent over to study the papers. "Interesting," he murmured. "I wonder . . . if these squiggles are routes."

"Like on a map? Do you think it's anything to do with the treasure?"

"Yes. If we plotted these routes over an old

map of Cooper, we might have ourselves a clue."
Theodore nodded. "Good work, Wilma."

Wilma beamed. She'd gotten something right
at last.

"What we need now," continued Theodore, "is
a map of Cooper that was drawn in the time of
Bludsten Blackheart. Wilma, Inspector Lemone,
we're going to see Dr. Flatelly. We shall need
snowshoes. Can you find Portious and see if he
has some we can use, please, Wilma?"

"Now then, is everyone ready?" Twenty minutes
later, the great detective brushed down his mustache and straightened up from a final fiddle with
his shoes.

Inspector Lemone, trussed to within an inch of
his life in winter coats, nodded. "Ready as ever!"
he shouted through three scarves.

"I know they're for table tennis, but they're
going to have to do, Pickle," said Wilma, tying
the small battered paddles to her despairing
hound's feet. "Portious didn't have snowshoes
small enough for you. And I can't carry you

all the way to Dr. Flatelly's office. And he only had two, so I'll put this tea strainer and cheese grater on your front paws. How's that?" Wilma stood back and admired her makeshift weather gear for dogs. Pickle gazed up at her with the sort of woebegone expression of defeat that only a beagle can muster. He looked like an idiot and he knew it.

"Good," said Theodore. "This shouldn't take long. Dr. Flatelly's temporary office is only a short walk from the main house. We need to take the path that goes around the ornamental gardens."

"But where is the path?" asked Inspector Lemone, shielding his eyes from the onslaught of snow as they stepped out of the door. "Can barely see a thing. Hang on . . ." he added, peering into the distance. "Is that someone coming?"

Wilma turned and looked. A hunched figure was trudging toward them carrying what looked to be a tray. "It can't be!" she gasped, eyes widening.

The woolly figure, covered in snow, shoved its second bobble hat upward. "Mr. Goodman," began the woman revealed beneath, narrowly avoiding skidding over in her knitted Wellingtons, "I thought I'd bring you some peppermint tea and a few corn crumbles. I've kept the tea in a hot-water bottle, so it should be fine. The corn crumbles have frozen solid on the way here, but stick them in your armpits and they'll be edible again in about half an hour."

"Mrs. Speckle," said an appalled Theodore, extending a chivalrous arm to stop her from slipping again. "You didn't need to come. The weather is atrocious."

"All the same," wheezed the no-nonsense housekeeper, "your mid-afternoon snacks are my responsibility, and I'll not have anyone else giving you substandard biscuits."

Inspector Lemone, who as we all know was always romantically overwhelmed in Mrs. Speckle's presence, gulped and took one of the biscuits from the ice-covered tray. Still staring at her, and without thinking, he put the rock-solid corn crumble to his lips and bit down. His face contorted. "Think I've broken a tooth," he whimpered. "And the biscuit's stuck to my lip," he added, giving it a tug to no avail. "Can't seem to get it off."

"You shall have to stay at the Hoo until this weather improves," said Mr. Goodman as he helped his housekeeper up the icy stone steps. "I'm sure Mrs. Moggins the cook can accommodate you."

"Mrs. Moggins?" Mrs. Speckle snapped. "*Miranda* Moggins? She can't even make a decent pea soup! And her corn crumbles! Well, the less said about *them* the better. Thank goodness I'm here. This is more serious than I thought." Inspector Lemone, biscuit still stuck to his bottom lip, watched awestruck as Mrs. Speckle slid sideways through the front doors of the Hoo. She had come to save him. He just *knew* it.

The walk to Irascimus Flatelly's shack was a struggle despite its short distance. The wind was howling and the snow was still falling in thick, soft flakes. As they finally stood at his door untying their snowshoes, Wilma stared upward. The sky was heavy and low. She shivered. There were so many things to think about: the mummy, the treasure, the fake spook and psychic, and now Barbu, up to no good as usual, and yet . . . She felt as if there was something more. Something obvious that she wasn't putting her finger on. This was what her textbook meant about Hunchy Instincts, she reminded herself. It was all very well having them, of course, but no good at all if you couldn't figure out what they were. As it was, it felt more like a mild case of indigestion than anything else. But one day, Wilma reasoned, she'd get to the bottom of her Hunchy Instinct. Until then, she'd just have to keep burping.

Dr. Flatelly's office was a jumble of archaeological flotsam. Old bones and broken bits of pottery were scattered across every surface, tall umbrella stands stood packed with rolled-up parchments, maps lay in heaps, and on the wall, much to Pickle's alarm, there hung a skeleton in full dinner dress and top hat.

Irascimus was on his hands and knees surrounded by open books and scattered documents, and as Theodore shook the snow from his over-coat, Wilma couldn't help but notice that the archaeologist looked a little put out.

"Mr. Goodman," he said, standing up, "I wasn't expecting you. Sorry . . . I've moved everything from my usual office on the other side of the island up here to the estate . . . wasn't sure what I'd need so I brought it all . . . er . . . everything's a bit of a jumble . . . I've been throwing myself into my work rather . . ."

"So I can see," said Theodore, bending down to pick up a plate and cup that were on the floor by his feet. "Here," he added, handing them to Iras-cimus. "Best to put these somewhere they won't get broken."

"Yes," answered the archaeologist, seeming a little rattled. He took the dirty crockery and placed it on the table, where there was another plate and cup and a ketchup bottle. "Anyway, what can I do for you?"

"I found Bludsten Blackheart's diary!" Wilma blurted out. Theodore shot her one of his more serious glances.

Dr. Flatelly's eyes widened. "Really?" he spluttered excitedly. "Where is it? Can I see?"

Wilma reached into her pinafore pocket and pulled out the battered red leather-bound book. "I can show it to you," she said, assuming a very serious tone, "but it is an official clue. In an official case. So I'll just keep one hand on it at all times, if that's all right."

"What we need," interjected Mr. Goodman, "is an old map of Cooper. One that was made during Bludsten's time. We have found some reference points in the diary and have a hunch about them."

Irascimus blinked and looked up from the diary, which he had been frantically flicking through while Wilma hovered possessively. "Old map?" he muttered. "Yes. Sure there's something here somewhere." He looked around him. "Sorry, place is rather a mess. Moved things about. Not quite sure . . ."

"Might it be in that tall basket that's got MAPS written on it?" asked Wilma, pointing toward a wicker bin stuffed with rolls of dusty-looking paper.

"Well spotted, Wilma!" said Theodore, twiddling the magnifying glass that hung from his waistcoat pocket.

"Silly me." Irascimus laughed a little nervously. "What with all this recent excitement, I'm forgetting the whats and wherefores! Right, then," he declared, extracting a handful of maps. "Let's have a look, shall we?"

Inspector Lemone helped clear a space on the large wooden table in the center of the room so that the maps could be unrolled and laid out. Flately frowned at him. "You seem to have a biscuit stuck to your bottom lip, Inspector," he said, pointing.

"Yes," mumbled Lemone, looking a little embarrassed. "I know."

Wilma, Bludsten's diary still in hand, moved a wooden stool over to the table and climbed up onto it so that she could see properly. Theodore and Irascimus were flicking through the large, brittle-edged parchments, discarding those that weren't what they were looking for. Gentlemen love maps. They can stare at them for hours. If ever you want a grown-up man to be quiet, give him a map. You won't hear another peep. This is why men often put maps in bathrooms. They're not washing when in there. They're just staring at the maps. Ridiculous!

"Ah-ha!" said Irascimus as they finally unfolded an ancient-looking map of massive proportions. "This looks like the thing. We need something heavy to hold down one edge."

Thinking quickly, Wilma hopped down from her stool and lifted Pickle onto the table.

Irascimus stared at the bedraggled hound. "Is that a tea strainer on his foot?"

"Oops! I forgot to take his snow gear off when we got here. Sorry, Pickle," Wilma said.

Pickle sighed. He liked to think of himself as a noble hound, brimful of destiny and digni-fied deeds. But here he was, soaked to the skin in his snow-covered knitted duffel coat, ears pinned back with pegs, booted into all manner of kitchen implements and being used as an over-sized paperweight. This wasn't how he thought his life would turn out. It really wasn't.

"Wilma," said Theodore, having a quick look at the map through his magnifying glass, "get out those reference points, would you? Dr. Flatelly, we're going to need a ruler, as long as you can find, and a pencil."

Wilma leaned forward onto the table and, resting on her elbows, opened up Bludsten's diary to the page that was doubled over. Pulling out the three scraps of paper hidden inside, she unfolded them and began to read. "The first one says That Place Under There to That Place Over There."

"Here you go, Goodman," chipped in Inspector Lemone, handing the great detective the archaeologist's ruler. "We couldn't find a pencil, but I have got this red crayon in my top pocket."

The detective gave his friend a quizzical look.

"I was making Mrs. Speckle a Brackle Day card . . . ahem! Well, never mind that now. Here you are."

Theodore took the implements and laying the ruler down on the map, drew a fine line between the two reference points. "Next one please, Wilma."

"Beach to Measly Down," replied Wilma, reading from the second piece of paper.

Theodore drew again. "And the last, thank you."

"Scraggy Point to Hare Forest, Mr. Goodman. That's it."

Wilma put the papers away, closed the diary, and lifted herself up so that she could see better. As Theodore drew the last mark it was quite clear that the three lines had created one small triangle on the map. "Drop Dead Gorge!" she whispered breathlessly as she realized what the triangle surrounded.

"Interesting," mumbled Irascimus. "Almost inaccessible, grisly place. I wonder . . . Hang on a minute. I was looking at something that mentioned Drop Dead Gorge before you arrived . . ." He turned and shoveled through a mound of papers on a sideboard. "Yes. Here we are. An invoice for a box of dynamite to be delivered to Drop Dead Gorge over a century ago. It must be connected! It must be the location of Bludsten's hidden gold mine!"

Theodore straightened up. "One thing's for sure: However deathly a place, we shall have to investigate. The treasure is unlikely to be hidden there, but it may yield more clues."

"And if by chance the treasure *is* there," whispered Inspector Lemone, "then the Fatal Phantom won't be far away . . ."

Pickle shifted uneasily. He hoped not. He REALLY did.

Mr. Goodman took out his pocket watch and looked at it. "This is all very promising, but I fear it's too late to do anything further today. We'll return to the Hoo and report to Lord Blackheart. Then I suggest we make a start at first light. Will you be returning to the house with us, Dr. Flatelly?"

"No," the archaeologist replied, looking fired up. "I think my time will be best spent here. See if I can find out anything more about the mine and that key. But I shall join you in the morning, if I may. I'm sure I can be of assistance."

"Then it is agreed," said Theodore with a nod. "Early tomorrow!"

Wilma said nothing, but that Hunchy Instinct feeling was coming back again. What did it mean? And why couldn't she work it out? She looked up from the ancient map and did a massive belch. Everyone turned and looked at her. "Sorry," she said, with a small, embarrassed grin. "My instincts keep repeating on me."

13

Dusk was drawing in and as Mr. Goodman and his companions arrived back at the Hoo, a strange, ethereal light bathed the main house. "Looks like a good evening for spooks," Wilma whispered to her shuddering hound. "If they existed, of course."

Pickle trembled and looked around anxiously.

The house was strangely dark as they entered. The gas lights that normally fizzed through the gloom were all extinguished. "Funny," commented Inspector Lemone. "Wh-wh-what's going on?"

Wilma, hearing footsteps coming toward them, spun in the direction of the sound and was startled to see the face of Portious looming over her, illuminated by a single candle. "I'm afraid the weather has knocked out our gas supply," he explained, his features exaggerated in the flickering beam. "Everyone is gathered in the upper sitting room. We have lit candles and Miss Daise is taking the opportunity to have a séance." Wilma and Inspector Lemone looked blank. "In an attempt to summon the dead," Portious added.

"Oooh," moaned Inspector Lemone anxiously. "Shall I go back to Flatelly's? He said he had work to do. He might need a hand."

"No," replied Theodore, glancing up the large staircase. "I need you with me, Inspector. I think this is something we ought to see." The butler led the way.

Wilma grinned with glee. A séance! She'd read about them. They were like party invites for spirits! Or fake ones, at least. Surely this would be the moment Mr. Goodman would be proved right—the séance would either be a flop because there were no ghosts, or whoever was faking it was bound to get caught. With Mr. Goodman in the room together with an expert apprentice detective like her . . . well, it was inevitable.

The upper sitting room was a small, dark place. As usual in the Hoo, heavy velvet curtains were drawn across every window and half-burned candles in dusty glass globes were dotted about. Nobody was speaking, and the eerie mood sent a chill down Wilma's spine. She shivered a little, despite her bravado. To distract herself, she looked around. The center of the space was dominated by a large circular wooden table around which sat Lord and Lady Blackheart, Tarquin, and Fenomina Daise. The psychic was wearing a dramatic flowing gown covered in stars (with matching eye patch) and had her one good eye closed while pinching the top of her nose. Between Tarquin and Fenomina, there was an empty chair. Wilma glanced quickly around the room. All the servants were there. Mrs. Moggins was standing wringing the hem of her apron anxiously, Portious was picking something from a fingernail in front of a half-decorated Brackle Bush, and Molly and Polly were huddled together in a corner. Wilma noticed that they were whispering and pointing in the direction of a small writing desk with a lock on it. There was no sign of Belinda or the ghastly Barbu D'Anvers and his gang. Nor could Wilma see any sign of Victor.

A knitted figure pushed her way through the assembled company. It was Mrs. Speckle and she was carrying her trusty tray. "Mr. Goodman," she puffed, "I took the liberty of bringing a few tea things to the séance for you. I knew you'd be chilled after your walk."

"There are sufficient tea things already laid out," hissed the cook, Mrs. Moggins, who was hard on her heels.

"I'm happy to eat both kinds of biscuits," proffered Inspector Lemone in a conciliatory fashion.

Mrs. Speckle shot him a deadly glance. "You'll do no such thing!" she barked. "You'll eat my corn crumbles or nothing!"

"Oh!" replied Inspector Lemone, startled. "I mean to say . . ." He gulped and ran a finger around the inside if his collar as he tried to back away slowly. Just then the door behind them all opened to reveal Belinda, flanked by Barbu D'Anvers and Janty. It was the first time Wilma had seen Barbu since the end of their last case, and he looked as dastardly as ever.

Lord Blackheart stood up. "Who in the blue blazes are you?" he demanded of the diminutive villain.

"These are my house guests, father," Tarquin blustered. "They came to visit me just as the snow was worsening. Naturally, I couldn't let them leave. Not when the storm is raging. I would have said something, but what with all this other unpleasantness, I never found the right moment and—"

"Lord Blackheart," interrupted Theodore, "house guests or no, I feel I must inform you that the man with your daughter is none other than Barbu D'Anvers, a notorious Criminal Element. I am not suggesting that he has as yet done anything untoward in this house, but his presence is a cause for concern."

"Well said, Mr. Goodman," announced Wilma, giving Barbu her crossest stare.

"Criminal Element? In my house? Then I shall ask you to leave, sir. Immediately!" bellowed Lord Blackheart.

"Oh, always sticking your nose in where it's not wanted, Goodman," said Barbu with a dismissive wave of his hand. "I'm afraid I can't leave," he went on, turning to address Lord Blackheart. "The thing is, your son owes me a great deal of money."

Tarquin reddened.

"And I shall remain here until I have my satisfaction." Barbu smirked. "I'm sure you wouldn't want all of Cooper to know that the Blackhearts can't pay their debts. The honor of your family name would be stained forever."

Lord Blackheart bristled. "You're playing a ghastly game, D'Anvers. That sounds dangerously close to blackmail, sir!"

"He has been frightfully kind to me, Father," piped up Belinda, stepping forward. "Don't be too harsh on him. It's not his fault Tarquin's an idiot."

"Easy now!" protested her brother.

Lord Blackheart, purple with rage, began to roar. "I don't care how kind he's been. He's threatening the good name of this family. And as for you, Tarquin, how dare you bring this man into our lives! Like a fox in the henhouse. Well, I shall teach you a lesson here and now. You are forthwith DISINHERITED. You shall get not one penny!"

"But, Father . . ." pleaded Tarquin.

"Oh, that's convenient," whispered Barbu behind his hand to Janty. "Though we'd better accelerate our plans with the girl before every Criminal Element on the island waltzes up with a bunch of daffodils."

"I would suggest," interrupted Fenomina loudly, raising a hand, "given that the spirit world is a volatile and tremulous place, that bringing a sense of calm to tonight's proceedings is of the utmost importance."

"Yes!" barked Barbu, waving his cane in the psychic's direction. "What she said! Let's all hurry up and find out where this treasure is that I've heard so much about!"

"For now it seems I have no choice," snarled Lord Blackheart, staring angrily at his son. "For the sake of the good name of this family, Barbu D'Anvers must stay. Now let's get on with this infernal séance. Belinda! Sit down!"

As the youngest Blackheart took her seat the room fell silent. You could hear a pin drop. The only sound Wilma was aware of was her heart thumping in her chest. She reached down and put a reassuring hand on Pickle's head. He was as stiff as a board and trembling. "There's no such thing as ghosts," she chanted under her breath. "No such—" Suddenly, behind the psychic, one of the heavy velvet curtains billowed out, sending a startled shock wave through the gathering. A terrifying chill entered the room. Wilma gasped.

"Probably just a draft," muttered Inspector Lemone, wiping his brow anxiously. "Everything can be explained. That's what Goodman said. Oh yes."

"If all gathered at the table could hold hands," Fenomina asked in a low purr, "I shall now attempt to commune with the damned. Darkness, please."

As Portious walked softly around the room extinguishing the candles, Wilma, realizing she was a lot more frightened that she wanted to be, slid into a side recess so as to keep her back to a wall. "As my Academy textbook recommends," she explained to Pickle. "It says, when in a tight spot, make sure you've got your back covered!" It WAS a tight space, but Pickle squeezed in with her and lay down with a paw over his eyes. The disquiet in the room was palpable. Wilma's nerves were on a knife-edge. This was the most disconcerting event she had ever attended.

Fenomina began to call out, asking for any nearby spirits to show themselves with a sign, to explain their presence, then leave in peace, when something touched Wilma's shoulder. She jumped and gave a small muffled cry as she twisted around to see who or what it was.

"Oh, thank goodness! Victor!" She heaved a sigh of relief. "I wondered where you were. I don't mind telling you, I'm positively petrified! And you believe in ghosts. Unlike me. Of course. So you must be feeling beside yourself."

Victor shrugged. "I've been hiding in this

alcove. It's so dark no one's noticed me. Was the diary useful?" he went on softly, taking the cap from his head and holding it in both hands.

Wilma's eyes widened. "Yes!" she answered eagerly. "We think we've worked out where Bludsten's gold mine might be! And if we find that, we might find the treasure! Although Mr. Goodman says we mustn't get our hopes up. It's what my Academy textbook calls a Proper Breakthrough. So thank you, Victor." Wilma looked up and caught the eye of Janty, who was staring at her with a strange look on his face. She tapped Victor on the arm and nodded in his direction. "That's Janty. He works for Barbu D'Anvers. He hasn't got any friends. He's probably jealous I'm talking to you." Wilma smiled in a conciliatory fashion but was met with one of Janty's dark scowls. "See what I mean? Anyway, I'm glad you and I are friends. You're much nicer than that grumpy boots."

Victor grinned shyly and reached into his pocket. "I'm glad we're friends too. And I want to help you prove yourself to Mr. Goodman, like I am proving myself to Lord Blackheart."

Wilma wrinkled her nose in puzzlement. But before she could ask more, Victor rushed on.

"I've got something else for you," he said, handing Wilma a small, crumpled piece of paper. "I found it in the library. I think it fell out of Bludsten's diary when you ran off."

Wilma took the piece of paper, but in the dark she couldn't quite make out what it was. By now Fenomina was asking the spirit world about the treasure. Her tone was becoming increasingly urgent. "Can't see . . ." Wilma said, frowning as she peered at Victor's paper. "They've blown out all the candles . . . Are they arrows in the corners . . . ?"

A sudden wail sounded from the direction of the séance table. Wilma snapped her head upward and let Victor's piece of paper fall into her pinafore pocket. Fenomina's mouth was wide open, her one eye wild and rolling. As her head flopped from side to side, a distressing hissing noise began emanating from her. It was one of the most evil things Wilma had ever heard. She clasped a hand to her mouth to stop herself from screaming. The room bristled with fear. Molly had buried her face in Polly's shoulder, Mrs. Speckle was doubled over in fright, and poor Inspector Lemone, at his wits' end, was actually in tears.

"So . . . cold." Wilma shivered. The room had turned icy as if the devil himself had breathed through the Hoo. A smell of sulfur filled the air along with a chorus of soft, horrible moans. It was the creepiest thing Wilma had ever experienced. For a moment she thought she felt Victor's own cold hand clutching hers reassuringly even as he whispered, "I told you ghosts were real."

Then Mrs. Moggins, the cook, suddenly exclaimed and pointed toward the ceiling. "Look!" she shrieked, gesturing desperately. "Look up there!"

Wilma looked. She gasped, as did the rest of the room. Because there, above everybody's heads, a strange floating golden claw had appeared from nowhere! And this time it was EXACTLY like the one in Bludsten's diary. A chair standing by the window skidded sideways and fell over. Screams broke out. Mrs. Speckle's tea tray was overturned, Inspector Lemone's hat was knocked from his head, and Pickle, in an alarming and unexpected turn, found himself cosmically booted into the air, where he did a full somersault and landed headfirst in a large bowl of nuts. The room was in chaos. Molly and Polly had both fainted, Portious was trying to hide behind the Brackle Bush, and Belinda was screeching as if her life depended on it.

Then a deep booming voice cut through the madness. "You shall not take that which is mine!" Wilma's mouth fell open and a cold, clammy wave of fear coursed through her. "If you try," it resonated on, "then REVENGE shall follow!" As the voice spoke, something began to solidify just over Fenomina's shoulder. It was a disembodied head wearing a dark cowl. A pair of red malevolent eyes burned out from within it. It gave a wicked, foul hiss, briefly displaying a set of vile fangs. Everybody screamed.

"Oh my!" Wilma murmured, half in shock. "It's actually true. There *are* ghosts at Blackheart Hoo! They *do* exist!" Instinctively, she turned to grab hold of Victor again, but he was gone. No doubt he had fled in fear. And then, as quickly as the apparition had formed, it vanished.

Fenomina slumped forward. "Light!" she moaned. "We must have light!"

Portious hastily relit a few candles. Everyone looked shaken and white-faced, even Fenomina.

"Mr. Goodman," Lady Blackheart wailed, fanning herself frantically, "perhaps you should call off your search for the missing treasure. Perhaps you should just leave and let Fenomina appease the spirits. I don't know if my nerves can stand much more of this!"

"Nonsense!" retorted Lord Blackheart, pulling himself together and thumping his hand hard on the séance table. "The sooner we find it, the better. Once we have it, all this madness will stop. I am sure of it."

"And the fact that he's so cross," shouted out Molly, clutching tightly to Polly, "proves the treasure must be MASSIVE."

"This is getting better with every passing moment," whispered Barbu, smirking.

As they all traipsed from the room, Wilma

skipped excitedly between a still trembling Inspector Lemone and her mentor. Now that she'd gotten over her extreme petrification, and rescued Pickle from the bowl of nuts, she was actually quite stirred up at the thought of becoming a ghost-hunting detective apprentice.

"Can you believe it, Mr. Goodman? There are ghosts after all—we've seen the proof needed with our own bare eyes!" she exclaimed. "So it is the Fatal Phantom causing havoc at the Hoo. All over its treasure. And Belinda probably IS possessed too."

"On the contrary, Wilma," replied Theodore forcibly. "I am more convinced than ever that ghosts and spirits are not real." And he looked more serious than Wilma had EVER seen him before.

"But . . ." Wilma trailed off. She was aghast. They had just seen proper proof with their own eyes, and here was Mr. Goodman refusing to accept it.

If you've ever spent any time with grown-ups, you'll have heard them talking about how their bosses are total idiots and how if they were in charge instead of their bosses, then their workplaces would be a lot better, thanks very much. Well, at this precise moment, that was a little bit how Wilma felt. There had to be some explanation. Perhaps Mr. Goodman had that thing when you're so cold you go a bit crazy. Surely he couldn't be possessed as well? She didn't know what to think. There was no criminal. There was a GHOST. Mr. Goodman MUST have taken leave of his senses. It was true he wasn't used to getting things wrong, so could that be it . . . ?

Wilma had to admit she didn't like it herself, but it was time to face the truth. Ghosts existed—however improbable that sounded. And it was now quite clear. The only hope for all of them—including Mr. Goodman (imagine his embarrassment if it was found out he'd gotten it all wrong)—was her. Someone had to do something to stop the spooks taking over at the Hoo. However scary it might be. "Nothing and nobody stops Wilma Tenderfoot," she whispered determinedly to Pickle. Besides, Victor would help her—hadn't he been trying to do so all along? HE believed in ghosts! Yes, apprentice detective she was, ghost hunter she would become. Because sometimes, if you want something done properly, you have to do it yourself.

A Fatal Phantom on the loose. Mr. Goodman gone crazy. Wilma up against it on her own. Surely this can't get any worse? Surely?

The morning was cold and unforgiving. Nobody had slept well. In fact Pickle, convinced that a spook was going to appear at any moment, had spent the night sitting bolt upright and barking at every creak, squeak, and bump, much to everyone's annoyance. Wilma and Pickle, Mr. Goodman and Inspector Lemone had been given a guest suite in the east wing of the Hoo, where there was a large four-poster bed with a set of bunks in an adjoining room. But after the terrors of the séance Inspector Lemone had insisted they all sleep in the same room, meaning they had been squashed toe to tail in the four-poster all night.

"I'm really tired." Wilma yawned as she pulled on her duffel coat and helped Pickle into his. "Still, no time for snoozing. We've got to get ready for the trek to Drop Dead Gorge." Trotting from the bedroom, she slid down the banister of the grand staircase and hopped across the marble floor of the hall, Pickle fast behind her. She had to find Portious and ask to borrow skis for them all.

Last time Wilma had been sent to find the butler, he'd been in the servants' quarters tending to his vegetable seedlings. If she remembered correctly, she needed to head toward the house kitchens. By now she had run past the dining room and the downstairs sitting room, scampered through a sun lounge, a study, and a washroom, and opened a door only to discover it was a broom closet. "I think I've gone the wrong way, Pickle," she admitted at last. "I think I should have turned left at the billiard room. Let's go back." But as Wilma turned, she stopped in her tracks.

There, coming out of a room and walking away from them up a corridor, was Belinda Blackheart.

Wilma raised a finger to her lips. "I know officially I'm supposed to be fetching skis, but unofficially we have got our own ghost investigation to think about. I was pondering on it in bed last night. I think I just need to *prove* to Mr. Goodman, beyond a shadow of a doubt, that it's ghosts up to no good. I'll have to find spooky clues and things. They have to be proper clues, though. It's my real chance to show him that I've worked something out correctly, all by myself. And we need a plan of action. That's like a list that reminds you what to do. So if we were making a plan of action for you, Pickle, it would go: scratch ear, sniff sock, snaffle crumbs." Pickle stood, rapt. That was a heck of a plan and he *liked* it! "So we have to do that, but for spooks. We probably won't find the treasure-guarding Fatal Phantom until we find the treasure, though we should keep our eyes peeled. But according to Fenomina, Bludsten Blackheart's troubled spirit is IN Belinda, so she might be a good place to start. It's sort of like Top Tip for Detecting number three—keep a sharp lookout for suspects and sometimes creep around after them—only this is a possession rather than a suspicion."

Reaching into her pinafore pocket, Wilma pulled out her notebook and began to read. "I wrote this last night—using what I could remember reading about spooks that first day in the Hoo library."

1. Summon the spook in question (nighttime is best).
2. If you have not already found it, ask it where the treasure is (be POLITE).
3. Put garlic on Belinda in case she's gone vampire like that book in the library said can happen when mummies are around.
4. If Belinda goes zombie, stick something pointy in her brain.
5. Try and exercise the spook. Try sit-ups. And jumping jacks.

"I think that's how it works. I definitely read you have to exercise people to get ghosts out.

Then once the spook is tired of exercising, it must come out of Belinda, or submit or something, and we can show it to Mr. Goodman. He'll realize then that my hunchy detective apprentice's instincts were right. Also, if Belinda really is smothered in ghost juice, then someone needs to help her. So seeing as we're here, perhaps we should follow her and see if anything possessed happens. Just for a while." Pickle blinked. He'd rather not. But a hound is at the mercy of his mistress. (Generally speaking, all boys have to do what girls want, really. It's written in stone. Don't fight it.)

They crept after the girl as she headed into the kitchens. Peeping around the door, Wilma could see Belinda standing with her back to them. She was bending over a plate and had a knife in her hand. Ushering Pickle in before her, Wilma caught sight of a large bunch of garlic hanging from the herb rack. Reaching for it, she draped it around Pickle's neck: "Just in case Belinda's gone vampire!"

At the sound of Wilma's voice, Belinda spun

around, a dripping orange in her free hand. "Oh, hello. What are you doing here?" she asked, moving toward them. "None of the servants will come near me, so I'm making myself some orange peel teeth with my breakfast. They're ever so funny. Look!" Belinda suddenly grinned hideously, revealing a row of orange fangs beneath her top lip.

Fighting the urge to scream, Wilma panicked and reached for an onion. "Oh no! She HAS gone vampire!" she yelled at Pickle. "I've run out of garlic! This will have to do! I'll have to chuck it at her!"

With that, Wilma pulled back her arm and threw the onion at Belinda with all her might. "If she's gone vampire," Wilma shouted, "she'll start melting or something!"

"What on earth are you . . . OW!" cried Belinda as the onion hit her in the eye. Half-blinded, she dropped the knife and orange and began to teeter toward Wilma and Pickle, one eye shut and arms held out in front of her.

"Oh no!" bellowed Wilma, frantically consulting her notebook, which she'd grabbed from her pinafore pocket. "Now she's gone a bit zombie! Don't let her bite you, Pickle. And don't bite her. It might go both ways. This is awful! My plan of action says the only way to stop a zombie is to stick something in its brain! But I'm not sure I can do that. Aaaaagh! She's coming!"

Stumbling against the kitchen table, Belinda stubbed her toe. "Owwwwwwwww!" she wailed, reeling backward and collapsing against a larder shelf, knocking a bowl of flour over herself. As she rose again, her face and hair were a ghastly white. Wilma grabbed two wooden spoons and, as Pickle barked encouragement, began to ward the now ghostly-looking Belinda off with them.

"It must be the spirit of Bludsten Blackheart!" Wilma shouted at Pickle over the racket. "I should commune with it immediately! Bludsten Blackheart, is that you? You must leave poor Belinda Blackheart immediately! Leave her, I say! But if you could tell us where the treasure is first, that would be good. Now do jumping jacks! Jumping jacks!"

Wilma poked Belinda in the back with her wooden spoons. "Quick, Pickle!" she yelled as she chased the limping Belinda around the kitchen. "Get ready to catch any spooky spirits that are thoroughly exercised!"

"What on EARTH is going on here?" said a voice behind them.

Wilma turned her head sharply. "Barbu D'Anvers!" she gasped, wooden spoons held aloft. "Oooh . . . umm . . . Mr. Bludsten!" she hissed back in Belinda's direction. "That thing I asked you about . . . doesn't matter now! Don't say a word!"

It was the first time since the end of the Case of the Putrid Poison that Wilma had been properly face-to-face with the dreadful Barbu D'Anvers. It's never pleasant encountering your deadliest enemy, especially one who has promised to kill you on several occasions, and at that moment Wilma was alone and outnumbered. He could kill her right here and now, and no one would be any the wiser. Pickle stepped in front of her, his teeth bared in a protective snarl.

"Oh no! It's Goodman's ghastly girl and her disgusting dog," sneered Barbu, scowling at Wilma and Pickle. "Why he has you hanging around I shall never know. What are you up to? Terrorizing . . . Whatsernameagain?" he continued, throwing a quizzical glance in Janty's direction.

"Belinda Blackheart," whispered the boy, leaning in.

"Yes, her. If there's any terrorizing to be done, *I* shall be the one to do it. So you can leave her alone. I have plans. And you won't be scuppering them. In fact, think yourself lucky that I am on a tight schedule and don't have the inclination to finish you off now—something I would *dearly* love to do. You're on borrowed time, Wilma Tenderfoot. You *and* your revolting hound," he added, waving his cane in Pickle's direction. "Now then, Janty, back to the task at hand. What are we supposed to be doing?"

"Helping the lady in distress, master. Phase two."

"Yes. Tully . . . help her."

The henchman pushed past Wilma to pick Belinda up off the floor, where she had collapsed in floury exhaustion.

"That enough?" Barbu raised his eyebrow questioningly.

"According to the book, yes, master," replied Janty, consulting the manual in his hands. "Although it does also say that you might like to offer the lady a cup of tea. To settle the nerves."

"Let's not go crazy." The villain shrugged. "We have saved her from this revolting child. I think that's plenty. Good. Right. Back to scouring those plans. Carry her out, Tully. As for you," he said, turning to Wilma with a sneer, "don't think I'll be forgetting you, because I won't."

As Barbu and his gang swept Belinda from the room, Wilma, covered in flour dust and still holding the spoons, could only gape in astonishment. "Why is Barbu D'Anvers being nice to Belinda Blackheart?" she asked Pickle, who had decided to have a quick bark at the villain now he was gone. "He's never nice to anyone. He's up to something more rotten than just finding that treasure, Pickle, mark my words. Unless he wants to cross-question Bludsten like we did? We'll have to think about this properly. After we've got the skis. Come on." Throwing the spoons down on the table, Wilma marched toward the door, still deep in thought. "It's almost as if he's in a romance. With Belinda Blackheart. But that *can't* be right, surely? She's about two feet taller than him for a start. The wedding portraits would look ridiculous."

But Pickle didn't have the answer to that. He was more worried about how he was going to get the smell of garlic out of his collar.

"And then Barbu came in and he was being all lovey-dovey. With Belinda Blackheart! What can it mean, Mr. Goodman?" asked Wilma, staring up at the great detective as she fastened her skis.

"What it always means where Barbu D'Anvers is concerned," replied Theodore, pulling a fur deerstalker hat over his golden hair. "That bamboozles and tricks are on the menu. We must keep an eye on this. Foul play is afoot. But in the meantime, we should be off."

"Now, stand still." Wilma turned back to Pickle. "You're the official expedition pack animal. That means you have to carry loads of equipment. According to my textbook, we're going to need climbing ropes, grapple hooks, ice picks, water, fruit cake, tea flasks, extra socks, and something slippery in case of mechanical mishaps. I got this saddlebag from Portious. I'm going to tie that around you. There. And now I'll pack everything into it. How's that?" She stood back and looked at Pickle. His knees were trembling slightly with the extra weight. "Hmm. Perhaps we'll leave the socks. Yes. That's better."

"A few more climbing ropes for you, Wilma," said the detective, handing them over. "We'll be facing a steep descent when we get to the gorge." She took them and slung them over her shoulder. "This is a dangerous mission. I wonder if you should stay here, in fact."

Wilma's eyes widened. "But I'm the apprentice. It's my job to go where you go. Unless . . ." She paused hopefully. ". . . unless you want me to stay here and do some Fatal Phantom investigating—if you've had a rethink about that at all . . .?

183

And I could follow Belinda Blackheart around—see if I can set off her possession again and—"

"Actually, I think you're right, Wilma," said Theodore hastily. "You should probably come with me after all. It might be . . . safer . . . for everyone. But stick as close as you can. Especially when we make our descent into the gorge."

"Is now a good time to tell you I'm not awfully fond of heights?" asked Inspector Lemone, stepping out from the dressing room. Wilma looked at him. He was wearing soccer cleats, long socks, a pair of terribly tiny shorts, an oversized sweater, and a pith helmet. The Inspector looked a little embarrassed and cleared his throat. "Mrs. Speckle laid out my adventure outfit, so I have to wear it. Let's say no more on the matter."

Sometimes, when fellows have been blinded by the love bug, they find themselves forced into sticky corners. Poor Inspector Lemone was dizzy with adoration for Mr. Goodman's irascible housekeeper, and given that this was the first time she had ever paid him any attention whatsoever, he couldn't bear not to wear what she had chosen for him, however . . . short. Never mind that the only reason Mrs. Speckle had waded in was that she was darned if a pair of flibbertigibbet housemaids were going to do what she quite determinedly regarded as *her* job.

"Are those shorts a bit . . . ?" began Theodore, frowning.

"No more!" cried Inspector Lemone.

"Here you go, Pickle," said Wilma, tying a small saucepan to the top of her beagle's head over his woolly dog-duffel coat. "That'll have to do as a hard hat. We don't want you falling off anything and hurting yourself, do we?"

Pickle caught sight of himself in the mirror. He hadn't thought his winter outfit could get any worse, but apparently it could. Much worse. At this rate he'd be happily throwing himself off any passing cliff, let alone falling off one.

A perilous gorge, a rogue phantom, and a dog in a saucepan. What can possibly go wrong?

15

"Mr. Goodman!" called Wilma, skiing skill-fully to catch up with her mentor (she had done lots of skiing when in the Institute for Woeful Children, where it had been her job to water the cabbages, even in snowy weather). "I just saw something that might change your mind about spooks, especially at the Hoo. As we were leaving, Pickle was doubling back to demonstrate some ski basics to Inspector Lemone, and he spotted a set of footprints in the snow. They went right up to the wall of the house and then just disappeared. I tried to call you, but I think your earmuffs must be on too tight and you didn't hear me."

"Interesting," said Theodore, stopping abruptly and looking down at his apprentice. "And you saw no footprints going away from the wall?"

"No, none," said Wilma with a small shake of her head. "They just stopped. The only other thing was two round holes in the snow on either side of the last set of footprints. And that was it."

"And where were these marks?"

Wilma pointed to the front of the house.

"The south side. Hmmm."

"So they could be actual spook prints, couldn't they, Mr. Goodman? Because only a spook can walk up to a wall and disappear. So now do you believe Blackheart Hoo is haunted?"

"I don't, Wilma, but you obviously do. And you seem determined to convince me. So I'll say this: If you CAN prove to me the existence of ghosts—with facts and solid clues that cannot be interpreted in any other way—well, I promise to be open-minded."

That was all Wilma needed to hear. Her own special spook case was well and truly on.

"Mr. Goodman!" Another ski-wearing figure emerged from the swirl of snowflakes. It was Dr.

Flatelly. "Good morning!" As the group drew closer to him he shot the Inspector a puzzled glance. "Aren't those shorts a bit . . . you know . . . ?" Inspector Lemone bit his lip and looked away. The archaeologist shrugged, then turned to the most famous and serious detective. "I'm here as promised. Glad to be of help. Especially with the diary. What with it being so hard to decipher. For someone as young as Wilma, that is."

Wilma's eyes flashed with indignation. She might be small, but she was certainly determined, and it was her job to assist, not his.

Seeing that his apprentice was a little rattled, Mr. Goodman gave her a quick pat on her bobble-hatted head. "I should caution you, Dr. Flatelly," he said with a grave look, "that our journey will be treacherous." The wind howled through his mustache. "And not necessarily just because of the weather."

"It's true. We are constantly in scrapes," added Wilma, trying to look official. "But we are trained professionals." Theodore raised his eyebrows. "Well . . . Mr. Goodman and Inspector Lemone are. But I will be too one day. So will Pickle."

"Not a problem," replied Flatelly with a wave of his hand. "As a boy I often climbed the one small hill, so I'm used to a bit of rough and tumble. And as for anything more sinister, well, I am an archaeologist. I'm not uncomfortable with the strange or unexpected."

"Then let's be on our way," said Theodore, handing Dr. Flatelly a length of climbing rope. "Onward to Drop Dead Gorge!"

Criminal Elements, as everybody knows, are a lazy bunch. If they can avoid hard work, they will, and as our intrepid team continued away from the Hoo, Barbu D'Anvers was watching from an upstairs window.

"There they go, master," said Janty, peering through a telescope as the team trudged away through the snow. "Shouldn't we be following them?"

"In this weather?" scoffed Barbu, snatching the telescope from the young boy. "My boots are the finest suede. They'd be positively ruined. No," he added as he took a long look at the traveling party before slamming the telescope shut, "I think it's a perfectly brilliant plan to let Goodman do all the hard work for us. If he finds the treasure, we shall simply steal it. If he finds a clue, we shall let him lead us to it and then steal it. That's a win-win. You should write that down, Janty—it's entry-level being-evil stuff. Only an idiot would follow him in these conditions. Which is why I'm sending an idiot . . . Tully. Obviously."

"Actually, you couldn't go anyway, master," replied Janty, consulting his notebook as he wrote down Barbu's wise words. "According to your evil schedule, you've arranged to meet Belinda for a follow-up romantic encounter."

"Have I?" snapped Barbu with a frown. "That sounds ominous. What is it again, Janty?"

"It may involve kissing, master," said the boy, checking his wooing handbook.

Barbu's face contorted. "Kissing? Is that the wet thing on the face?"

"Yup."

"How utterly revolting. Now then, Janty, while I am engaged in repulsive romance, I would like you to get on with that stealing we talked about. Poke around at the same time. Make yourself a nuisance. Find anything interesting—bring it to me."

As Wilma and her companions approached the top of the gorge, squalls of snow spiraled all around them and heavy clouds grumbled overhead. The storm, if anything, was getting worse. Wilma tied one end of her climbing rope around her waist and the other around Pickle. "Just in case!" she shouted over the gale. "Climbers have to buddy up for safety. And you're my best buddy, so that's why we're tied together! Now we have to climb down into the gorge. But it's almost a sheer descent!" The ground before them dropped away dramatically, and as they edged closer to the gorge edge, the wind buffeted them from every side so that each step became an effort.

"We must take care!" yelled Theodore, shielding his eyes from the onslaught of snow. "Stand back! I'm going to test the brink!" Taking the ice pick from his belt, the great detective skied forward gingerly.

As she watched Mr. Goodman, virtually holding

her breath with tension, Wilma suddenly felt a prickling sensation on the back of her neck. It was the Hunchy Instinct again, the one that left her stomach so unsettled. She couldn't explain it, but she couldn't shake the feeling that they were being *watched*. She turned to look over her shoulder and something caught her eye—a small flash of movement in the distance. Lifting one of her mittened hands to her brow, Wilma strained to see through the ever-thickening snow. There it was again! Someone large and lumbering. But then, behind that, something else, dark and indefinable. "Mr. Goodman," she yelled, a little concerned. "Something's moving behind us!" But even as he turned, the shadows began to withdraw and the detective was left staring at nothing.

Inspector Lemone, who was at his wits' end with fear as it was, whimpered. "Probably a branch falling from a tree or a deer leaping to shelter. Yes, that's probably it. Just an animal. Or the light playing tricks on you."

Wilma nodded. All the same, that feeling in her neck hadn't gone.

"Okay!" called out Theodore. "Let's have you and Pickle first. I'll lower you over the edge. And then I want you to use your rope to rappel down the gorge wall. Make your way toward me! And tread carefully!"

Wilma thrust one ski deep into a large drift of snow and pushed her weight forward carefully, but as she did so, Pickle took a corresponding step, skidded sideways, and before anyone could react, he was careering, skis paddling like crazy, toward the edge of the gorge.

"Oh no!" shouted Inspector Lemone, making a lunge for the dog. His bare legs were so frozen, however, that he couldn't move quickly enough. "He's going over, Flatelly! Do something!" Irascimus threw himself at the sliding hound. But he was too late and Wilma, horror-struck, could only watch as Pickle's startled face slid slowly but surely over the cliff edge and disappeared from sight.

Seconds later, she remembered the rope joining them. "Pickle!" she yelled, grasping for the end at her waist. She felt it jerk as Pickle fell to the limit of its length, and found herself sliding toward the cliff edge. Grabbing at a large root that was sticking out of the ground, Wilma pushed her skis up against a boulder for leverage, and heaved on the rope with all the determination she had in her small body. The cliff edge began to crumble where the rope chafed and debris showered down on Pickle, but it was working, and before long the hound's saucepan hat and little face appeared back over the top of the gorge edge. Mr. Goodman scooped him up and delivered him to Wilma's waiting arms.

"Thank goodness you were wearing that saucepan, Pickle." She gulped. "Or those falling rocks would have been the end of you!" It was a small comfort, but right at that precise moment, Pickle didn't care. He just wanted a cuddle.

Behind them, there was a loud tearing noise. "Oh no!" said the Inspector, who had backed up onto a patch of snowed-over thorns. "I seem to have ripped my shorts. I'll have to make the rest of the journey in my underpants." He stared down at his hairy, exposed legs and overly large and slightly baggy underpants billowing in the breeze.

"I say, chaps," he whispered, looking humiliated. "Let's never speak of this again, eh? Never."

Having set up some grappling hooks and made a strong and sturdy hold point, Theodore lowered a trembling Inspector Lemone and an excited Dr. Flatelly to the gorge floor before rappelling down himself with Wilma secured tightly to his back. As they bounced down Wilma couldn't help reflecting that despite the fact that she was halfway down a sheer and dreadful drop, held on only by ropes and Mr. Goodman's grip, she had never felt safer. Or happier. Pickle was rappelling down professionally just below them. Mr. Goodman had been about to lower Pickle after the archaeologist when the little dog had given his saucepan helmet head a shake, stepped into his rappelling harness, and made a flying leap into the air, the rope arcing outward behind him like an elongated tail, before executing a perfect flip-twist and coming back in toward the gorge wall, from where he had begun to bounce toward the valley floor with aplomb. Dogs are actually excellent rappellers. It's a skill they like to keep quiet.

That and quilt making. Brilliant at it. You'd never know to look at them, would you?

As Wilma was unstrapping herself at the bottom of the cliff and giving Pickle an impressed thumbs-up, she caught sight again of something—or was it two things?—moving through the snow farther along the upper rim. Then they were gone again. She frowned.

"Inspector Lemone," she muttered, tugging at his oversized sweater sleeve, "I don't want to look silly in front of Mr. Goodman again, but I think . . . we're being followed."

Lemone's eyes widened. "By something alive?" he asked anxiously.

"I'm not sure," she whispered, giving his hand a squeeze.

There are some relevant words that you might like to try in this situation. PERIL is one of them and FOREBODING is the other. Whichever you prefer, they both mean the same thing: UH-OH!

16

The valley was a desolate place: Icicles hung from every crevice, dead trees stood petri-fied, and the odd upturned carcass of a frozen mule did nothing to improve matters. The wind whipped through the gorge, bouncing off the echoey canyon walls so that the sound of its howling was amplified again and again. Skis now strapped to their backs, Wilma and her compan-ions were looking for the mine's entrance point, but as they didn't know exactly where that was or what it looked like, and the snow was coming down heavily, the challenge was on. Added to this, the gorge was a mass of twists and turns, with craggy outcrops that loomed over them and rough gravel underfoot. It was no easy task.

"Crumbs!" said Wilma as she passed the skeleton of an upturned horse. "They don't call this place Drop Dead Gorge for nothing, do they?" Pickle stared at the bones and drooled. He hadn't eaten in hours. He sidled toward them. Perhaps if he just had one tiny lick? "No, Pickle," warned Wilma, seeing what he was about to do. But Pickle had already lost interest in the bones. He had stiffened in the wind, nose straight and true, and with one paw aloft, he gestured upward. Wilma followed Pickle's gaze. "What is it? A yellow rock . . . Hey, is that . . . ? Of course—it's in the shape of an eagle! Like the rock pictures in Bludsten's notebook, like the golden bird claw treasure itself. This MUST be the mine entrance. Look!" she yelled to the others. "And well done, Pickle!"

The strange eagle-like formation seemed to be flying at them from the gorge wall, huge wings unfurled and beak gaping as if about to scoop them up and swallow them whole. Wilma shivered a little and pulled her scarf tighter. The rock here was yellowed by a strange lichen, adding to the golden-eagle effect.

Mr. Goodman had made his way toward a fissure just below the bird rock. "Yes, I think we've found it," he yelled, brushing snow aside to reveal some old planks of wood nailed between the two rock walls.

"Bludsten must have boarded the place up," shouted Irascimus, holding on to his hat.

"Help me break through," called Theodore, turning to Inspector Lemone. "The wood is quite rotten. It shouldn't be too difficult."

Wilma, who had never been on a proper outdoors adventure before, was, she had to confess, finding all of this incredibly thrilling. She was up to her knees in snow, she had almost tumbled off a cliff top, she had rappelled with Mr. Goodman, and now here she was, on the cusp of exploring a disused gold mine that might be jam-packed with missing treasure. Or clues. Or spooks. She looked down at Pickle and grinned, but he was still thinking about those bones. Oh, those lovely bones!

"Wilma!" called Theodore, having broken through the rotten planks. "Light that lantern we brought with us, will you? It's pitch-black in here."

Wilma untied the small lantern that she'd attached to Pickle's back. Taking a candle from her duffel pocket, she slotted it into the lantern. Pulling off her mittens and blowing on her freezing fingers, she was able to reach into her pinafore pocket, take out a box of matches and strike one, her back to the wind. The lantern flamed into life.

"Shall I carry it for you, Mr. Goodman?" she asked, hurrying to the mine's entrance. "I haven't done much apprenticeship stuff on this trip and I expect lantern holding is probably something I should take a turn at."

"All right, Wilma," said Theodore, his voice slightly muffled because his mustache had frozen solid. "But hold it high. And tell me if your arm gets tired."

Wilma nodded. Yes! This meant she got to go first, which technically made her the pioneer proper of this particular adventure. Everyone knows that the person who goes first is officially the person who finds stuff. The person credited with finding America, for example, is Christopher Columbus but actually, the whole idea of turning left at Greenland was down to a woman named Zoop Erkins, the real leader of the expedition. Does she get the credit? Oh no. Christopher Columbus does, because he was the one holding the lantern, so he got to go first. That's just how it works.

The tunnel that spread ahead of them was cramped and dark. An abandoned cart lay on its side, a few lengths of frayed rope hanging from its harness points, and to the right of it Wilma could just make out what appeared to be a side chamber.

Clambering over a broken wheel and holding the lantern as high as she could, Wilma shone the light into the smaller cavern. "Mr. Goodman," she gasped, "you might want to see this!" Shelves covered one wall, most of them bare except for a small pile of papers. "They're instructions for a kind of magic box and . . . old jokes," said Wilma, scanning them quickly. "What's brown and taps on your window?" she read. "A poo on stilts." She blinked and quietly returned the paper to the shelf. To their left, a large copper boiling pot was sitting on what appeared to be an old furnace. A few chains lay scattered on the floor, and on the wall, in a frame, was a strange-looking map. Wilma held the lantern closer to it so as to get a better look. "It looks like a map of the mine," she said.

Theodore raised his eyebrows. He took a pen-knife from his pocket. "Let's take this with us. It could be useful." With a few deft flicks, the great detective prised the map from its fixtures. "There you go, Wilma," he added, handing it to his young apprentice. "You know what to do."

"Bag it and tag it, Mr. Goodman." She nodded, trying to take it in her left hand. But the lantern was so heavy, she'd been using both hands to keep it high and as she took the map it fell from her fingers, nearly plunging them into darkness.

"Why don't you give that to me?" offered Dr. Flatelly. "I'd be happy to hold the lantern for you."

Wilma blinked. She quite liked being the one to go first, thank you very much. Being the one to go first meant you found stuff, like the map on the wall. So there was no way she was going to let

Dr. Flatelly take the lantern. No way at all. "It's all right," she said, smiling sweetly. She pocketed the map and swung the lantern up again.

"Hang on a moment," Theodore said excitedly. "Wave the lantern back that way again. I thought I saw something on that far wall."

Following Theodore's pointing finger, Wilma took a step forward and dangled the lantern to the left. "Oh my," she whispered as the light hit the other side of the chamber. The wall before them was covered in a series of strange pictures and scrawls.

"Looks like ancient Cooperan," said the detective seriously (and greatly), stepping closer. "You wrote a paper on that once, didn't you, Dr. Flatelly? Can you translate it?"

The archaeologist stood in front of the wall and gazed up, taking his glasses off as he did so. There was a picture of a large golden claw, then below it a series of drawings: a cherry, something that looked like a maggot, some mathematical symbols between them, then an arrow that pointed to a question mark with two map scrolls next to it.

"What do you think that all means?" asked Wilma, peering to see better.

"Not sure," replied Theodore. "Quite interested in those mathematical symbols, though. Is it ancient Cooperan or is it made up? Mind you, it's not uncommon for people to make up things in order to get what they want. You should remember that, Wilma." He gave her a meaningful look. Wilma hoped he was onto something and it wasn't his cold coming back and affecting his judgment again.

"So, Dr. Flatelly, can you make head or tail of it?" she said.

The archaeologist frowned and shook his head. "I'm afraid I can't identify the script. It's not Cooperan, ancient or otherwise."

"They look a bit like those symbols and pictures in Bludsten's diary," said Wilma, remembering what she had seen the day before.

"Perhaps Bludsten wrote a code of his own devising," suggested Flatelly. "Wilma, do you still have his diary with you?"

"I do, yes," she said. "It's in my pinafore pocket."

"Thank you," said the archaeologist, reaching into her pocket and taking it. Wilma gulped. She didn't like the fact that Dr. Flatelly had taken evidence from her own pinafore without asking, but she couldn't hold the lamp and take the diary back.

"There was a small table in the entrance," Dr. Flatelly continued. "Perhaps if I could just borrow the lantern I can study this quickly and see if there's a key page." He edged in that direction, Wilma glued to his side and keeping a careful eye on the diary.

"I thought keys were made of metal, not pages," she remarked, still wondering how she was going to get the diary back.

"Well, keys normally are made of metal, yes," explained Mr. Goodman as Irascimus gently prised the lantern from Wilma's fingers. "But a key page is like a code breaker. It tells you how to decipher something that on first glance may appear unreadable. However, Dr. Flatelly," he called after the archaeologist's already receding back, "I—"

"Oh no!" Dr. Flatelly screamed from just beyond the chamber. "Oh please, NO!"

Wilma spun around. Suddenly the air around them seemed even colder. Dr. Flatelly was now framed in the side chamber's doorway, lantern aloft, backing away from something and trembling. A huge, shadowy mass rushed at him, flinging him sideways into the beam supporting the entrance. Knocked unconscious by the impact, Flatelly collapsed to the floor and the lantern rolled sideways back into the room.

"Take the lantern, Wilma!" shouted Theodore as he raced toward her. "Try to see its face!"

Wilma swallowed, grabbing the lantern from the floor near her feet and holding it up. There, looming above her, was a monstrously tall figure, hooded in black. Wilma stared upward to see a set of vile fangs glistening in the candlelight. "The F . . . F . . . Fatal Phantom . . ." she whimpered, rigid with fear. With a loathsome hiss the form began to move toward her, two horrifying claws extending to grab her, two dark red eyes burning out from within the depths of its cowl.

"Noooo!" she wailed, flailing at it with the lantern. Pickle barked and ran forward, but as he did so, Wilma stepped backward into him and stumbled sideways into a wooden prop supporting the ceiling beam. As she struck it, it shifted suddenly and the wood gave a groan. The monster screamed and edged closer, and Wilma and Pickle scrabbled farther back, this time colliding with Mr. Goodman as he raced to their rescue. Wilma bounced forward as the Phantom, with a dreadful shriek, lunged and struck the edge of the ceiling beam, which began to topple. The ceiling gave way and with the creature's startling screech ringing in Wilma's ears, the doorway collapsed in on itself.

Dust filled the room. Wilma was coughing violently. She could hear Theodore and the Inspector coughing behind her, but the room had been plunged into darkness as the candle in the lantern was smothered. Was the Fatal Phantom still in the room with them? As soon as the thought struck her, Wilma found herself frozen to the spot—literally. What was happening? Was it the ghoul casting a spooky spell on her? Would they all die here, unable to move as the spirit wreaked its terrible revenge on them for daring to go after its treasure? Was this the end for Wilma Tenderfoot, detective apprentice extraordinaire, and the serious and great Detective Goodman? Just then Pickle, who had been sneezing on a loop since the collapse of the doorway, finally gave a loud snort and sent a plume of sticky nose-dust all over Wilma. "Ew!" She wiped herself down frantically. Still spluttering, she reached into her pocket and found another match. She blew into the lantern to clean it, relit the candle, and held it aloft. The doorway out into the rest of the mine was completely blocked. The ghost was gone. But they were trapped. Still coughing, Wilma turned to Theodore, who was just visible through the haze of dust. "Oops!" she said.

"Don't worry, Wilma," Mr. Goodman reassured her, pulling a handkerchief from his pocket. "It wasn't your fault . . . exactly."

The young apprentice pushed against the floor to stand up. "OW!" she exclaimed as something sharp pressed into her hand. "Ooh!" she added when she saw what it was. "Mr. Goodman, I think one of the Phantom's talons broke off in the scrabble. It's stuck here, in the floor. It's even got ectoplasm under the nail." She shuddered. "Yuck. Now I've touched it, does that mean I'll be possessed too?!"

"I very much doubt it, Wilma." Theodore reached once again for his pocketknife and levered the long, strangely flimsy nail from the floor. He held it briefly in the lamplight, made a note in his notebook, then tucked it into his pocket. "Well found, though."

Wilma was delighted—she was really proving her apprentice detective mettle on this expedition, even if she had also helped to trap them in a very dark and scary mine. "Well," she said, brushing dirt from the hem of her pinafore, "I don't suppose you think there's no such thing as ghosts now, eh, Mr. Goodman?"

The detective patted his pocket and his mustache twitched. "Oh, there is no doubt the Phantom is our newest culprit, Wilma. But not in quite the way that you mean."

Well, that was that, Wilma thought. He still

didn't believe in ghosts, even after everything that had just happened. Mr. Goodman had obviously gone quite mad.

"Besides, we have more urgent matters to deal with right now," the great detective continued.

"Like whether Dr. Flatelly's been killed by that Phantom, you mean?"

"It doesn't look good," interrupted Inspector Lemone. "But more importantly, how are we going to get out?"

Wilma turned to Mr. Goodman, knowing he would have a grand plan.

Wiping the dirt from his mustache, the great detective stood and faced his companions. "I'm about to make a very rare deduction," he declared, even more serious than when at his most serious. "I think we might be in a vast amount of trouble."

Wilma gasped. Pickle whimpered. So did Lemone.

You don't say?

17

Very slowly Inspector Lemone heaved sideways into the rack of shelves, put his head in the crook of his arm, and started wailing. "I don't want to die," he blubbered. "And I'm not even wearing trousers. They'll find our bodies in hundreds of years. And an archaeologist will look at me and think, Why was he only wearing underpants? Baggy underpants at that. WHY? Maybe I can make myself a pair of trousers using this dirty bit of rope."

"Don't worry, old friend," soothed Theodore, placing a reassuring hand on his colleague's shoulder. "At least we're in this together."

Wilma had gotten out her apprentice detective's notebook and was on her hands and knees flicking through it by the lantern light. She looked up. "I'm trying to find the newspaper cuttings I've got of all your old cases, Mr. Goodman," she said. "I used to have them on my Clue Ring, but I stuck them in here when I got my official notebook. There was that time in the Case of the Damaged Drainpipe where you were trapped in a barrel but you rolled yourself down a hill to get out of that scrape. Although we're not in a barrel. And we haven't got a hill. Then there was the time you were stuck in a dungeon but you had a lock to pick, which we don't. We've just got rubble. I could start moving the rocks and things. Shall I do that, Mr. Goodman?"

"I don't think the structure is stable enough, Wilma," pondered Theodore, examining the debris that blocked their path.

"And Dr. Flatelly had the diary," added Wilma, face falling. "When the Phantom got him. So we can't look at that. You know, for secrets."

"We'll have no more chat about the Phantom

right now," said the great detective sternly, brushing dust from the sleeves of his overcoat. "But I have just realized that we still have the map we took from the wall. Hold up the lantern, Wilma, and let's take a look at it."

The three of them crowded into a huddle around the map. "Interesting," said Theodore, frowning with concentration. "That doorway was the only exit, but look here." He pointed. "There's a chamber on the other side of that far wall. And according to this map, there would appear to be a shaft from there that leads to an underground water source. Beyond that, there seems to be a way out."

"So we need to get into the other chamber," said Wilma. "But how are we going to do that? There's a solid wall there. Only spooks can get through it."

"Oh no!" wailed Inspector Lemone. "Does that mean that dreadful thing can waft through and get us too?"

"I doubt that very much, Inspector," assured Theodore, rolling up his sleeves. "We are clearly in a highly unstable environment, but we can make that work to our advantage. If the ceiling can collapse to our left, then we should be able to get the wall to collapse to our right. If the measurements on this map are correct, I estimate that wall is probably no more than six inches wide. And what is more," he added, picking at it with his fingers, "it's made of talcum rock. That's the softest rock there is. We'll dig through this in no time."

"But how?" cried Inspector Lemone. "We've got no proper tools, and I've had nothing to eat since breakfast. My sugar levels are code red. That's verging on critical."

Wilma blinked. This was precisely the sort of situation where an apprentice needed to think on her feet. "Number one, I've got some dog biscuits in my pinafore pocket." Pickle's ears cocked upward. Dog biscuits? Here? Now? "They're chicken-flavored. They're no corn crumble of course, Inspector, but if you close your eyes you can probably pretend." Wilma held out two chicken-shaped biscuits. Pickle licked his lips . . .

then watched, dumbstruck, as Inspector Lemone took them both.

"Close my eyes, you say?" answered Lemone, popping the biscuits into his mouth. "Imagine they're corn crumbles? Ooh!" He chewed, eyes clamped shut. "They are . . . meaty! Dry as a bone! Slight gristly texture! Mrs. Speckle! Oh dear," he panted as he struggled to swallow the last bits down. "That was AWFUL."

Pickle blinked and stared. This was an OUT-RAGE.

"Number two," continued Wilma, hitting her stride, "we don't have any proper tools, but my Academy textbook says that you should always try to make the best of things with what you've got. There's a proper word for it, but I can't remember."

"Improvise," chipped in Theodore with a solemn smile.

"Yes." Wilma nodded forcefully. "That. So I think we can impy . . . that thing . . . with Pickle's saucepan helmet. We can use it to scoop and dig." She untied the pan from under her beagle's chin, marched toward the wall, and began to scrape at it. "There you are," she said, beaming. "It's working already! I may be small, Mr. Goodman, but I'm very determined!"

"That you are, Wilma." Theodore smiled. "Good work. Now then, Lemone! Help me move this shelving unit out of the way. You carry on with the pan, Wilma; I'll use this bit of broken plank; you can use one of your shoes, Lemone, and Pickle, you can dig with your paws! If we work together, we'll be through and out of here in no time!"

Some people like to do things on their own. That way they get all the credit and they don't run the risk of losing their temper with anyone or having to chat about terrible holidays or unpleasant skin complaints for hours on end. And some problems are often best dealt with by one person—constructing flat-pack furniture or trying to work out the mystery of soufflés, for example. However, other things are best tackled in a cheerful group, and it just so happens that escaping from a certain slow and terrifying death in an underground mine is pretty much at the top of the list. Which was fortunate for everyone concerned.

Working together, the team dug furiously and within an hour they had a big enough hole in the wall to be able to see another chamber beyond. "A few more scoops," panted Wilma, "and I'll squeeze through!"

It wasn't long before Pickle, Wilma, and Theodore had wriggled their way through the hole and were standing in a vast cavern filled with stalagmites. Now the latter two had hold of Inspector Lemone's arms and were pulling with all their might to get him through as well. It's a basic law of physics that round things generally can go in holes, but when the round things are as rotund as Inspector Lemone, a gentleman with a woeful weakness for biscuits and buns, this is how things end up. "Pull . . . a . . . bit . . . harder!" shouted Wilma, throwing her head back and tugging.

"Breathe in, Lemone!" panted Theodore, putting one foot up against the wall for extra grip.

Pickle looked on and did nothing. Maybe if

Lemone hadn't eaten his dog biscuits he might be slipping through that hole like a greased banana. But he did. As far as Pickle was concerned, he had only himself to blame. The lesson to learn from this, children, is NEVER eat a dog's biscuits. Ever. Especially when the dog is watching.

The Inspector was well and truly stuck and, finally, they had to admit it. Theodore stopped pulling and wiped his brow, his mustache twitching as he thought. "We need some sort of lubricant," he announced.

"Looby what?" asked Wilma, hands on knees and gasping for breath.

"Lubricant," explained Theodore. "Anything that makes things feel slippery. Like grease, or oil."

"Oh!" said Wilma, brightening. "That! Well, I packed a can of crushed slugs with the adventure gear. In case of mechanical mishaps!"

"We haven't got anything mechanical with us." Mr. Goodman frowned.

"Well, it was a just-in-case thing. So I thought I'd pack it nonetheless."

"Good job you did, Wilma!" Theodore beamed, bending down and extracting the can of crushed slugs from Pickle's saddlebag. Wilma could hardly contain her pride. She was on a roll. Being trapped underground in perilous circumstances obviously suited her. "Now then, Lemone, you might want to hold your nose," Theodore continued. "This does have a rather powerful odor."

Try to remember the worst smell you have ever smelled. Perhaps it was a dead rat stuck under some floorboards? Or a large rotting mackerel stitched into some curtains? Or, heaven forbid, the stinking feet of any teenage boy who likes to wear the same socks every day for a year without washing them. Imagine that smell now. Then multiply it by a hundred. Even then you are nowhere near close to experiencing the foul stench of crushed slugs. It is literally the worst odor known to man. Or woman. Especially woman.

"Ohhhhhhhh!" Inspector Lemone gagged as the foul, gloopy gunk was poured all over his head and shoulders, then spread around his sides by Wilma, using a large spoon from Pickle's saddlebag. "Smells like a skunk's armpit!"

"Actually," said Theodore, holding his nose, "it's worse than that. Now breathe in again!"

Wilma and her mentor grabbed hold of Lemone's hands and pulled with all their might and at last, with a shuddering pop, out slipped the Inspector. "Oh, thank Cooper!" he gasped. "Thought I was going to be stuck in there for all eternity."

Mr. Goodman was already scanning the cavern's far recesses with the lantern. "There!" he called out, pointing toward a shimmering mass in the distance. "Water! That must be the rock pool we're looking for! There's a low arch on the far side and the water flows through it. We're going to have to swim under the arch, so we'll be totally submerged, but according to this map, the way out should be just on the other side."

Wilma gulped. As small ten-year-old girls go, she was extremely brave, of that there was no doubt. But the fact of the matter was, she couldn't swim. In fact, she didn't have the first clue how to do it. She looked down at Pickle. "Can I hold on to you, please?" she whispered, chewing her lip. Pickle gazed back at her. Of course she could. There was no scrape on this earth that

Pickle wouldn't want to get Wilma out of and, given that his day thus far had been just about as bad as it could get, it would be a pleasure, nay, an HONOR to *finally* do something noble.

Theodore had removed the skis from his back, waded into the water, and was up to his chest by the time he reached the arch. Placing the lantern on a rock ledge, he took a gulp of air and dived from sight. Wilma and Inspector Lemone looked at each other as they unstrapped their own skis. "Do you think it's going to be very cold?" asked Wilma anxiously.

"Positively freezing, I expect," Lemone replied. "It'll still be better than being dug up as a relic with no trousers on, though," he added with a firm blink. "And smelling of slugs."

A splash sounded and Mr. Goodman reappeared, gasping for air. "We were right!" he shouted, tossing his wet hair from his face. "There's a stairway carved into the rock on the other side of this arch. The tunnel is a little longer than I would have hoped, but with one big lungful of air you'll be able to make it. Come on in,

Lemone. Wilma, you follow the Inspector, and I'll bring up the rear."

Wilma twisted the bottom of her pinafore into a knot. Pickle had already padded into the pool and was treading water just in front of her. Giving her a small bark of encouragement, he paddled after Inspector Lemone, who was now wading toward the arch. Wilma dipped one foot into the water. Oh, it was icy! "Just jump in, Wilma," shouted Theodore as he shoved the Inspector down into the underwater tunnel. "You know how it is with swimming . . . the sooner you're in, the less you feel the cold!"

Wilma didn't know this because she couldn't swim. But she was sure that a good apprentice detective would be an excellent swimmer, so she didn't like to say anything. "What did I read in my textbook about adventures?" she whispered to herself. "Nothing ventured—nothing gained! I'm not quite sure what that means, but I think it's about how you'll never get anywhere if you don't try. Well, it's time to venture! Here I come, Pickle!"

Worried and a little frightened, Wilma threw herself into the water. A blast of cold so intense as to be almost blinding took her breath away. She gasped in short, sharp pants as the chill stabbed at every part of her body. Still able to keep a foot on the rock pool floor, she moved toward Theodore and Pickle. "All right?" the great detective said gently. "Keep your eyes open and your hand on the tunnel wall. And take a deep breath, Wilma! You're going to need it! Don't worry, I'll be right behind you."

Wilma nodded and tried to look as if she swam through pitch-black tunnels every day of the week just for fun. But of course she didn't. She'd never swum in her life. Taking hold of the leather saddlebag she had tied around Pickle that morning she took three deep breaths and threw herself downward behind her faithful friend. As they dived, all Wilma could hear was the muffled gurgling of rushing water. Ahead of her, she could see Pickle's back legs kicking through the dark and murky water. With one hand on her beagle friend and the other on the tunnel wall, she pulled herself along while copying Pickle and paddling as hard as she could with her own feet. But suddenly, she felt something snag. Fumbling around, she realized that the knot on her pinafore had gotten itself hooked on an underwater stalagmite!

Desperately Wilma struggled to hold on to Pickle, but not realizing she was in trouble, he kicked onward and slipped from her fingers. Frantically she tried to pull herself free, her cheeks puffed out into small balloons as she tugged at the knotted pinafore, but it was stuck fast, twisted around a rocky hook. Where was Mr. Goodman? Her lungs felt as if they would burst. Panic burned through her and she knew that she couldn't hold her breath for a moment longer. Exhausted, she felt her body go limp. Her hands could no longer work the knot, her feet stopped kicking, and her eyes began to glaze over. Any moment now she'd breathe in water and . . .

From nowhere, Pickle appeared at Wilma's side. Biting through the knotted pinafore, he grabbed hold of her sleeve, and at the same time she felt Mr. Goodman's hands on her feet propelling her forward. At last Wilma burst from the tunnel of water and felt a fresh wind on her cheek. With one incredible gasp, she filled her lungs with air. "Thank you, Pickle," she said as Mr. Goodman scooped her from the rock pool to catch her breath on its rocky shore.

"Yes, thank you, Pickle," he added in his most serious tone, giving the small, brave beagle's head a rub before checking Wilma over.

"I don't know what I'd do without you," Wilma panted. Pickle gave his best friend a quick lick. He didn't know what he'd do without her either.

"Starlight!" shouted Inspector Lemone, who was standing at the foot of the rock staircase, dripping and pointing toward a hole in the rock above them. "We've made it! Thank goodness," he sighed. "Now we've just got to trudge back to the Hoo in freezing temperatures. And with no trousers on."

Piece of cake. Eh, readers?

18

Back at the Hoo, the evening was drawing in. Theodore and the others had not returned and the Blackhearts had gone their separate ways around the house. Belinda was alone in the sitting room, in a large armchair by the fire, her head resting on her hand, staring at the flickering coals. Everyone was behaving strangely around her: Tarquin was barely speaking to her, her own mother screamed every time she entered a room, and Mrs. Moggins had opened the door a fraction, shoved a tray of food across the floor, and run off again. Everybody thought she was a Spook Beacon. Perhaps she was. She did have a slight fizzing sensation in her left ear. Was that a symptom of a ghostly possession? Either way, she was thoroughly miserable and would be glad when this business was over.

"Just leave the tea by the door," she sighed, hearing it open again behind her. "You don't have to come in if you don't want to."

"Is that her?" she heard a man muttering. "The one in the chair?"

"Yes, master," she heard a boy whisper back.

"At last! I can't believe we've wasted so many hours just looking for her!"

Belinda turned around. Striding toward the fireplace was Barbu D'Anvers, followed by Tully and Janty. The boy had several large cards tucked under his arm, and the henchman seemed to be carrying a wilted bunch of flowers and a box of some sort.

"I have business to conduct. Now then," Barbu announced, placing himself in front of Belinda, "I shall stand here. Janty, if you could . . . yes . . . just behind her chair . . . left a bit, no, I can't see the cards . . . back a bit. There. And Tully, you crouch there. Good." Barbu cleared his throat. "Right. First card please, Janty."

The boy held up a large card above Belinda's head and Barbu began to read. "Belinda Blackheart. Hello."

"Hello," answered Belinda, a little puzzled.

"In brackets, shake her hand or something. Hmm. Quite non-specific. Just put a glove on . . ." Barbu stepped forward, took Belinda's arm at the wrist, and shook it a few times. "That's enough," he muttered, stepping back. "Right, next card, next card . . ."

Janty held another one aloft. Barbu peered at it. "I think you're very . . . what does that say? Fat? I think you're fat?"

"Fab, master," corrected Janty.

"And I got you a gift. Dear me. Appalling grammar," Barbu declared as he read on. "Hand him the chocolates. Oh. Tully—that's your card. Yours!" he shouted, giving his stupid henchman a sideways kick.

Tully crept forward and handed Barbu a box. "Sorry, Mr. D'Anvers," he whispered.

"Yes, you've got plenty to be sorry about— giving up following Goodman because it was 'too cold,' for a start. Anyway, that'll do," replied the tiny villain, shooing him away again. "These," he added, gesturing toward the box in his hands, "are for you."

"For me?" gushed Belinda, eyes brightening. She took the box and opened it. "Oh," she added quietly. "They seem to be half-eaten."

"Really?" asked Barbu, assuming an innocent face.

"Master!" mouthed Janty, waving another card. "Give her the flowers!"

Barbu stared angrily at his henchman again. "Flowers! Come on! No! Don't give them to me! Give them to her!"

Tully crawled across the floor on his knees and proffered Miss Blackheart a rather drab-looking handful of tulips.

"Weren't those in the vase outside in the hall-way?" asked Belinda, brushing a few fallen petals from her skirt.

"Never mind that now, we're getting to the important bit. Right, you!" Barbu began. "Hold it up a bit, Janty . . . can't quite see . . . yes, that's it . . . Belinda Blackheart! I have come here to tell you that I lo . . . oooh." Barbu stopped suddenly. He shook his head and cleared his throat. "I lo . . .

ach, hrrrmph! Sorry. Feel a bit sick suddenly."
He gagged, swallowed, took a deep breath, and
carried on. "I love you. Oh, Cooper! Seriously,
I think I might be allergic . . ." He grabbed the
chocolate box on Belinda's lap and threw up into
it. "You might not want those now . . ." he added,
handing the box back again, panting. "Anyway,
let's cut to the chase and get this over with. Will
you marry me?"

Belinda's eyes opened to the size of saucers.
"Me? Marry YOU?"

"I know," Barbu sighed. "It's ridiculous."

"YES!" she screamed, leaping from her chair,
arms wide open. Barbu let out a small screech.
Dodging to the left, he ducked and dived around
the room, Belinda hot on his heels.

"Stop her, Tully!" he yelled, throwing a chair in
her path. The henchman, who was secretly enjoy-
ing the spectacle, nonetheless picked Belinda
up when she next passed him and dumped her,
unceremoniously, on the chaise longue.

"You have to do the wet thing on the face
now, Mr. Barbu," said Tully as the villain cowered
behind an armchair.

"Really?" Barbu grimaced, closing his eyes in dread. "Oh, all right!" he yelled at Belinda. "Just stand up, keep still, and I'll do the kissing."

Clearing his throat, Barbu came out from behind the chair and approached his expectant fiancée. She had her eyes closed and her lips pursed in readiness. This really was beyond the call of duty, but a villain has to do what a villain has to do. With a heavy sigh, he leaned forward to kiss her, but found himself staring at the end of her chin. "Footstool, Tully," he hissed. "Quickly. Though I am not small. It's merely for *gravitas*."

Tully slid a small wooden box in front of Belinda's feet. Stepping up onto it with a revolted scowl, Barbu leaned toward Belinda's cheek and, very swiftly, stuck out his tongue and licked it. "Right!" he yelled, jumping down from the box. "That will do. That's that. We're now engaged. But don't get any funny ideas. I don't want to be bothered again until the wedding."

Belinda clutched her hands with joy. "I'm engaged!" She beamed. "Engaged! I must run and tell Mother and Father immediately. You've made me the happiest girl on Cooper, Barbu!"

"That's Mr. D'Anvers to you," snarled Barbu, wiping his tongue clean with a handkerchief.

As Belinda skipped from the room, the ghastly criminal turned to his cohorts. "It would have been very nice to have avoided all this distastefulness by finding the treasure quicker so we could have been on our way by now," the villain snarled. "That dreadful Goody-Goodman always seems to thwart my plans. Anyway, that's phase one of the marriage plan complete. Let phase two commence. Now we just have to get rid of Lord and Lady Blackheart. Is there some sort of deep well anywhere on the estate?"

"Why, Mr. Barbu?" asked Tully, scratching his head. "Do you need some water?"

"No!" yelled Barbu, rapping Tully on the forehead with his silver cane. "So we can push them down it! OBVIOUSLY!"

So there it is. Barbu D'Anvers engaged to a lady. Hell has frozen over.

"There you go, Inspector Lemone!" Mrs. Moggins smiled, handing the shivering policeman a large and steaming bowl. "My heavy soup made with our very own butler's homegrown vegetables will warm you through in no time."

"He'll eat nothing of the sort!" snapped Mrs. Speckle, snatching the bowl away again. "Heavy soup? Revolting! Here," she added, handing the Inspector a pie dish. "Fish tart. That's the breakfast you need. Heavy soup! I ask you! It's a wonder anyone in this house is *still alive!*"

Inspector Lemone didn't dare respond. After

their terrible trudge through the night, he was frozen to the bone, and with icicles hanging from his nostrils, he was in no fit state to be coping with the unexpected attentions of not one, but *two* cooks, especially as one of them was his beloved Mrs. Speckle. Wilma, who had been hanging Pickle up by his ears in front of the fire to thaw out, now pulled off her mittens and slumped into a chair. Her braids were frozen solid, her shoes were full of snow, and her teeth were chattering nonstop. Theodore opened the oven door and stuck his bottom into it. "Oh, that's better!" he groaned with a grateful sigh. There was no doubt about it, they had had a horrible hike.

Once Wilma had defrosted enough to turn her head again, she looked around the kitchen. She'd quite like to put her hands around something hot, like a just boiled kettle or a steaming potato. Above her, hanging next to Pickle, there was a large square of cloth. She reached up and touched it. It was warm from the fire. Maybe she could wrap her hands in it for a few minutes until the blood started pumping again? She slipped the cloth from the line and began to wrap it about her frozen fingers. The fabric felt warm and toasty, and as life flooded back into her ice-battered hands, she looked down and noticed that there was a mark stamped into one corner of the rag. Hang on—she'd seen that mark before. On the muslin that she was wrapped in when she was left on the orphanage doorstep as a baby! "Mrs. Moggins!" she cried excitedly, leaping from her chair. "This cloth—where did it come from?"

Mrs. Moggins, who was still glaring at Mrs. Speckle, gave the cloth a quick glance. "That old thing? That's what the hams come wrapped in. I wash them out and dry them. They make good tea cloths."

"Yes," urged Wilma, "but where do you buy the ham?"

"From the butcher's over in Arewenearly-thereyet," the cook replied with a shrug.

Wilma stumbled backward into her chair again, her mouth agape. "Mr. Goodman," she whispered, staring at the crest of the crossed lamb chops. "Look at that! It's the same mark as the one on my missing relative clue. Oh my! Do you think I might have found my missing relative? A butcher?"

The great and serious detective, who was still thawing his backside in the oven, frowned a little. "Take care, Wilma," he warned softly. "It's certainly an excellent new clue and you should definitely follow it up as soon as you can, but remember what I told you about speculating. It's best not to get your hopes up. I suspect you will need many more clues before your particular mystery is solved. And besides, you still have to speak to Kite Lambard, remember?"

Wilma's eyes widened. "How could I forget, Mr. Goodman? It's the one thing I am most looking forward to! Even more than Brackle Day!" What a wonderful surprise! Thoughts of her own mystery were never far from Wilma's mind, and the unexpected discovery of an enormous new clue thrilled her to the core. What with everything that was happening at the Hoo, she hadn't given Miss Lambard's impending arrival much thought, but this sudden find had jolted her back to her own reality. In a matter of days, Wilma might have the answers she'd been looking for.

"So you made it back?" came a voice from the doorway. "Thought you might be goners. Flatelly came back, heck of a state, had to be sedated, mumbling something about a phantom and a cherub. Said you were all trapped. Was going to rustle up a rescue committee, of course," Lord Blackheart added, "but it turned out you'd taken all the skis. According to Portious."

"Dr. Flatelly's here?" said Wilma, smiling. "So the Phantom didn't kill him? Well, thank goodness," she added with a relieved sigh. "That would have been terrible and sad and I would have been up to my eyes in paperwork."

"Thank you, Wilma," interrupted Theodore. "Where is Dr. Flatelly now, Lord Blackheart?"

"I left him with Tarquin," Blackheart explained. "He was gibbering about some painting of a cherub. Only cherub I know of around here is the big stone one in the chapel opposite the family pew."

"Of course. The cherry and the maggot-like

thing on the wall in the mine . . ." mused Mr. Goodman. Then, seeing Wilma's bemused look, he continued. "Those pictures—one was of a cherry, the other of a grub. And what if the strange symbol between them meant 'to merge'? What do you get if you mix a cherry and a grub, Wilma?"

"A disgusting mouthful of grossness?"

"A cher-ub," the detective exclaimed, starting for the door. "If that isn't a clue, I don't know what is."

"So you think the cherub in the chapel is the one that's in the picture, Mr. Goodman?" yelled Wilma, leaping from her chair and unhooking Pickle from the drying line. "And it's a clue as to where the missing treasure is?"

The great detective nodded, wiggling his mustache to free it of the last chips of ice. "Lemone! Look sharp! To the chapel!"

Wilma frowned as she followed her mentor to the door. "Dr. Flatelly must have used Bludsten's diary key to work it out, but he shouldn't have told Tarquin all those clues, should he, Mr.

Goodman? Because proper detectives always save what they're thinking till last—Top Tip for Detecting number nine. This is what happens when untrained people try and go detective. He's not the apprentice. I am. Come on, Inspector Lemone!"

Inspector Lemone, who was only halfway through the fish tart Mrs. Speckle had given him and had yet to find himself a pair of trousers, looked up and gulped as he watched his companions racing out through the kitchen door. "Sometimes," he mumbled as he stuffed the tart into a pocket and chased after them, "I can't help thinking we've got our priorities all wrong in this job. Never mind top tip number nine, what about number ten—never go detecting on an empty stomach, eh?"

The family chapel was in the west wing of Blackheart Hoo. The storm clouds that had hung so low were starting to lift, and for the first time in days, blue sky and a bright winter sunshine began to appear, sending shafts of light through the chapel's stained-glass windows. Wilma glanced up. The decorated panes were filled with familiar Brackle Day images: the discovery of the first Brackle Bush, the fateful encounter between Melingerra Maffling and Stavier Cranktop, and the moment the island was divided between the Lowside and the Farside forever—all were beautifully rendered. But there was something even more startling to draw the group's attention—in a far corner Tarquin was attacking the church floor with a pickaxe.

"Aaaarrrgh!" he yelled, tossing the heavy tool to one side and running a frustrated hand through his hair. "Nothing here! Where is it? WHERE IS IT?" Suddenly realizing he was not alone, Tarquin froze. "Oh, it's you. I was just . . . trying to assist Dr. Flatelly." He waved his hand in the direction of the stone cherub that looked down on the very spot he'd been demolishing. "And find the treasure for Father, of course."

Theodore fixed him with a penetrating stare. "Have you told Barbu D'Anvers about the cherub yet?" he asked in a low tone.

"No," replied Tarquin sheepishly.

Wilma looked down at the heap of broken tiles on the floor and peered into the empty hole beneath them, Pickle sniffing at it from behind her legs. "Nothing buried there, then," she said, getting her apprentice's notebook from her pocket. "This looks like it may require some wonky thinking, Mr. Goodman," she added, tapping a pencil against her bottom lip. "And as for you . . ." She turned toward Tarquin, trying to look VERY serious. "If I hadn't seen the Fatal Phantom with my own eyes, twice, this would push you RIGHT up my Likely Suspects list. In debt, running off, digging things up—it doesn't look good. Doesn't look good AT ALL."

"Thank you, Wilma." Theodore reached for his magnifying glass. "And this is the only cherub on the estate?" he asked the Blackheart boy as he took a closer look at the statue.

"As far as I know." Tarquin nodded, slumping down onto a wooden pew. "Perhaps this treasure thing is just a wild-goose chase."

"Oh, I don't know about that," muttered the detective, giving the cherub's wing a little rub.

"Actually, I think we're dealing with an old-fashioned treasure hunt, odd as that seems. And here we have our next clue, there, on the edge of the cherub's wing. A small engraving showing a question mark like the one on the mine wall, then an equals symbol and a picture of some coins and a key with that same 'merge' sign. So if we apply the same logic as to the cherub clue— 'coins' plus 'key' doesn't mean much, but what about 'money' plus 'key,' Wilma?"

"A monkey, Mr. Goodman!" Wilma scribbled frantically in her pad as she spoke.

"That's what we're looking for next. And I'd say, on the basis of the mine wall, that it will lead us to the two map scrolls it pictured—and they'll give us the treasure location. If it really exists."

"Makes my head hurt," Inspector Lemone grumbled, "but good work, Goodman!"

"What was that?" asked a tired voice from behind them. "A monkey? Heard you'd made it out. Thank goodness! I hit my head when that terrible thing came at me. Then it must have left me for dead. I came around a while later. I called out for you, but perhaps the walls were too thick. I was so worried you were all goners . . ."

Everyone turned to see Dr. Flatelly making his way toward them.

"I'm ever so glad you weren't killed, Doctor," said Wilma.

"Why, thank you." Irascimus smiled. "That's most kind."

"Because you've still got Bludsten's diary," she continued, holding her hand out. "And it's official evidence."

"Oh." The archaeologist blinked, a little taken aback. "Well, I'm happy to hang on to it for further analysis, if that's helpful."

Wilma's upturned palm remained steadfastly thrust toward him. "No, thank you. You're not the apprentice detective. I am."

"You'd better let her have it, Dr. Flatelly," interjected Theodore, tucking his magnifying glass back into his waistcoat. "Wilma is nothing if not determined."

"Even if I am small to look at," agreed Wilma.

Dr. Flatelly pulled the diary reluctantly from

the inside of his overcoat. "As you wish . . . there. Now then, Mr. Goodman, what's this about a monkey?"

"Perhaps Tarquin knows where it . . . Oh!" Wilma looked about her. "He's gone."

"Must have sneaked off!" blustered Inspector Lemone, spinning about to see if he could catch a glimpse of him. "Dang it all, Goodman! That feels slippery to me!"

"Quickly," urged Theodore, heading for the doorway. "We must seek Lord Blackheart's counsel immediately. He may be able to tell us the location of the monkey!"

Tarquin was creeping silently along an upstairs corridor toward the small reading room on the second floor. The monkey, he was positive, was a small bronze statue that sat on a decorative drinks table to the left of the fireplace. Hearing a noise, he stopped where he was and slipped into a dark recess so as not to be discovered. Carefully, he peered out and saw Molly and Polly leaving the reading room. "What're they up to?" Tarquin said, frowning. "Oh, of course—setting out Father's midday cocoa as usual," he realized. "Which means Father's due here any moment. I've got to act fast."

As soon as the maids had disappeared into the gloom of the corridor, Tarquin slipped from his hiding place and into the reading room. For some reason the curtains were drawn and the lamps unlit, so the only light emanated from a small fire in the grate. Tarquin shivered. Why was it so cold in here even with the fire lit? And why did he have a funny feeling that he was not alone? With his eyes still adjusting to the dim light, he told himself he was imagining things and stumbled across to the ornate stand next to the hearth, checking over his shoulder the whole way. The table was bare.

"Where's the monkey?" Tarquin yelled, slamming his fist down. "Who has taken it?"

Suddenly, from above, there came a short, sharp cracking sound and Tarquin looked up to see a heavy marble bust that had been standing on a nearby pedestal come crashing down toward him. He leaped backward just in time and the bust shattered over the fireside table and chair. It had missed him by inches. He scrabbled to his feet, wild-eyed and terrified. "What is this?" he screamed. "Hocus-pocus? Well, you won't scare me, Fatal Phantom! You won't, I tell you!" And with that he made a mad dash for the door, fumbled with the handle, and ran for his life.

Somewhere, in the shadows, a dark form stirred . . .

Frightened now? You *should* be.

Things were not progressing quickly enough for Barbu D'Anvers. The Blackhearts were still the picture of health and they were no nearer finding the treasure. It wasn't all bad news, though.

"That's quite a reasonable haul." Barbu smirked, tossing a candlestick into the large wooden crate in Tully's arms. "Good work, Janty. Your light fingers should bring us a tidy sum. Take it down to Arewenearlythereyet market—it's on today and not far from here. You can unload the stuff there. Though be careful the deadly dull Goodman doesn't catch you. You know what he's like about trying to sell things that aren't yours. So boring."

"Yes, master." The young boy nodded, taking the box from the henchman.

"Tully, I want you to continue your sneaky spying on Goody Two-Shoes. And do try and *keep up* this time. Plus, remember your dodgy demises duty," Barbu went on.

Tully blinked. "Dodgy what?"

"Demises!" yelled Barbu, rapping him on the forehead with the end of his cane. "Assassinations! Slaughters! And general carnage! In short, bump off the Blackhearts! I don't care how we do it—the fortune SHALL be mine!"

"Yes, Mr. Barbu." Tully sniffed, rubbing his eyebrow. "Though, that really hurt."

Barbu stared at him with incredulity. "Look at your contract!" he yelled, producing Tully's Contract of Employment from his inside coat pocket. "Subsection B! 'The henchman will receive raps to the head from time to time. These may *smart*.' It's there in black and white! I'm perfectly within my rights. End of discussion."

Tully pouted.

* * *

"Gone?" boomed Lord Blackheart, staring at his squirming son. "What do you mean it's gone?"

"The monkey just isn't there, Father," answered Tarquin nervously.

"And what's all this Mr. Goodman tells me about you sneaking off? Trying to pull a fast one, are you? Take the treasure for yourself so you can gamble that away too?"

Tarquin gulped. "No . . . I mean . . ."

"Lord Blackheart," interrupted Portious morosely, entering the tea room, where everyone was gathered. "I'm afraid I have some startling news."

"Oh, not more spookings," sighed Blackheart. "What now?"

"Several of Mrs. Moggins's saucepans have gone missing, m'lord," explained Portious in his usual flat tone.

"My best milk pan!" yelled the fuming cook, leaning out from behind the butler. "And a frying pot! Valuable they are! I'll wager it's that Speckle woman—out to sabotage my cooking."

"Ooh now, steady on," piped up Inspector Lemone. "That's a serious allegation."

"Aloysius!" wailed Lady Blackheart, wafting in through the doorway. "A pearl box has gone missing from my boudoir! Miss Daise thinks it's the treasure-hungry ghoul adding to his stash!"

"Like the monkey too," Wilma said, reaching for her notebook.

"I'm not so sure about that," Mr. Goodman interjected. "A spook doesn't have much need for cooking implements. But it would appear," he went on, reaching for his pipe and tobacco, "that seemingly random objects *are* going missing around the Hoo. However, I would suggest there is a pattern emerging."

"Oh!" piped up Wilma, who had been scribbling down a list of the missing things. "I love a pattern! Is it swirly? Or curly?"

Theodore cleared his throat. "It is my opinion that the presence of a notorious Criminal Element and the sudden disappearance of several *valuable* objects are not unrelated."

"Oh, wait," Wilma said, scratching her head. "That's one of those double nots, isn't it? If it's a not it's a no, but if it's a not-not it's a yes."

"A double negative," explained the great detective patiently. "Correct."

"In this patterny thing, you said they're not *un*-related. That's one not for the not and the second not for the *un,* so that's definitely a not-not. So that means they ARE related. Ah-ha! Golly. Not-nots are quite dizzy, aren't they, Mr. Goodman?"

"What my apprentice is accurately, if a little excessively, explaining is that yes, I think it's safe to assume that the person behind these thefts is none other than Barbu D'Anvers."

"So Barbu's got the monkey!" said Tarquin, standing up suddenly. "But if he gets to the treasure first, then I still owe him all that money!"

"The good thing is," said Theodore, holding out a steadying hand, "that if he does have it, there's every chance he doesn't know what he has, so there may be no cause for alarm. Besides, if he has it, then Inspector Lemone can arrest him. It is stealing, after all."

"It'd be a pleasure," burst out Lemone, puffing his cheeks. "Has anyone seen the scoundrel? I'll chase him down!"

"Actually, wasn't that him?" exclaimed Dr. Flatelly suddenly, pointing out of the window. "I'll see if I can grab him, shall I?"

"What? Where?" blustered the Inspector, also peering out of the window. "I'll come with you, Doctor—oh, he's already gone."

"Yes, let's go after him," Mr. Goodman agreed, but Lord Blackheart stepped in front of the door.

"So are you saying"—he narrowed his eyes—"that as far as the treasure hunt goes, without that monkey you've drawn a blank?"

"Lord Blackheart," the great and serious detective began, "there's something important I need—"

"Blanks!" Wilma yelled suddenly. "In Bludsten's diary!" She held it aloft.

"Yes, a very useful document, Wilma," Mr. Goodman agreed, slightly baffled by the outburst. "I did indeed plan to turn to that next, in lieu of the monkey statue. But that's not what I was going to say."

"No," Wilma gabbled desperately. "I've just had a Hunchy Instinct moment and remembered the chapter on top secret messages in my Academy textbook. And it said that sometimes a blank page isn't a blank page at all but an invisible message, and I know revealing the message had something to do with pancakes . . . but I can't quite remember—do you add sugar or eat it? But my textbook also says that if you munch up the evidence, that's sort of destroying it, so that can't be right . . ."

"Hmm," said Theodore, taking the diary and flicking through it. "You're right, Wilma." He gave her a proud look. "Only I think you mean add lemon and cook it. Mrs. Moggins," the great detective went on, turning to the cook, "would you have some lemon juice at your disposal?"

"Never mind her," shouted Mrs. Speckle, marching in with a tray of corn crumbles. "I've ALWAYS got a lemon in my knitted sock pouch. Never leave home without one."

"Oooh, biscuits . . ." murmured the Inspector, dribbling a little.

Taking a knife from the tea tray, Theodore sliced the lemon in two. Then he squeezed one half gently so that a few drops of lemon juice dripped onto the blank pages of the diary. "Some-times," the famed detective explained, walking over to the fire, "secret things are written in ink that is invisible to the naked eye. But if you add a little acidity—the lemon—and a little heat—the fire . . . come here and see . . ." He held the diary pages toward the flaming coals. Wilma trotted over and peered at the blank pages. As if by magic, faint brown lines began to appear on one of them right before her eyes. She let out a small gasp. "And there you are," continued Theo-dore as the picture revealed itself further. "We have a . . . map!"

"Oh my!" whispered Wilma, who was ever so impressed. A little bit with herself as well, for working it out. Sort of. "Is that it, then? Is that the map to the treasure?"

"Not sure. It looks incomplete," pondered Theodore. "I've seen this before. It may be half of a double map—it's a common trick, two maps needed to make one complete map. By the look of it, Bludsten was making rough drafts in his diary of the two map clues he planned to hide as part of the treasure trail. Like the two map scrolls shown on the mine wall. Although annoyingly, there is a page missing here. It may be the second part we needed."

Wilma, who had gone a bit cross-eyed with all the "this map, that map" business, shook her head. "There's an awful lot to take in, isn't there, Pickle? We're on a treasure hunt with a map that needs another map," she explained. "I hope you're keeping up." Pickle stared back at her. He didn't have a clue WHAT was going on.

Suddenly there was a shattering noise and a scream rang through the house. Lady Blackheart leaped out of her skin. "Not again!" she cried, running to the door. "That sounded like Miss Daise! Oh, Aloysius! We must hurry!"

Wilma followed closely behind Mr. Goodman as they all ran toward the continuing screams. She had to admit that although part of her couldn't wait for another spooky clue to add to her Clue Board, she was also more than a little petrified about what ghoulishness they might face. She hadn't forgotten her terrifying encounter with the Phantom in the mine. In fact, she wasn't sure she ever would. It had tried to kill them, after all!

When they finally arrived in the lower hall they found Fenomina collapsed in the arms of Dr. Flatelly. Both looked extremely rattled.

"What has happened?" asked Theodore with some urgency, glancing quickly about him. On the floor, next to the psychic, there was an upturned table, a broken vase, and some plant stems . . . and three arrows were embedded in the wooden floor.

"It must have been the crossbow up there," muttered Irascimus, visibly shaken. "Something must have set off the mechanism. But how . . . I can't explain. Missed us by a whisker."

"I was adding to your latest flower arrangement, Lady Blackheart," Fenomina wailed, indicating what looked like a bunch of thorny weeds at her feet, "and the doctor here had stopped to admire it, when those arrows came at us out of nowhere!"

"Someone just tried to kill me too," admitted Tarquin, following hard on Theodore's heels. "With a marble bust."

"Really?" the butler exclaimed, a shocked expression on his usually droopy face.

"It's the Fatal Phantom again!" whispered Lady Blackheart, gripping her husband's arm. "And now it's so angry, it's trying to kill us all!"

Theodore turned and squinted toward the firing mechanism on the weapon mounted high on the wall. "Hmm," he pondered. "It seems we have progressed beyond attempted theft and scare tactics to something much worse, what with the attack on our lives in the mine as well!"

"Oh my goodness!" Wilma exclaimed, her eyes widening. "And there's proof the Phantom is feeling Fatal again. Look at this, Mr. Goodman. Something terrible's scratched into the wallpaper over here." While everyone else had gathered around Fenomina, Dr. Flatelly, and the arrows, Wilma and Pickle had been doing their own sniffing out of the scene—and just around the corner from the last arrow, they had found another spooky scrawl.

The great detective reached for his magnifying glass and followed Wilma's shaking finger toward the message gouged into the wall.

"'DEATH TO ALL IF YOU PERSIST IN THIS HUNT,'" he read in a solemn tone. Everyone gathered gasped.

"The Phantom probably did it with its terrible talons, right, Mr. Goodman?" Wilma urged.

"Definitely something curved," the detective continued.

Wilma looked at him hopefully—was that a yes, he believed in ghosts and their talons now? She wasn't sure.

"The dead are truly walking among us!" cried Belinda, clutching her hands to her mouth. "And what's more, they want us dead too!"

"I didn't come here to be *murdered*," moaned Fenomina. "Portious, arrange for my sled to return me home immediately."

"Are you sure, madame?" the butler rumbled. "I—"

"YES!" the psychic screamed hysterically.

Dr. Flatelly staggered to his feet and, taking a handkerchief from his pocket, he wiped his brow. "First the mine, now this . . . If anyone needs me I shall be in my office. I need to calm down."

"Wilma, Inspector," said Theodore, looking purposeful, "to the Clue Board. We need to have a rethink."

"But what about my pan?" yelled Mrs. Moggins as the detective paced away. "What are you going to do about that?"

"I think he's decided there are more pressing matters to be dealt with, Mrs. Moggins," stated Portious, pulling one of the arrows from the floor.

"Not for me there aren't!" declared the angry cook. "Well, if you want something done, do it yourself!" And with that, she barged down the corridor.

Goodness, this is a hullaballoo. An incomplete map, a hidden treasure, a milk pan stolen, a missing monkey, a villain on the loose, and a murderous ghoul with a fondness for writing on walls—it's a positive *commotion*. Steady your nerves, children, and let's crank up the heat . . .

21

"I know it was you!" shouted a livid Mrs. Moggins, hands on hips. "That's my best pan for sauces! And I want it back!"

Barbu, who had been cornered, grimaced and looked a bit baffled. "And you are?" he demanded. "I'm generally not used to being told what to do by anybody, let alone rough-skinned women who look like boiled hams. OW! What the . . . OW!" he yelled again, recoiling as Mrs. Moggins came at him with her rolling pin.

The bully cook wasn't standing for any sort of nonsense. "I don't care what you are used to, I want my pan back," she hissed in his face.

"Ugh!" Barbu protested, wiping his cheeks frantically. "You're actually spitting on me! All right! You can have your stupid pan back. My boy has it. He's down at Arewenearlythereyet market on our stall."

Mrs. Moggins straightened up and tucked her rolling pin back under the top string of her apron. "Right, then. And let's hope for your sake that he *still* has it. And that monkey. Or they'll never find the treasure."

Barbu's ears pricked. "What monkey?" he pressed.

"A brass monkey they're all moaning about. Got some scribbles on it or something. Clues for the treasure."

An evil smirk spread across Barbu's lips. "Let me accompany you to Coop. We'll take my carriage. I wouldn't *like* it if you slipped on some ice . . ."

Mrs. Moggins's face softened. "Oh well, thank you very much," she answered, turning and stomping down the corridor.

Barbu watched her as she galumphed away from him, his smirk turning to a deep scowl.

"I'd *LOVE* it . . ." he muttered, before heading off after her.

Janty had set up a stall in a prominent position in the middle of Arewenearlythereyet's small but bustling market. It was well-known for its broad range of goods, everything from bobble hats to porcelain mice. And despite the snow, people bustled back and forth buying hiding holes and last-minute Brussels sprouts and parsnips for their Brackle Day celebrations. A small crowd had gathered at Janty's stall and so far, trade had been brisk. He had managed to sell a silver prawn, a wooden nutcracker in the shape of a pig, and one decorative plate with a badger on it. With his jacket buttoned up tightly and his scarf wrapped around him, Janty hopped on the spot and blew on his fingers. The weather might have started to improve, but it was still freezing cold.

"How much for that pan?" asked a woman in an enormous balloon-shaped hat.

"Five groggles," replied the boy, pulling the saucepan from the box.

"Not so fast!" came the voice of Mrs. Moggins as she dashed toward him, Barbu hot on her heels. "I'll take that, thank you! Ooooooooh!" she cried out as she slid violently to the icy ground.

"Oh dear," said Barbu, staring down at the flailing figure of the oversized cook. "Fallen over? Have you broken anything?"

"No, I don't think so," groaned Mrs. Moggins, trying to get up.

"Too bad. I should have pushed a bit harder. Now then, Janty." He grabbed the boy by the shoulder and hissed into his ear. "Please don't tell me you've sold anything looking like a monkey?"

Luckily for Barbu, he hadn't. It was still in Janty's box and within moments, after handing back all the cook's pans, they were examining it for clues.

"Look—there, engraved on the bottom. Symbols and pictures," Janty exclaimed seconds later.

Barbu grabbed the monkey and narrowed his eyes. "So there is. There's a fly—no . . . a bee, some squiggles, then a picture of an ear. Interesting. Wonder what it means?"

Wilma had never seen Mr. Goodman so agitated. He was pacing back and forth in front of the Clue Board, hands clasped behind his back, deep in thought. Perhaps, Wilma pondered, he was upset because it was *obvious* now that there was a ghost at Blackheart Hoo and he'd been proved wrong. She would have to tread carefully. Even though she was delighted that her deductions had proved correct, she didn't want to make her mentor feel foolish.

"Shall I stick some more clues up, Mr. Goodman? It's been a while since we updated the Clue Board," she said, reaching for her own notebook and making a few pertinent drawings. "There's the cherub, the monkey, and our half a map on the treasure front; and the spooky footprints in the snow, latest ghoulish message, talon, and the Phantom's murder attempts on the ghost hunt, whodunit front. And Bludsten's diary gives us clues on both fronts—what with the symbols key AND the cursed ramblings. Do you think . . ." Wilma paused, blinked, and continued, ". . . that Fenomina's in danger from the Fatal Phantom because she's got powers to get rid of spooks? And Tarquin and Dr. Flatelly because they're hunting the treasure, like us?" Wilma held up her notebook to show Mr. Goodman her picture. "I've given the Fatal Phantom antlers, but that's only because I can't draw talons. And Bludsten Blackheart's ghost—I've done him too since he is inside Belinda—probably doesn't wear a skirt. But still—it's a two-spook case, after all."

"Which is something along the lines of what I've been thinking, Wilma." Theodore nodded. "Only now . . ."

Wilma swallowed. *Did* Mr. Goodman finally believe in spooks? "Really?"

"Yes, really?" Inspector Lemone echoed nervously.

"Not the spooks bit. There's still no *proof* of that! But the rest—though it suddenly seems not quite as clear as I believed. No matter!" Theodore continued, scribbling in his notebook. "It simply means that more digging and evidence are required. Besides, that part of the investigation will have to wait. Our priority once again is to find that treasure as quickly as possible. If Barbu D'Anvers, or whoever is doing all this, gets hold of it first, then Cooper or the Blackhearts are done for. So, what do we *know* of its where-abouts?"

Wilma screwed her lips sideways. She wasn't quite sure what Mr. Goodman was talking about. He was displaying classic confusion—up to their eyes in spook clues and he still couldn't see it. Instead, his mind seemed to be racing hither and thither. "Not much, really. There's probably a clue on a monkey that we haven't got. And we *have* got half a map. That's about it."

"Let me have another look at that map in Blud-sten's diary please, Wilma." The young appren-tice scooped it from her pinafore pocket and presented it to the great detective. "Yes." Theo-dore sighed. "Look here at the corners. Placer markers. That's where the second part of the map needs to be laid so that the two merge and become the complete picture. Maybe we need to find Barbu and that monkey after all."

As they headed toward the door, they passed the window, and in the courtyard below Wilma suddenly spotted Victor. Seeing her appear at the window he waved up. Wilma smiled. Hang on! Her churning thoughts suddenly crystallized. She'd seen those map marker arrows before! On the bit of paper Victor had given her at the séance! She stuck her thumbs up in Victor's direction. She knew he had promised to help her prove herself to Mr. Goodman, but how was it he always knew when she needed him? She reached into the bottom of her pinafore pocket and took out the crumpled ball of paper. She had totally forgotten about it—in fact, she'd barely looked at it. Opening it out, her eyes widened. It was a mass of scribbled lines that made no sense, but in the corners there were four small black arrows. The same black arrows that appeared on the map in Bludsten's diary! "Mr. Goodman!" she squealed excitedly, grabbing him by the arm. "Victor, the boy who works in the stable, gave me this at the séance!" She was so grateful to him, she couldn't keep his part in her recent discoveries a secret any longer. Besides, Mr. Goodman and the Inspector wouldn't rat him out! "It's the missing map page from the diary."

"Stable boy?" quizzed Inspector Lemone now. "Why haven't I seen him around the place?"

"He's not supposed to come into the main house. Anyway," Wilma pressed on, handing the famed detective the crinkled paper, "see what happens if you put that on the secret map!"

Theodore took the paper and began to line up the arrows so that all four matched. "Oh no!" whimpered Inspector Lemone, eyes darting about the room anxiously. "This might be it. We might be about to find the treasure's location. Don't let the spook hear us . . ." He loosened his tie.

"Do we know what we're going to do when the Fatal Phantom appears?" asked Wilma. "I suspect handcuffs won't work. We might need a net or an enormous jam jar or a—"

"There," interrupted Theodore, triumphant. "Just as I thought." As the great detective held the two pieces of paper together, the map, which had previously seemed higgledy-piggledy, suddenly made sense. Wilma grinned and pointed. "Oh my goodness! The treasure! There it is!"

All pathways were now complete and the words "It Lies Here" came into sharp relief. From the words, a long thin arrow pointed upward and ended at the picture of a casket with a lock. "It's buried under the gazebo on the boating lake," whispered Theodore, getting out his magnifying glass. "And that," he added, pointing with his pen toward the casket, "looks like the padlock that the mummy's key is for."

Suddenly the lights went out, a terrible chill drifted into the room, and there was a strange, spooky creak from behind them. Twisting around, Theodore dashed toward the cupboard the sound had come from and opened the door. But there was nothing there. "Thank goodness," mumbled Lemone, who was looking over his friend's shoulder. "Thought it was the Phantom come to get us. Again."

"It's worse than that," Theodore rumbled.

"Really?" worried Lemone as the great and

serious detective poked urgently at the back of the cupboard with a finger.

"Yes. This has a false back. Someone has been eavesdropping and has heard every word we just said. Hang on, where's Wilma?"

For as the lights came back on it was very clear that Wilma and Pickle were . . . gone.

There's a word for this sort of situation. Can you guess what it is? No? Then I'll tell you. It's OMINOUS. Go and look it up now in a dictionary and then start quaking.

arquin was getting desperate. He had to find that treasure first! If Barbu did have the monkey, then he had to get to him and take it. With all eyes watching him, it had been virtually impossible to get away, but now that Mr. Goodman and his crew were in a case conference, all Tarquin had had to do was wait for his father to slip into his inevitable post-lunch snooze and he could creep away.

As soon as his father had slumped sideways and started snoring, Tarquin had tiptoed from the room. Now he headed quickly toward the main staircase, but before he could reach the grand descent he stopped. Molly and Polly were standing in the hall, huddled together and whispering. They had something in their hands. Tarquin's eyes narrowed. "What are you two up to?" he asked, rushing toward them.

"Nothing, Master Blackheart," answered Polly, hiding the thing behind her back.

"What have you got there?" barked Tarquin, grabbing the girl's arm.

"Just a casket we were polishing," interrupted Molly, taking the small locked chest from Polly's hand and placing it down on the nearby shelf.

Tarquin, wild-eyed, snatched at it. "Probably think the treasure's in it, don't you? You're all after it! Don't think I don't know!" He shook it. "Empty. Blast!" Throwing it to the ground, he turned back to Polly. "Where's D'Anvers?" he asked urgently. "He must be around somewhere."

"I don't know, Master Blackheart," answered the shaken girl. "Though I think I saw him going into the pistol parlor about an hour ago."

"Out of my way," yelled Tarquin, pushing past them both. Running down the main staircase and along the narrow twisting corridors, Tarquin sped past ancient Blackheart portraits of infamous pigs, all of them staring down accusingly.

The pistol parlor was in the north wing, a dark, menacing room used to keep weapons old and new, and that was rarely visited except by Lord Blackheart. "Where are you, D'Anvers?" Tarquin shouted, striding around it frantically. But the room was empty. "Dash it all!" he yelled in frustration. But a sudden movement to his left made him turn just in time to see the door slam shut seemingly of its own accord, an ominous shadow, then something long and pointed flying through the air toward him. It was a spear! Tarquin let out a yell and veered sideways, but he wasn't quite quick enough and the spear caught the edge of his cheek before thumping into the wall behind him. Tarquin raised a hand to his face and looked at the blood left on his fingers. His eyes, wide with fear, darted around him, but there was no one there. He looked up at the spear vibrating in the wall and stumbled backward toward the door. "I'm not afraid, I tell you!" he screamed. "Not afraid!" But he was. He was *terrified*.

* * *

Barbu and Janty had been brainstorming for over an hour, but the closest they'd come to an answer was to find something that buzzed and listen to it for . . . who knows what?

"What can it mean?" pondered Barbu, eyebrows knitted in angry thought. He spun around and threw his cane at Tully's head as the henchman joined them. "You'd better be able to tell us something useful, with all the spying and sneaking around you've been doing."

Tully blinked as he put his hands to his battered head. "I couldn't get close to their operations room, Master Barbu, but I did get to listen in when they were in the kitchen—all they were talking about though was a clue of cherries, grubs, and stone cherubs. Didn't sound very treasure-y to me."

Janty sat back in his chair and thought. "Hang on! 'Cherry,' 'grub'—say those words together quickly enough and they turn into 'cherub.' What if this clue is the same? Yes," he went on excitedly, jumping up. "Bee and ear—it's easy. Beer!"

Barbu looked at his young charge. "Well, well," he jeered. "If I didn't know you were rotten to the core, I'd have you down as a detective's apprentice!"

"What?" sneered Janty. "No way. Like that revolting Wilma Tenderfoot, you mean? Not me. I don't even like her."

"Hmm, yes, well. Good work, Janty, though there's not a moment to lose. We have the advantage over Goodman and speed is of the essence." Barbu ran to the window and stared out over the Hoo grounds. "There!" he shouted, pointing toward a low wooden structure. "The shed that leads down into the beer cellar." Barbu looked triumphant. "Let's go!"

"Can't see a thing," complained Barbu, taking the steep steps down into the cellar. "Light that lantern, Janty. Can either of you see anything vaguely TREASUREY?"

"There, master! There's a small cupboard in the wall behind that beer barrel," Janty cried, pointing.

Barbu went to reach up, but then retracted his hand swiftly. "I forgot," he said with a small cough, "I don't *do* reaching. Tully, get it."

The hefty henchman lumbered forward and opened the tiny postcard-sized door that was halfway up the wall. Reaching in, he pulled out a strange-looking blackened cube and a charred and crumpled piece of paper. He handed both to Barbu. "The paper's a map," Barbu explained, giving it a cursory examination, "although it seems a bit half-baked to my eye. There're a couple of crosses, some weird lines, and some odd arrows in the corners. Perhaps one of these marks the spot where the treasure's buried! Besides, there are no more clues, so this must be it. This cube doesn't seem to do anything," he added, tossing it aside. "Well, there's nothing for it—I can make enough out and we shall start digging! By that I mean you, Tully. My hands are far too sensitive. That treasure will be mine by the end of the day!" With a triumphant laugh, Barbu swung about only to find himself face-to-face with Belinda Blackheart.

"Boo!" giggled Belinda, smiling.

Barbu stared at her blankly. "Who's this?" he mumbled out of the side of his mouth.

"Belinda Blackheart," Janty whispered back. Barbu still looked blank. "She's your fiancée, master."

"Oh yes," muttered Barbu. "What do you want?"

"Well," began Belinda, "I came down to choose some wines for our reception. You must have had the same thought. Anyway, now I've got you here, we could decide what wedding cake we want and whether the bridesmaids' dresses should be in cream or mauve and . . . OH!"

With one sharp shove, Barbu barged past Belinda and sent her collapsing into a large barrel. He strode off up the wine cellar steps. "Don't mind Mr. D'Anvers," Janty explained to a shell-shocked Belinda. "He's just overexcited."

Meanwhile, the strange cube the teeny villain had tossed aside earlier lay unnoticed on the floor. Its fall had caused it to spring open, revealing the other half of Barbu's map clearly visible within it. He had thrown away the one bit he needed! And the lesson to be learned here, readers? ALWAYS check the packaging!

* * *

Wilma leaped down the front steps of the Hoo, Pickle fast on her heels. One of the best things about being an apprentice detective was getting to do things that felt urgent and important. They would need the mummy's key to open the treasure that they now had a location for, and showing initiative by hurrying to fetch it from Dr. Flatelly was exactly the sort of urgent thing Wilma had in mind. "Mr. Goodman will be ever so pleased with me," she told Pickle with a grin. There's nothing worse than having to do boring jobs. A lot of grown-ups spend all their time moaning about how dull their lives are precisely because of this problem. That's why they always look miserable, are prone to grumpiness, and sometimes develop a sudden and inexplicable desire to go cycling on mountain bikes or run marathons. Keep your eyes peeled. Those ones are bored STIFF.

Wilma ran through the snow, her Wellingtons leaving deep footprints behind her as Pickle bounced along at her side. The sunny afternoon air was crisp and cold so that their breath puffed out before them. Wilma felt excited. As soon as they had the key they could unlock the Blackheart treasure and when that was done, they'd get to the bottom of the hauntings. Never mind that Mr. Goodman still thought it was a heap of hocus-pocus! She knew otherwise, and would be ready to impress him with her spook-exercising regimen when it appeared. She'd tire out the Phantom in no time, catch it, and banish it once and for all. The case would be solved on two counts, and all thanks to Mr. Goodman and her! She'd be a proper detective before she could say "Fatal Phantom."

They had run around the front of the Hoo and were heading past the kitchens when Wilma skidded to a halt. In the courtyard, beside the back door into the delivery area, stood a cart. The breath caught in Wilma's throat and she could feel her heart thumping against her rib cage. Pickle, who actually *had* to bounce along because the snow was so deep and he wasn't wearing his snowshoes, suddenly realized she had come to a standstill and, trying to turn back mid-bounce, flipped sideways into a pile of wooden buckets. The clatter of falling buckets echoed around the courtyard. Hearing it, a man's face popped up from behind the back of the cart. Wilma's heart beat faster. Emblazoned on the side of the cart was the exact same crest that had been on the ham cloth in Mrs. Moggins's kitchen and on the muslin Wilma had been found wrapped in when she was a baby! Was that man Wilma's responsible person . . . even relative?

"Afternoon!" said the fellow with a nod.

Wilma gulped and clutched her mittens together tightly. "Hello," she said quietly, walking a little closer. "Are you the butcher?"

"Stanley Brisket!" said the man, pointing to the name under the crest. "That's me! Been a butcher on Cooper for eleven years!"

Wilma stared at him. He was a short, wide-looking fellow with cheeks like meatballs. He was bald apart from a few stray wisps of hair blowing in the chilly wind, and his apron, slightly bloodied, was pulled tight over the sort of belly that showed an incredible dedication to both pints of beer and pies. He didn't *look* like Wilma, but then, family members don't always have to bear a resemblance. There was nothing else for it, Wilma was going to have to bite the bullet. She took a deep breath. "The thing is, Mr. Brisket," she said, "I was left at the gates of the Institute for Woeful Children when I was a baby. And the reason I'm telling you is because I was wrapped in one of your meaty muslins." She stopped and flashed her green eyes upward, waiting to see if there was a moment of recognition.

Stanley Brisket stared back. "Wrapped in one of my muslins?" he asked eventually, scratching the top of his head. "And how long ago was this?"

"Well, I'm ten years old," replied Wilma. "So that long ago. And then Madam Skratch, who runs the orphanage, told me that I have a relative still alive. And there were some letters. So I was wondering . . ."Wilma stopped and took a massive gulp. ". . . because I was wrapped up like a ham, whether you might be my missing relative?"

Stanley Brisket looked rather taken aback, almost as if someone had slapped him about the face with a large greasy liver. This was not what he had been expecting when he left his butcher's shop that morning. He thought he'd be making his weekly routine delivery to the Hoo, but here he was, cornered by an abandoned child and being quizzed as to whether she was a member of his family. It's fair to say that most people would remember having a baby in the family and then mislaying it at the front gates of an orphanage, but even so, Stanley Brisket stood for a long while deep in thought. Then he looked back at Wilma, whose eyes were full of hope, and placed a large ruddy hand on her little shoulder. He shook his head. "I'm sorry that you had such a rough start in life," he began softly. "And I'm even sorrier that one of my ham cloths was involved with it. But I can tell you now, it was not I who deserted you. I can't explain how you came to be there or how you came to be so wrapped, but I can tell you this: I only wrap my large hams for delivery. And the only places I delivered to ten years ago, when I was just starting out, were here and to the Twelve Rats' Tails on the Lowside. So if you were wrapped in my muslin all those years back, then I reckon someone from one of those two places had taken my ham, unwrapped it, and wrapped you up instead."

Wilma felt a little crestfallen. Stanley Brisket was so nice, but he was clearly not her relative.

Still, if there was one thing she'd learned since becoming an apprentice detective, it was that every fresh piece of information is useful. Even so, the two options sent her mind reeling. Was she a Blackheart? They all seemed to have enormous teeth, which she did not, so perhaps that was unlikely. Of course, if the muslin had come from the Hoo, it could also have been used by one of the servants. As for being related to someone at the Twelve Rats' Tails, the notorious hangout for all Criminal Elements on Cooper—well! It didn't bear thinking about. That would make *her* a Criminal Element too. And where would that leave her, what with being an apprentice detective and all?

Wilma smiled bravely and thanked the butcher. She was in a bit of a daze, to be honest, and as she wandered off she began to think about how all of this fit in with the letter from her headmistress, Kite Lambard. The handwriting matched the handwriting of the person who had written to Madam Skratch all those years ago looking for Wilma. Miss Lambard didn't seem to have any connections to the Blackheart estate, not that

Wilma knew of, anyhow. Perhaps she was investigating a crime involving someone at the Twelve Rats' Tails at the time of Wilma's birth? Wilma felt her heart sink again. Every new clue seemed to create more confusion. "Sometimes," she said quietly to Pickle as they approached Dr. Flatelly's office, "it's a bit rubbish being an orphan. What with all the mystery and what-nots. Still. At least I've got you, eh, Pickle?" He barked up at her and wagged his tail. He'd never leave her. Never.

Arriving at Dr. Flatelly's shack, Wilma gave her head a little shake to clear her mind and concentrate on the matter at hand. Then she knocked twice. To her surprise, there was no reply. "That's funny," she said, scrunching her nose up. "I thought he'd be here, researching. Maybe he just didn't hear."

She banged again, this time a little louder, and called out, "Hello! It's me! Wilma Tenderfoot! Mr. Goodman's apprentice detective! I'm totally official! And I've come to get the key! Which is evidence. So I should have had it in the first place! We found the treasure! We sort of need it!" Then she stopped and listened, cocking her head to one side. She heard a bump. "Hello?" she called out again, but still no one came to the door. Pickle had his nose to the gap under it, however, and began to paw at the doorstep with some urgency. The bumping sounded again.

"Strange," said Wilma. "Do you think we should go in?" Pickle barked and pawed at the door once more. Gingerly, Wilma pulled off one of her mittens and tried the front latch. It was unlocked. Opening the door quietly, she poked her head into Irascimus's office. Again she heard the bumping noise. "Where is that coming from?" she said. Pickle ran to the rug in the center of the room, struck a stiffened pose, and pointed his nose downward to draw Wilma's attention to something. Tiptoeing over, she stood beside the alert beagle, looked down and listened. There it was again! A muffled bumping! And it seemed to be coming from under her feet!

Pulling back the rug, Wilma gasped. "A trap-door!" she exclaimed. "Get back, Pickle—I'm going to open it." Taking hold of the large brass ring that was inlaid on its surface, Wilma heaved the door open. It fell backward with a bang. And there, in the dark cavity below, was a man in a large-brimmed hat, bound and gagged. "Goodness!" Wilma cried, getting down on her knees to untie him.

"Th-thank you," the man spluttered as his mouth and hands were released. "Thank goodness you've found me! I managed to work my feet free so I could kick on the door, but I wasn't sure anyone would hear me."

"But who are you?" Wilma asked, staring.

"I am Dr. Irascimus Flatelly!" he declared with some force. "And the man claiming to be me is an imposter!"

"Oh my!" exclaimed Wilma, clamping a hand to her mouth. She paused for a moment, trying to slot everything into place in her head. Then she burped. "Sorry about that—it's my Hunchy Instincts repeating on me again. Gosh. The false Dr. Flatelly is after the treasure too! And he's got the key! Ooooh, I hope he hasn't worked out where the treasure is. It's in the gazebo, Real Dr. Flatelly. The one at Folly Island, in the Blackheart boating lake. Mr. Goodman is probably there already, guarding it. You'd better get there as quickly as you can and warn him about the false Dr. Flatelly. This has all suddenly become very serious. And I'd better go and fetch Miss Daise back from the Swamp of Heavy Sighs. Because what with Mr. Goodman knowing where the treasure is, it's only a matter of time before we're overrun with spooks."

The real Irascimus Flatelly, who was sitting on a chair now and rubbing his wrists, looked up and frowned. "What are you talking about? What spooks?"

"No time to explain!" Wilma cried, making for the door. "I need to get to the swamp. Miss Daise's exercising skills are much better than mine. Tell Mr. Goodman I've gone to fetch Fenomina. Come on, Pickle! There're spooks to catch!"

Not possible to be more shocked. Simply not possible.

23

"Not here either, Mr. Barbu," shouted Tully from the bottom of the hole he had been digging.

"Curses," growled the diminutive villain, getting out the map they had found and looking at it again. "We've tried that squiggle there and that blot and that swirly thing that looks half like a worm. Still nothing. One of you had better come up with an idea quickly or I shall start to administer random blows."

"Maybe I could dig some more holes, Mr. Barbu," Tully suggested.

Barbu scowled. "We don't have FOREVER, Tully!" he snapped. "In case you've FORGOT-TEN," he added, rapping the henchman on the forehead with his cane, "we're trying to get to the treasure before Goody-Goodman."

"Talking of which, master," piped up Janty, pointing, "there he is! And look, everyone's following him. And they're running!"

"They must have found something!" barked Barbu, flinging his cloak over his shoulder. "After them! If we can't find this treasure first, then we shall have to take it by fair means or foul! Though to be perfectly honest, it'll probably be foul. Remember that, Janty!"

Folly Island was a small, round, raised piece of ground in the middle of the boating lake. On it stood an ornate stone gazebo, slightly crumbling, its pillars in the shape of fat pigs standing on their hind legs. At the edge of the lake, there was a line of abandoned rowing boats dragged up onto the shore. Panting and shielding his eyes against the late afternoon sun, Inspector Lemone looked out toward the island. "Nobody there, Goodman," he puffed. "Perhaps we made it in time? Though no Wilma either, from what I can see. We can use one of these boats and row out to check."

Theodore jumped into the nearest boat and took up an oar. "Come on, Lemone!" he yelled. "You take the other!"

"Hold on!" shouted Tarquin, who was running toward them, hand on top hat. "Wait for me!" He looked frantically along the line of boats. Nearest to him there was a paddleboat in the shape of a duck and a small canoe tied to the rickety wooden jetty. He looked from one to the other before jumping into the paddleboat, but just as his feet touched the pedals, a large hand grabbed his coat collar and yanked him back onto the snow. "Out of our way!" yelled Barbu, leaping into the paddleboat instead. "Tully, Janty, GET IN!"

Spitting frozen soil from his mouth, Tarquin scrabbled to his feet and squeezed himself into the canoe. Both Theodore's boat and Barbu's paddleboat were now racing toward the island. He had to beat them!

Suddenly Belinda appeared from nowhere and threw herself at the end of the canoe, where she hung on for dear life. "Wait for me!" she yelled. "I need that treasure for my dream wedding!"

"And I need a new set of pans!" shouted Mrs. Moggins, shoving Belinda out of the way.

"And we need it so we can start our String Emporium!" cried Molly, who was running with Polly toward the lake's edge.

"Hang on!" yelled Lord Blackheart, who was struggling to keep up with everyone else. "That treasure is mine! I'm the head of this house and I hired Mr. Goodman!"

"And I am the lady! And I have pearls to replace!" cried Lady Blackheart, who was right behind him.

Portious brought up the rear, looking as somber and disinterested as ever but following nonetheless.

"Everyone's gone treasure-CRAZY! And that devil D'Anvers is catching up with us, Goodman!" wailed Inspector Lemone, pulling on his oar with all his might. Theodore looked over his shoulder. The duck-shaped paddleboat was indeed gaining on them.

"Ram them!" shouted Barbu at Tully, who was pedaling like fury. "Ram them in the side!" Janty, who had his hand on the tiller, swung it away from himself, sending the paddleboat veering to its left. The beak-shaped prow missed the tail end of Mr. Goodman's rowing boat by inches. "Blast!" yelled the villain. "Come around again and smash them in the other side!"

"Get away!" bellowed Inspector Lemone, standing up and swinging his oar at the fast-approaching paddleboat. "You're a dastardly scoundrel, Barbu D'Anvers!"

"Now isn't the time for compliments, Inspector Lemone!" jeered the diminutive rascal as they bore down on the small rowing boat for the second time. "Prepare for a dousing!" As the vessels collided, there was a mighty crunch and the rowing boat toppled sideways. The lighter paddleboat, propelled by its own speed, skewed skyward and flew over the top of the rowboat rear end first, where it caught the wind and in one almost balletic movement flipped and dumped everyone in it into the lake.

"Yes!" shouted Inspector Lemone, standing once more to cheer as their enemies splashed into the water. But as he stood, the rowboat gave a deep and troubling cracking sound and with one shuddering snap, fractured in two.

"Quick!" shouted the great and serious detective, still frantically rowing. "Jump onto this half and pull as hard as you can, Lemone!" With only a few more feet to go, Theodore and the Inspector dug into the water with their oars and made it to shore just before the boat sank into oblivion.

Inspector Lemone crawled onto the shore and lay there panting and dripping, looking out toward the overturned paddleboat. Just behind it, Janty was standing up to his chest in water. "It's not so bad," he heard him shout to Tully. "I can reach the bottom. Hang on! Where's the master?" Tully looked around him, but there was no sign of the villainous D'Anvers. Then a small plume of bubbles broke the water's surface to his left. Plunging a hand downward, he pulled up a spluttering, coughing Barbu. He could reach the bottom too, but unfortunately his head couldn't reach the surface at the same time.

"Get off!" yelled a voice behind them. "It's mine!" The others, taking advantage of the mid-lake battle, had reached the island first and discovered the casket. Mrs. Moggins was scrabbling with Molly and Polly, while Lord Blackheart was wrestling his wife. Belinda, crawling out from the tangle of bodies, stretched a hand toward the infamous casket but suddenly Tarquin climbed over his sister, grabbed it, and held it aloft.

"I have it!" he declared in triumph. "Finders Keepers! Finders Keepers!" Breathing heavily with exertion, everyone stopped and stared. "Where's the key?" Tarquin demanded, looking toward Mr. Goodman. "Don't be a sore loser— hand it over!"

"Actually . . ." the great detective began.

"Oh, be like that," Tarquin snapped. "I've no time for chit-chat. I'll just break it open, spook or no spook!" He looked about his feet for a large rock, but suddenly his face, which moments before had been so smug and joyful, fell. "The . . . the mummy's key." He pointed down to where it lay discarded beneath some leaves. "How . . . why . . . ?" Slowly, he looked back at the casket in his hands and shook it. Nothing. With trembling fingers he touched the lid. It opened smoothly. The casket had evidently already been unearthed and unlocked, and it was empty. "Nooooooooooooo!" Tarquin screamed.

"Beaten to it!" groaned Mr. Goodman as he took the casket from the young Blackheart to examine it.

"But who by?" wailed Inspector Lemone.

"Maybe I can help with that!" shouted out a tussled figure who was frantically rowing toward the island. "Allow me to introduce myself," he added as he reached the shore and stepped out from his boat. "I am Dr. Irascimus Flatelly. The real Irascimus Flatelly."

"It's as I suspected all along!" exclaimed Theodore, his eyes flashing. "And yet . . ."

Then as Barbu and his cohorts dragged themselves ashore and Belinda sidled toward them, the great and serious detective hit himself in the forehead and shouted, "Of course! How could I have been so blind?"

"I'm sorry," said Lady Blackheart, shaking her head and staring at the crumpled fellow in front of her. "You're Irascimus Flately? Then who was that other chap?"

"My assistant, Oscar Crackett," explained the real Irascimus. "He's had me locked up for weeks, ever since he found out about the Blackheart treasure. He threatened to kill me too, once I was of no more use to him—he's been picking my brains on Blackheart history for days. And as he had the key, I fear it must have been him who beat you all to it."

"No idea what's going on," declared Mrs. Moggins, throwing her arms in the air. "But this treasure-chasing is playing havoc with my cooking timetable. I've got onions to peel and peas to shell. I'm off!"

"Peas!" yelled Goodman, throwing the casket to the floor. "And so it comes together!"

"I am VERY confused," boomed Lord Blackheart, scrambling up from the ground. "Have the ghosts gone? Were there ever any? Who's got the treasure? And what's all this about peas?"

"Don't worry, Lord Blackheart," cried the detective, making for the doctor's rowboat. "I'll explain everything later. But it's imperative that I try and arrest this fellow before he makes off with what should rightfully be yours. And I know exactly where he'll be now he's got what he was after. Hang on a minute," he added, looking around him, "we still don't know where Wilma is."

"Your able apprentice was the one who released me," explained Dr. Flatelly with a smile, "and she did ask me to tell you she's gone to the Swamp of Heavy Sighs to track down some psychic or other. Something to do with needing her for spooks."

"Oh no," sighed Theodore. "There isn't a moment to lose. We must get to the swamp immediately. Portious, everyone else, I shall need you to accompany us—we may need some strong hands on our side!"

"Wilma's not in dire peril again, is she?" wailed Lemone as Lord Blackheart ushered a reluctant butler after the dynamic duo.

"Just jump in and row, man!" yelled Goodman. "Wilma's life may depend on it!"

"Help! And it's going to get spooky!" whimpered Inspector Lemone, wading back into the lake after his friend. "And handcuffs won't work on ghosts!"

No. No they won't. Oh dear, I do hope everyone's going to be all right. Don't you?

24

There are some places where people with any sense should never go, and on Cooper that place was the Swamp of Heavy Sighs. Very few who entered ever left, and unless you knew every twist and sticky turn, you were more likely to end up lost in a maze of vines and roots or sucked downward to a muddy end than reach your destination. Damp quagmires and bubbling bogs lay on either side as Wilma and her intrepid hound picked their way along the narrow path. The young apprentice detective couldn't help but shiver. No birds sang. Instead, the only sounds were the deep rumblings of toads on slimy pads and the occasional slithering of snakes in the shallow waters.

Fenomina's shack was deep in the center of the swamp, completely surrounded by water and with a wooden bridge connecting it to the patch of dry land they found themselves on. It had a porch adorned with the skeletons of dead animals, marsh gas surrounded it with a permanent rolling cloud of fog, and candles set in rodent skulls lit the way across the wobbly bridge. As Wilma and Pickle began to cross the water, something large and scaly broke the surface below them, only to disappear back into the murky oblivion from whence it came. "Why on earth does Fenomina want to live out here?" wondered Wilma as she flicked something slimy off her hand. "It's revolting! And more than a little eerie." She strode on bravely while Pickle crept even closer to her and quivered.

When they reached the porch, Wilma looked down at her companion. "Do nothing unless I say so," she whispered. "It may be about to go all spooky and precarious."

Pickle threw his best friend a troubled glance. Wilma gulped. "We have to persuade Fenomina to come back with us so she can exercise the spooks now that we've found the treasure. Only that will definitely, once and for all, be the proof Mr. Goodman needs. We can't give up now. Besides, he might be in trouble if the spooks attack and there's no expert exerciser on hand."

As Wilma raised her hand to knock, she realized she could hear loud sounds on the other side of the door as if things were being moved in a hurry. She rapped hard. The sounds stopped but no one answered. Wilma looked down at Pickle. "We've got no time to waste," she whispered, and burst through the door, Pickle tumbling in behind her.

There was a strange smell inside the shack, of old incense and worse. A large suitcase stood in the center of the room and Fenomina, startled by the sudden intrusion, had dived behind it momentarily. "My goodness!" she cried, staring up at them. "I wasn't expecting . . . I mean . . . Has there been another phenomenon? Must I intervene? Sorry! You have caught me unawares. I was just packing some things. For a psychic's convention. Over in Bleeuuurgh. In fact, I'm quite late!" Scrambling to her feet, Fenomina slammed the case shut, dress sleeves still hanging out of it, and picking it up, made a dash for the door.

"I've got news, Miss Daise," said Wilma, stepping into her path. "We need your help. Mr. Goodman thinks he knows where the treasure is and only you can fend off the spooks."

Fenomina rose to her full height. "Are you . . . alone?" she asked, peering around the young girl.

"Yes," said Wilma, nodding, "apart from Pickle . . ."

Suddenly, a strange moaning sounded through the shack. Wilma looked around, but in the gloom she could see nothing except the almost imperceptible trembling of a curtain to their left. Fenomina, her one good eye ablaze, dropped her case and held a hand to her forehead in apparent terror.

"Oh my," mumbled Wilma, backing into a coat stand that was dripping in snakes. "OH MY!" she yelled, realizing that they were crawling over her shoulders. She brushed them off with some urgency only to notice a strange bulge behind the curtain. "There's something going on over there. What is it, Miss Daise? Is someone else here? Or some*thing*?"

Wilma turned to look at Fenomina, who was pointing wordlessly at the ceiling. Just then a great wind rushed through the shack, extinguishing all the candles. The place was pitched into darkness and Wilma was left staring up at the glowing, dis-embodied head of the Fatal Phantom! "I warned you to leave what was mine!" it hissed. "AND NOW I SHALL KILL YOU BOTH!"

Suddenly, the apparition disappeared, and from out of the shadows swept the Fatal Phantom made flesh. Fenomina screamed and recoiled from it. Then, as it pursued her across the shack, she dropped down in a dead faint and it turned its attentions on Wilma.

Wilma looked around to see if there was any-thing she could protect herself with. Grabbing a mounted set of antlers, she cowered, waving them defensively, but the Fatal Phantom, red eyes burning and hissing evilly, knocked the makeshift shield to one side and raised its talons to strike. Wilma was defenseless. But as the Phantom lunged forward, Pickle leaped up, bit down on its arm, and twisted the talons away from Wilma's heart. The spook was too strong for the small hound, however, and shook Pickle violently, sending the poor dog careening into the wall. Winded, the brave hound slumped to the floor.

"Pickle!" yelled Wilma, trying to get to him, but the Phantom had hold of her. She could feel its hot breath on the back of her head as the Phantom raised its talons once more . . .

Click! A handcuff snapped shut around the Phantom's wrist and as Mr. Goodman swept Wilma from its clutches, Inspector Lemone wrestled the ghoul to the floor and cuffed its second wrist. The shack door was still swinging wildly from where they had burst in.

"Well, I never!" declared Inspector Lemone, panting. "Handcuffs *do* work on ghosts! And spooks or no spooks, no one attempts murder on our young apprentice detective on my watch!" He wiped his eyes discreetly. "I'm so glad you're all right, Wilma."

"You have to believe in ghosts now, Mr. Goodman," breathed the small girl determinedly. "We've only gone and *caught* one."

"Ohhhhhh!" moaned Fenomina, coming to and gingerly standing up. "Sorry I wasn't of much help . . . Shall I wave a few crystals?"

"You're in no way guiltless in all of this, Miss Daise," Mr. Goodman retorted. "Portious, would you mind standing guard over her for the time being?" Fenomina grunted and stood, looking sheepish, as the butler planted himself at her side expressionlessly.

"Pickle!" cried Wilma as the shock of nearly being murdered by a ghost for the second time that week wore off and she remembered what had just happened. She rushed to her hound's side.

"It's all right, Wilma," said Theodore, taking a quick look at him. "He's still breathing, just stunned. Stay with him. There's something I need to do."

The great and serious detective leaped to his feet and striding toward the long black curtain at the shack's one window, pulled it dramatically to one side. There behind the drapes was a kind of projector. "As I suspected!" he declared. Then, turning, he grabbed hold of the Phantom's hood. "And if I just pull this off," he added, yanking it backward, "the true identity of the ghost will be revealed!"

"False Dr. Irascimus Flatelly!" gasped Wilma as she stared wide-eyed at the man before her. "That means YOU just tried to kill me . . ."

"Also known as Oscar Crackett!" yelled the real Irascimus Flatelly, who was standing behind Inspector Lemone as the rest of the Blackhearts and their servants piled in behind him. Barbu, Tully, and Janty hovered on the porch, determined not to miss anything either.

"Curse you, Mr. Goodman!" yelled Oscar, spitting with defiance. "If it weren't for you and your infernal apprentice, I'd be away with the treasure by now!"

"I can't believe it," said Wilma, staring at Oscar Crackett. "You were pretending to be Dr. Flatelly

AND the Fatal Phantom. But how can that be? The Phantom attacked you at the mine. You can't be in one place twice."

"You are right, Wilma," said Theodore, reaching for his pipe. "But I'll get to that in a moment. Let's go back to the beginning first."

"Oh good," said Lemone, finding a chair, hooking Oscar's cuffs over the back of it, and sitting. "The explanation bit. At last."

"This case began when a body was discovered in an excavation pit at the back of Blackheart Hoo," began Theodore, tucking a thumb into his waistcoat pocket. "Apparently frightened to death."

"It was planted there," interjected the real Irascimus. "That mummy came from my offices. It was the over-a-century-old body of a farm worker, according to my research—a man called Taver Cester. He was petrified of spiders. When I dug his body up while doing some basic swamp research, I found it preserved and wrapped about with a massive spiderweb. My guess is that he stumbled into a black reaper's web. They're enormous but perfectly harmless. He panicked and died, scared to death."

"That would explain the build-up of adrenaline that Penbert found," Wilma interjected helpfully, looking up from tending Pickle.

"Exactly so, Wilma." Theodore nodded. "I thought it must have been something like that. What you stumbled across when I sent you to fetch a new Brackle Bush was Oscar digging an excavation hole to *bury* the planted mummy, not dig it up. I suspect he wanted the body to be found by someone else. Your intervention simply made him speed up his plans. Oscar had learned of the legend of a hidden treasure and saw an opportunity to investigate and steal it for himself, but he needed access to the Blackheart estate. He did so by getting close to and then masquerading as Dr. Flatelly, planting a false body and making it seem that it was Bludsten Blackheart . . ."

"With the tooth and the ring?" asked Lord Blackheart.

"Yes." Mr. Goodman nodded again. "He must have knocked out the appropriate tooth and taken the ring from the real Flatelly's office."

"Quite so. I had borrowed some Blackheart artifacts, including the ring, from the island museum—I believe they'd been sold to the collection over the decades to raise funds for the Hoo's upkeep . . ." The doctor trailed off tactfully.

"And the body gave weight to the legend of the treasure, which finally won Oscar the access he needed. But he also needed something more dastardly," Theodore continued, "something that would stop every man and woman in the household from trying to find the treasure too. And that was when he introduced the story of the curse."

"So . . . so that wasn't true either?" asked Wilma. "No ghosts. AND no curse."

"Well, really!" Lady Blackheart exclaimed.

"No, Wilma, I'm afraid not," Mr. Goodman said, looking rueful. "As you know, I was always certain there was no Phantom. But it was your diary find that enabled me to question the curse story and the supposed Dr. Flatelly, so in many ways you were on the right track nonetheless."

Wilma blushed with pride. Besides, even though it meant she had been wrong all along, it was a relief to discover that Mr. Goodman hadn't been. The idea that the great detective wouldn't always be right had felt most unsettling!

"Because if Bludsten wanted the treasure to remain hidden," Theodore continued, "why did the diary appear to have the makings of a classic treasure hunt enclosed within it? Why so many clues? Besides, without it, we never would have found the treasure in time to stop Oscar getting away—so, well done again, Wilma."

"But what about his crazed rantings about death . . . a curse . . . ?" Wilma persisted.

"My guess now is that they are part of the story too. But I imagine Dr. Flatelly might be able to answer that better than me."

The doctor nodded. "I advertised and took on an assistant specifically to help me with my research into the ancient legend of the Blackheart treasure. I had discovered stories about a great golden claw that had been commissioned by Bludsten Black- heart and buried somewhere on the estate. But the treasure wasn't buried because Bludsten was mean or crazy. By all accounts, he was a bit of a practical joker with a fondness for adventure—hence his finding of the mine in the first place."

"The jokes I found in the mine." Wilma nodded.

"But if it was for fun, then why was the treasure not found?" she pondered.

"Because the night before the hunt, a terrible fire swept through the Hoo," explained Dr. Flatelly. "A young boy was killed—a lad who had been taken in as an orphan by the Blackhearts. He was helping Bludsten to lay clues and had been sent to the beer cellar to do so, but the fire took hold and the boy was trapped. The fumes killed him. If he hadn't been in the beer cellar, he would have lived. Bludsten was heartbroken and never forgave himself, so the treasure hunt was called off, and he went slowly crazy with grief, as you saw in his diary. Then he disappeared. Where to? No one knows to this day. That was one of the main reasons I wanted to research the story."

"But the treasure remained?" asked Tarquin eagerly.

"When he disappeared, the treasure was still buried. And with the passing of time, it was forgotten. There were rumors of it, of course, but it became the stuff of legend."

Wilma shook her head in disbelief as she stroked Pickle's ears. "Yet the haunting and the spooks seemed so real! How did Oscar do it?"

"Yes, how?" chimed in several of the others.

"I'm a genius, that's how," the crook retorted.

"I have Penbert's results here." Theodore reached for a piece of paper in his waistcoat pocket. "As I suspected, the blood used for the ghostly threats was, in fact, ketchup, a bottle of which I saw in Dr. Flatelly's shack."

"And the ghost at the séance, Goodman?" said Lemone, still puzzled.

"Tricks of the mind," replied Theodore with a shake of his head. "You saw what you already believed. You weren't looking with the eyes of a detective. You were speculating—always dangerous! And the séance was skillfully done. Tripwires knocked people and things over, recordings of strange noises were played, stink bombs were set off, and a pump plate sent Pickle spinning through the air. All of this created the illusion of ghastly chaos. If you look in Miss Daise's suitcase there, I imagine you'll find most of this equipment inside."

Fenomina promptly sat on her case so that no one could do so.

"The ghostly head, however, was a more complicated trick of the light," continued the great detective, walking over to the strange contraption behind the drawn curtain. "This is an aphengoscopic lantern. It projects the image of anything you place before it and magnifies it. Watch."

Theodore picked at something on his sleeve and dropped it into the lantern's beam. Suddenly a giant spider appeared in the air above them. Everyone gasped.

"Hey, that's mine—I usually use it for looking at my slides in greater detail," the real Dr. Flatelly explained indignantly.

"It was this, along with a handheld loudspeaker, that allowed Oscar, disguised as the Fatal Phantom, to appear and speak seemingly in midair. My suspicions of the man calling himself Dr. Flatelly started when we first went to visit him in his makeshift office. There were two sets of plates and two mugs, both of which were still warm, yet there were no departing footprints outside. So where was the other person—hidden? Hiding? My suspicions were aroused, but it wasn't proof enough. Then Wilma saw a set of seemingly ghostly footprints leading up to the south side of the Hoo. They stopped at the wall and on either side of them were two round indentations in the snow. You will recall at the séance that there was a sharp blast of cold air that made the curtains billow out. The reason for this was that someone—and I soon realized it must have been the pretend doctor—had climbed up a ladder, opened the window, climbed in, and pulled the ladder up behind him so that he could help create the illusion of a haunting."

"So the footprints weren't spooky, but they were a useful clue, Mr. Goodman," Wilma said, jumping up. "I got that right at least, didn't I?"

"That you did, Wilma," the great detective acknowledged cheerfully. "But I was still left wondering WHY the famed archaeologist would be doing all this. His long-standing reputation belied such behavior, and I knew he was comfortably well-off because of all the award-winning papers he has published. It was at the mine soon after that when I finally got the answer. The so-called Dr. Flatelly took *off* his reading glasses to examine the drawings on the wall. Nobody who really wore glasses would have done that."

At this, Oscar tutted loudly. "And nobody who isn't an annoying attention-to-detail detective would have noticed!"

Mr. Goodman gave him a stern silencing look and continued. "He was obviously a fake! He went to great lengths to take Bludsten's diary from Wilma too, and as soon as he had it, the Fatal Phantom appeared and the attempt on our lives was made."

"But what about that Fatal Phantom?" called out Inspector Lemone. "If the fake doctor was with us, how was he acting the Phantom too?"

"He wasn't," declared Theodore. "At that moment I realized that his accomplice was! There was more than one person at the Hoo up to no good."

More than one person? But is it a human? Or a SPOOK? Turn the page, quick! QUICK!

25

Everyone in the room gasped. Oscar went pale and stared at the floor, and Wilma couldn't stop herself looking from face to face, trying to see someone's guilt in their eyes. How had she missed this? She couldn't help feeling a little disheartened that she had gotten it SO wrong.

Seeing her glum face, Mr. Goodman bent down toward her. "And it was Wilma's keen eyes again," he reminded her as he continued to address his audience, "that spotted said accomplice trailing us down to the mine. In fact, she saw two separate people on our tail, but the other was merely

Barbu's spying henchman, so I was less concerned about that."

"What? No, er maybe, er . . ." Tully blustered from just outside the shack door.

"Shut up, you idiot." Barbu's cane popped up from behind the thug and rapped him on the knee.

"So," Theodore continued, "I knew the accomplice had to be a real insider—someone with easy access to the house to help with the ghostly scrawls and keep abreast of developments while Oscar was stationed outside; someone who could have planted that ectoplasm, since the fake Dr. Flatelly was sitting next to me, so I knew it wasn't him. And motive was, as ever, at the forefront of my thoughts. Most of you here needed money: Lady Blackheart with her penchant for pearls, Tarquin with his terrible gambling debts, and Belinda with her lavish dream wedding. Then there were the servants. All of you needed the money the treasure would bring."

"Well, really!" Lady Blackheart exclaimed.

"Exactly, Mother," Belinda pitched in. "I think I might faint at the impertinence of the man."

Tarquin remained sheepishly silent whilst the servants simply huddled closer together nervously.

"Fret not, Miss Blackheart. I am no longer, in fact, accusing any of you," Theodore went on. "But the presence of Barbu D'Anvers did slow my deducting down in this respect. For one thing, it made finding the treasure of the utmost importance and distracted my attention from getting to the bottom of the hauntings."

"Yes." Barbu nodded, twirling his cane smugly. "Yes, it would."

"More importantly, it was *his* attempts to FINISH OFF LORD AND LADY BLACKHEART that led me to doubt myself."

"What?" Lord Blackheart roared as Belinda's eyes widened.

Barbu froze. "That's an outrageous slander! Anyway, they're both still alive, so I've done nothing wrong. You can't arrest me. You've got no proof!"

"Sadly, no," Mr. Goodman acknowledged quietly. "But I know I am right. At first, after the attempt on our lives by Oscar and his accomplice in the mine, I took the murder attempt on Tarquin to be the work of Oscar and his friend—perhaps they were trying to protect the treasure?"

"But it wasn't," Oscar interrupted. "You can't try and pin that on me too!"

"Quiet!" Lemone snapped. "I need to concentrate in these explanation scenes. Especially when I haven't had a biscuit in hours! Carry on, Goodman."

"Thank you, Inspector," the great detective said, inclining his head. "So before I could accuse or arrest the fake doctor and force the name of his accomplice from him, the next trap—the crossbow—was sprung. It seemed to target the fake doctor, and he was genuinely shaken by it. Suddenly, all my theories were thrown into disarray. Why would the fake doctor or his accomplice try to kill Tarquin? Had I gotten the wrong person all along? It wasn't until we were at Folly Island and I saw Barbu D'Anvers hanging around Belinda that I realized the first murder attempt was not meant for Tarquin but for Lord Blackheart, who had been about to drink his hot cocoa in that very seat. The second one was intended for Lady Blackheart, when she was next arranging her famed flowers. Instead Miss Daise sprang the mechanism—which only someone as tall as Tully could have set up with the crossbow so high up the wall—by lifting the vase from the table, and Oscar simply got caught out when he stopped to talk to the psychic on his way back from scratching the latest fake-phantom message into the wall."

"So the spear in the pistol parlor was meant for Father too," Tarquin added. "What a relief. Er, I mean . . ." He trailed off as Lord Blackheart's already reddened face turned puce.

"And who would want Lord and Lady Blackheart dead? It's obvious—our old friend Barbu D'Anvers, though I am sure Tully was doing the dirty work. Barbu had engaged himself to Belinda, and with Tarquin disinherited, all he had to do was bump everyone else off. Thankfully, he failed."

"I feel almost disappointed that I can't openly take the credit for all that," admitted the villain, arching an eyebrow. "It is a splendidly dastardly sequence of events, even if it didn't quite succeed!"

The great and serious detective shook his head in disgust.

"But hang on," Wilma piped up from where she was sitting on the floor, Pickle in her arms. "So after Folly Island you were back to thinking it WAS Oscar, but does that mean you still don't know who the accomplice is?"

"In fact, Wilma, that fell into place almost at the same moment!"

"So who was it? It must be Fenomina Daise!" cried Belinda, pointing to the gasping psychic. "And she tried to turn everyone against me with her possession nonsense. I say arrest her immediately!"

Portious made a dutiful move in her direction, but Mr. Goodman waved him back.

"She was an obvious choice," he agreed, "especially when I learned that her card was left in Lady Blackheart's room anonymously at such a prescient time. But it was *too* obvious. And I saw her face at the séance when the fake Phantom materialized—she was genuinely shocked. There is no doubt that Fenomina was brought in to advance the illusion of a haunting, and like most psychics she was a willing participant in a sham. It was in her interests to pretend that the haunting was real—it could only mean more business for her. But she was not expecting an attempt on her life, and that is why she rushed back here to pack her things and leave. She knew she was in danger, and she was right. Oscar's presence in this shack proves one thing: He might not have been responsible for the crossbow near-miss, as Miss Daise believed he was, but he had come here to kill her."

The evil crook shrank further into himself, but he did not try to deny the great and serious detective's words.

"It's true." Fenomina nodded shamefacedly. "I received a note from someone tipping me off about a legend of a haunting at the Hoo. I was told I'd be paid handsomely but that I wasn't to question anything and to go along with everything I saw. Someone at the Hoo would help me. But then I was almost killed and it made me realize that no amount of money was worth losing my life over. I knew that the very note that had hired me made me a liability—I held one of the case's biggest clues."

"A clue as to the person on the inside who was in cahoots with Oscar Crackett," Theodore continued. "Someone with access to all areas of the house, who could easily leave a psychic's card in Lady Blackheart's room, who knew all the secret passageways and closets with false backs perfect for listening in from."

"Ooh." Wilma suddenly twigged. "All that sneaking and creaking outside the official operations room!"

"Indeed," Mr. Goodman agreed. "And it was the person who had bamboo planting sticks aplenty with which to fashion strangely light phantom talons like the one you found, Wilma, the person with curved pruning shears perfect for scratching talon-like messages into walls, the person who was standing right next to Belinda when she got covered in ectoplasm—actually mashed peas—the person who tended the Hoo's award-winning vegetable patch. And the person who longed to retire but thanks to the Blackhearts' poverty couldn't afford to do so comfortably. It was . . . Portious!"

"Thank goodness that's finished." Inspector Lemone sank back into his chair, panting.

"What did I say?" yelled Wilma, punching the air with her fist. "It *is* always the butler!"

"What?" Lord Blackheart roared again—now he was even pucer than puce!

"If you look in his pocket, I believe you'll find a letter of notice already typed out," Mr. Goodman explained. "Miss Daise and the doctor were the last loose ends before Oscar and Portious were due to disappear blamelessly and forever."

Realizing the game was up, the butler made a dive for the shack door, but Tarquin wrestled him to the floor. "Oh no you don't!" he said.

"I thought I had covered my tracks and that Fenomina would take the blame," grumbled Portious, his long face becoming even longer.

"Ironically, it was almost the first thing you said to me that gave you away in the end," Mr. Goodman said, addressing the butler seriously. "You complained that the snow was preventing you from planting your favorite vegetable: peas. And what do you need to plant peas? Bamboo sticks and hedge clippers. I had completely forgotten about it until Mrs. Moggins mentioned peas at Folly Island."

"Admit it, brother dear," Oscar said, looking up for the first time in several minutes. "You were going to let me take the rap alone."

"I'd have kept the treasure safe till you were out!" Portious retorted even as Wilma registered what had just been said and yelled, "Brother?"

"Hence my moment of recognition when I first met Oscar in the guise of Dr. Flatelly," Theodore conceded. "Note the same droopy eyes on both of them."

"That's not the only reason you recognize me," sneered Oscar Crackett. "I'm a notorious criminal! A rapscallion of some repute! My face will appear on every newspaper in Cooper!"

Barbu, bemused, turned to Janty and muttered, "Never heard of him. He's clearly delusional. Beware the wannabes, young apprentice, they're tedious beyond belief."

"But I'm afraid I have heard of him," interjected Theodore, fingering his magnifying glass. "Though he looks quite different now he's grown up. You see, many years ago, when Oscar was a boy, I was just starting out—and was called upon to solve the Case of the Pinched Partridge. An award-winning game bird had been stolen, pilfered by, it turned out, the young Oscar. As soon as Dr. Flatelly here mentioned his name, I recognized it. I have heard he has been in and out of prison since, his crimes growing in immensity each time. It just goes to show," continued Theodore, shooting Janty a quick glance, "that a life of petty crime as a lad can turn to graver trouble later."

Wilma nodded in agreement. She hoped Janty had taken note of that bit about graver trouble. Although as Mr. Goodman was speaking, she noticed he had been picking his nose, which was a disappointment. Boys, eh?

"But why, Portious? Why?" Lady Blackheart wailed, still staring in disbelief at her once faithful manservant.

"I hated you all," the butler sneered angrily, his face animated for the first time since they'd arrived at the shack. "Waiting on you hand and foot year in, year out—a threadbare existence. No pension to speak of and never a word of thanks. Then Oscar got out of prison and approached me and we hatched the perfect plan! Where's being good and respectable all these years gotten me? I just wanted some peace and luxury in my retirement—it's not too much to ask, is it?! It was only a matter of time before we had the treasure from under your noses." He spat on the floor.

"And we would have been away with it if it hadn't been for you two!" yelled Oscar grumpily, narrowing his eyes at Mr. Goodman and Wilma.

"Hang on," said Wilma. "Speaking of the treasure . . . where is it?"

Just then Oscar tossed Lemone and his chair aside and made a sudden lunge for a bundle left at the foot of the aphengoscopic lantern. "I did everything to get this," he yelled, "and you won't take it from me! Sorry, brother." And tapping twice on a square in the floor, he abruptly disappeared from view.

"What in the blue blazes!" yelled Inspector Lemone.

"It's my trapdoor!" cried Fenomina. "I use it to spooky effect when people come for readings. It leads outside!"

"Keep an eye on the butler, Lemone!" yelled Theodore, making for the door. "I'll go after him!"

Pickle, whom Wilma had been tending gently for the past half hour, suddenly raised his head a little and struggled up. He might not have quite saved the hour, but he was determined to save the day. Nobody could run faster than him. Using every last scrap of strength he had, he dashed through the door after the fake archaeologist, overtaking the great detective. Wilma jumped to her feet and ran after him. Oscar, the treasure tucked under his arm, had almost made it to the other side of the bridge and into the cloudy swamp when Pickle caught up with him and dashed between his legs. The villain staggered, stumbled, and finally tripped . . . and as he fell, the bundle that he had held so tightly tumbled to the edge of the bridge and landed at the feet of . . . Tarquin Blackheart. The cloth unrolled and the golden claw was at last revealed in all its magnificence.

"Finally!" yelled the errant young man, holding the golden claw above his head triumphantly. "I have it! It's mine!"

"Not so fast!" shouted another voice behind him. It was Barbu D'Anvers, still dripping wet and running at him with Tully and Janty in tow. "Grab it, Tully! Grab it!" The large henchman flung himself forward and landed on Tarquin, bringing him to the ground. As they rolled, the golden claw was tossed into the air. "Catch it!" screamed Barbu, trying to jump up, but he wasn't tall enough. And the claw, skimming across the tops of his fingertips, rotated in midair before landing squarely in the middle of a patch of wet sand.

Everybody watched as the treasure of Bludsten Blackheart was sucked downward. Forever.

Glaring, Barbu swung his cane into the nearest tree and screamed, "NOOOOOOO! NOOOOOOOO! NOOOOOOOOO!"

"Well done, Pickle," said Wilma as her brave dog hobbled back to her. "Though I think you've had enough excitement for one day."

I think everyone has. Don't you?

26

"So let me get this straight," boomed Lord Blackheart as the family and servants all stood around the fireplace back at the Hoo. "There were no ghosts? None at all? And after all that, the golden claw is gone as well?" He picked up a large steak pie and bit into it aggressively.

"I'm afraid so." Theodore nodded, his hands clasped behind his back. "And Oscar Crackett and Portious are in custody at last."

"I can't believe I had it in my grasp," wailed Tarquin. "I had the claw! And I lost it!"

"Which is bad luck on you," snapped Barbu

D'Anvers, who was standing, scowling, in a corner. "You still owe me a vast amount of grogs."

Lord Blackheart put down his pie and stood up. "I've just about had enough of you, D'Anvers," he said, pushing his chest out. "A man's home is his castle and for another chap to come in and rattle around it unwanted is the worst sort of bad show there is."

"Well, you'd better get used to it," sneered the diminutive villain, twirling his cane, "seeing as I'm going to be marrying . . . hang on . . . which one is it . . . that one there?"

"No, that's the maid Polly, master," whispered Janty. "The one you want is there. The one waving at you and smiling."

"Oh yes. Sorry, what's her name again?"

"Belinda, master. Belinda Blackheart."

"Yes!" declared Barbu forcefully. "Blah-Blah Blackheart is my betrothed and I shall be moving in permanently and taking her inheritance."

"Ah yes," said Lord Blackheart, sticking his chin in the air. "I'm glad you brought that up. You won't be marrying my daughter."

"But Daddy!" wailed Belinda. "We're engaged!"

"Yes," Lord Blackheart went on, nodding toward his daughter. "You are engaged, but not to D'Anvers. You have been engaged to your third cousin twice removed, Septimus, since the age of three. I was going to tell you on your twenty-first birthday, as a treat. So that's that surprise ruined. There it is. You can't be engaged to two people. You're already taken."

Barbu let out a small explosive scream. "All right! You can keep your buck-toothed, wonky-eyed daughter. I don't really care. I JUST WANT THE MONEY TARQUIN OWES ME!"

Belinda burst into tears.

"I am quite aware of that debt," continued Lord Blackheart, "but it has come to my attention that you have spent your time here pilfering my possessions and trying to kill us."

"Correct." Theodore smiled, lighting his pipe. "Which means Inspector Lemone is perfectly entitled to arrest you *unless* you forfeit your right to the debt in return for amnesty. I'm afraid you leave with nothing, Barbu. Yet again."

"Toss them out, Goodman," roared Lord Blackheart. "Immediately!"

"This is an outrage!" yelled Barbu as Inspector Lemone grabbed him by the collar and bundled him to the door. "Torn asunder from the woman I love! Surely you want me to stay?"

Belinda, wiping the tears from her eyes, walked across the room to look down at Barbu. "Even when I discovered you'd been trying to kill my parents I was prepared to forgive you in the name of true love. And having someone to marry. But I see now I meant nothing to you. You just wanted the money. However, if you can get my name right ONCE, I shall ask my father to forgive you."

Barbu grimaced. "Oh, COME ON! Can't I have an easy one?"

"WHAT IS MY NAME?"

Barbu's face contorted into a myriad of ghastly shapes as he racked his brains in thought. "B . . . B . . . B . . ." he began desperately. And then, in a tiny whisper, "Barbara?"

Belinda raised her hand and slapped Barbu

firmly about the face. "OWWWWW!" he yelled. "That STUNG!"

"There's a manure cart that leaves for the Lowside in five minutes, Inspector," she said imperiously. "Make sure they're on it!"

"My pleasure," replied Lemone, bustling the villain from the room.

It had been a very long day. Pickle was still a little concussed after his tumble at the shack and so, as they waited for a carriage to return them to Clarissa Cottage, Wilma had tucked him into a small bed with a warm hot-water bottle and a bobble hat. Inspector Lemone, exhausted, was fast asleep and snoring in the chair by the fire. Wilma's mind was whirring. It felt like it had been a difficult case of highs and lows in terms of her apprenticeship, and she wasn't sure what to make of it. Theodore, noticing that his apprentice looked a little crestfallen, put a hand on her shoulder. "Come and walk with me while I take a pipe, Wilma," he said. "I want to have a chat with you."

"Yes, Mr. Goodman," she answered, reaching for her woolly duffel coat.

The night sky was clear and sharp and as they walked into the yard behind the kitchens, Wilma looked up at a bank of stars that seemed to go on forever. "Know what that one is?" asked Theodore, staring upward and pointing to a particularly bright constellation. Wilma shook her head. "That's the Big Badger. If you ever get lost on a clear night, look for it and it'll give you your bearings. Follow the snout. It always points north."

"Thank you," she replied in a small voice. Then she looked up at her mentor. "I'm sorry I didn't believe you that there weren't any ghosts, Mr. Goodman. I got a bit carried away. Having a case go all spooky was a bit giddy-making."

"No apologies required, Wilma," replied Theodore, giving her a pat. "With every case, you are learning new skills, and that's what being an apprentice is all about. Besides, part of learning how to do things properly is allowing yourself to get things quite wrong sometimes. Everyone makes mistakes, but what we can do is strive to improve and do our best all the time."

"I would like to get things COMPLETELY right one day, Mr. Goodman," said Wilma quietly.

Theodore smiled and put his hand on his young apprentice's back. "I know, Wilma. And your enthusiasm for the task is commendable. Your Hunchy Instincts, as you call them, were often spot on, as were a lot of your observations. But enthusiasm isn't all that's required. It must be tempered with thought and calm contemplation of the facts—not speculations, remember. If you can manage that, then you have the makings of becoming a very great detective, Wilma."

Wilma gave a small but determined smile.

As the pair walked, they found themselves next to a derelict building. Wilma looked up and frowned. "That sign there, Mr. Goodman," she said, pointing, "the one hanging off its hook. It says 'Stables.' But that can't be. These stables look ruined, but Victor told me he worked in them."

"Victor?" asked Theodore, puzzled.

"The boy I told you about before," answered Wilma, looking around. "The one who helped me with the case. If it wasn't for him, I wouldn't have found the diary or the second piece of the map."

"But there is no stable lad at Blackheart Hoo, Wilma," said the great detective seriously, stopping and putting his pipe away. "Are you sure?"

"Definitely, Mr. Goodman. He must be here somewhere. He's not allowed in the house."

Wilma ran forward and looked about her. "There he is!" she cried, pointing toward a thicket to the right of the stables. She could see Victor standing in the moonlight. He looked straight at her, smiled, raised a hand, and . . . melted into the cold night air. Wilma blinked. "How did he do that?" she whispered. "Where did he go? Did you see that, Mr. Goodman?"

"I'm afraid I saw nothing, Wilma," said Theodore, scanning the horizon in the direction Wilma was pointing in. "Hang on, what's that . . ."

The pair walked toward the point where Victor had stood. There, among the long grass, was a single gravestone. Theodore bent down and pushed the undergrowth to one side so as to read it. "'Here lies Victor,'" he said. "'Buried near his adored horses. Killed in the great Hoo fire. Greatly loved. Sadly missed.' "

"Oh my," gasped Wilma.

Mr. Goodman looked up as the leaves in the trees above them shifted gently, as if the spirit of a sweet boy finally at rest—his last treasure hunt for his dear mentor, Lord Bludsten Blackheart, completed at last—was playing among them . . .

27

Pickle was feeling much better and was enduring the fitting for his Brackle Bush costume as best he could. "It'll need letting down a bit there," Mrs. Speckle grumbled, pins in her mouth. "The traditional Brackle Bush doesn't have a tail sticking out of it." Pickle gave a snort. He was of the opinion that a Brackle Bush would be vastly improved by the presence of a tail. Still, there was no accounting for taste. Most humans deserved nothing but his endless pity. He needed to remember that.

Wilma had been hard at it trying to learn all her lines. The Brackle Day play was in a few hours, and what with the Case of the Fatal Phantom and being stuck at the Hoo, there had been precious little time for rehearsals. Given that the only part Pickle could play was the all-important bush, it fell to Wilma to take on all the other parts. After mixing up her porpoise lines with her Melingerra Maffling lines and forgetting about the beard change for Old Jackquis, she decided that the best thing for it was to go for a brisk stroll to clear her head. But it wasn't just her lines that were causing her to feel troubled. Her headmistress, Kite Lambard, would be back that very afternoon and finally, after a long and interminable wait, she would be able to ask her about the letter she was sure Miss Lambard had written to Madam Skratch mentioning her all those years ago.

But there was something else Wilma had to do before she saw Miss Lambard. She wanted to prepare herself for the worst, should the worst come. Stanley Brisket had given Wilma what any young detective would refer to as a "golden lead." After determining that she was not Lady Blackheart's and working out that neither Molly nor Polly were old enough to have left her at the Institute ten years ago, and that Portious and Mrs. Moggins had absolutely no recollection of absentmindedly wrapping a baby in a ham-smelling blanket, Wilma was forced to come to the conclusion that the Twelve Rats' Tails was her next port of call. There was no point in pretending otherwise—the thought that she might have started life as the very worst sort of Criminal Element filled her with dread. But she had promised herself that she would get to the bottom of her own story and do it she would, even if the answers were murky and mud-splattered.

"This," explained Wilma as she and Pickle walked along the front pier of the Cooper Docks, having crossed the border from the Farside to the Lowside of the island, "is called killing two birds with one stone. That means we're being super-efficient and doing two things at once. So in this instance, we are taking a brisk stroll in fresh-aired circumstances to prepare ourselves for this afternoon's performance, but at the same time we are going to the Twelve Rats' Tails to investigate the next development in the Case of the Missing Relative. What do you think? No, don't eat that," she added, bending down and pulling a crab's leg from Pickle's mouth. "Beagles shouldn't touch shellfish."

The Twelve Rats' Tails was the island's most notorious hangout for Criminal Elements. As inns of ill repute go, it was the absolute worst and was full to the brim with rapscallions and desperadoes all hunched over flagons of bubbling beer, grumbling about evil deeds and misdemeanors that they had every intention of committing. Generally speaking, low dives and hidey-holes aren't to be recommended for ten-year-olds. Firstly, there is always the danger of falling in with the wrong crowd (which is never advisable). Secondly, you'll probably catch something. So avoid them. Thank you.

As she pushed open the door, Wilma coughed and tried to clear the air in front of her with a hand. "Goodness, Pickle," she said as they wandered through the murk of pipe smoke. "You'd think they'd open a window or something. Stinks a bit, doesn't it?" As she spoke, a villainous-looking type sneered in her direction while his raggedy-looking bulldog snarled at Pickle. They were clearly not welcome.

The barman, an ugly fellow with a nose that looked like a burst tomato, stared down over the bar at her. "Detective types don't do well here," he grumbled, spying the apprentice badge on Wilma's pinafore. "If I was you, I'd turn around and leave."

Wilma gulped. This was what her Academy textbook referred to as a "hostile environment": not one where conditions are tricky, like a desert or an ice cap, but one where nobody in your immediate vicinity wants to be in the least bit helpful. You know, like supermarkets the day before Christmas. She needed to be brave. So taking a big breath, she began. "Do you get your ham delivered here by Stanley Brisket?"

The barman nodded. "Yes. What about it?" he snarled.

"And does that ham get wrapped in a muslin like this?" she added, holding up the piece she had been wrapped in when she was a baby.

The fellow looked at it and put down the tankard he was wiping. "Yeah," he said, narrowing his eyes suspiciously.

"And can you remember someone from here taking one of those hammy cloths and wrapping a baby in one? And then taking that baby to the Institute for Woeful Children?"

The innkeeper thought for a moment. "About ten years back?" he asked eventually, leaning forward.

Wilma's heart leaped to her throat. "Yes, almost exactly ten years ago. Do you remember?"

"Yes I do." He nodded. "And it was I what done it. A baby was left here, so I took it up to the Institute. Left a note with it an' all."

"This note?" asked Wilma, her hand shaking as she showed him the luggage tag with the words "Because they gone" that had been left tied about her neck.

"That's the one." The fellow nodded again. "My handwriting too." The man rested back on his heels and squinted at Wilma. "Hang on a minute—that baby. Weren't you it?"

Wilma looked up at him, her green eyes brimming with emotion. "Yes," she whispered, putting the tag back in her pinafore pocket. "It was me. I was the baby you left at the gates." She stopped.

Was this the moment she had waited for all her life? Gathering her courage, she continued. "Can you tell me where I came from?"

"Don't know about that, but I can certainly tell you who left you here," said the barkeeper. And then, leaning right over the counter, he looked Wilma straight in the eyes. "The person who brought you here and told me to get rid of you whatever way I chose was . . . Barbu D'Anvers."

Pickle yelped and Wilma stumbled backward. She felt dizzy and sick. She shook her head slowly. "I don't believe you!" she muttered at last. "I DON'T BELIEVE YOU!" Filled with anguish and with tears running down her cheeks, she pushed through the crush of scoundrels and ran from the Twelve Rats' Tails as fast as she could. Not Barbu D'Anvers, the man she despised the most on all of Cooper! It was the worst news possible. She couldn't be related to him! But what if she was? What if he was . . . her father? It didn't bear thinking about. She had to get to Mr. Goodman—he would know what to do.

Blinded by tears, Wilma stumbled back to

Clarissa Cottage. She had never experienced such a feeling of despair. It was as if the sun had gone in forever and she would never be happy again. As she pushed her way through the front gate of the cottage, Wilma was so miserable that she failed to notice the small horse-drawn carriage parked outside. Her eyes were so filled with tears that as she fell into the cottage kitchen, she paid no attention to the leather deerstalker hat sitting on the table. Racked with sobs, she made her way to Theodore's study, opened his door, and she collapsed to the floor with emotion. Pickle instantly flopped down beside her and began to lick her face sympathetically. "It was Barbu D'Anvers," she wept, her face hidden in the crook of her elbow. "He was the one . . . who left me . . . at the Institute."

Suddenly Wilma was lifted up, and as she opened her eyes she realized it was by her headmistress, Kite Lambard. Wilma buried her face in Kite's shoulder. "I thought it was you," she wept. "Because of the letter . . . I thought you were my . . . missing . . . relative."

Kite stroked Wilma's hair and held her tight. "Wilma," she whispered eventually as the small girl's crying began to lessen, "I've come here because I have something important to tell you. Before I was the headmistress of the Academy of Detection and Espionage, there was someone in charge called Maximillian Blades. He was a brilliant man and was married to my sister, Prudence."

"And he was my best friend, Wilma," said Theodore, coming forward to comfort her too.

"But eleven years ago, both Maximillian and Prudence disappeared and I haven't seen them since."

"What has this to do with me?" asked Wilma, rubbing her eyes and gulping.

"Well, I've never told anyone this before, but the last person I know of to have seen them . . . saw them with a baby. Very fleetingly and from a distance, but with a baby nonetheless. The baby disappeared too, and I think it was taken to the Institute for Woeful Children. The question for me is whether the baby they were seen with was theirs at all. I made inquiries at the Institute, as I had discovered that a baby was sent there at around the same time as Max and Pru went missing. May be unrelated, of course, but it was a lead I needed to follow up. Sadly, I got little if no help from Madam Skratch. And, now Theodore has told me about you being given MY letter to Madam Skratch, I think that baby might have been you."

Wilma shook her head. "But I don't understand . . ." she whispered, blinking. "The innkeeper told me Barbu D'Anvers gave me to him."

Kite shot a quick, worried look in Theodore's direction. "And we need to get to the bottom of that," she replied. "It seems somehow you, Barbu, and the disappearance of my sister and Maximillian are all tied together."

"Do you . . ." Wilma began, her arms still around Kite's neck. "Do you think *they* might be my parents? That would make you . . . my aunt . . ."

Kite smiled slightly as she stared into Wilma's eyes. "I don't know," she said. "The last time I saw my sister she wasn't pregnant, so you still could be anyone's. Especially as Theodore tells me someone else has been writing to Madam Skratch about you too, sending payments for your upkeep—and that wasn't me. On the other hand, I didn't see Prudence for a whole year before you were even born . . . so you could be hers. We just don't know. But there's more," she added, putting Wilma down gently. "The reason I have been away is because I've been following some new leads about my sister's disappearance. And yesterday, I found this. It was in a bottle in Filthy Cove." She reached into her leather satchel and pulled out a crumpled piece of paper. "Here, Theodore—read that."

The great detective's eyes flashed as he read the note, "'All is not lost. Maximillian.' It's dated only two months ago." He put a relieved hand on Kite's shoulder. "We have hope at last. They're still alive."

"But where?" asked Wilma, wiping her eyes.

"I don't know," replied Kite. "But I'm going to do everything I can to find out."

Wilma didn't know what to think. Maximillian and Prudence? Barbu D'Anvers and her? All connected in some ghastly and underhanded business that left two people missing and her abandoned in a basket? This was as sticky a muddle as she could ever imagine. "Well, there's only one thing for it," she said at last, with a determined nod. "I shall have to help you. It's time to find out what's what and who's who. We haven't known each other long, Miss Lambard, but nothing and nobody stops Wilma Tenderfoot!"

Theodore looked down at his apprentice and laughed. "Then let's get started. Mrs. Speckle! Some corn crumbles, if you please! And a pot of peppermint tea would do very nicely."

And you will have to wait till the next book to see exactly what they do about it. Goodness. I do hope Barbu D'Anvers ISN'T Wilma's father. Don't you?

THE COOPER BRACKLE DAY PLAY

NARRATOR: In the middle of an ocean deep, there was once an island with one small hill. And on it lived a maiden, Melingerra Maffling.

[Enter Melingerra. She is dressed in rags and is shivering.]

NARRATOR: Melingerra was from a poor family. There had been a harsh winter that year and with no crops to eat, the girl was cold and starving. That morning, Melingerra was determined to find food for her brothers and sisters, and so she left her village and began to walk.

MELINGERRA: Oh, my poor belly! How it rumbles! My poor mother is dead! My poor father is dead! And now I am the only hope for my brothers and sisters. If I do not find food, then we shall all surely die! But wait! What is this? Why, it is a Brackle Bush!

[Enter Brackle Bush]

MELINGERRA: But how did it get to be here? Brackle Bushes only grow in summer! And yet this one is not only in bloom, but it is bearing fruit! Tell me, dearest Bush, how do you come to be so unseasonably ripe?

BRACKLE BUSH: *(shakes leaves)*

MELINGERRA: I have no idea what you are saying, but then, you are a bush. Come, let me pick some of your juicy fruits so that I may feed my brother and sisters!

[Enter Stavier Cranktop. He is dressed in fine clothes.]

STAVIER: Hold, young maiden! Hold! This is my father's land and you are trespassing upon it! And what is more, you are stealing from my precious Brackle Bush! Only I can eat the sweet fruits it yields!

MELINGERRA: I am sorry, sir. I did not know that this Brackle Bush was yours. I was taking the fruit for my brothers and sisters, who are most hungry during this foul winter. They have had nothing to eat for five days.

STAVIER: Five days, you say? That's almost a week! I am sorry for it. Now I am closer to you, I see you are a fair maiden indeed. But you are poor and I am rich. We can never be romantically paired!

BRACKLE BUSH: *(shakes leaves)*

STAVIER: What's that, Brackle Bush? Love knows nothing of grogs and groggles? Why, you are right! Come then! Let us be betrothed, fair maiden! My name is Stavier, by the way. Stavier Cranktop.

MELINGERRA: And I am Melingerra Maffling.

[They embrace]

[Enter Old Jackquis and The Porpoise]

OLD JACKQUIS: Stop, I say! Stop! The Porpoise of Fortune has told me of your intentions!

PORPOISE: Eep! Eep! Eep! Eep!

OLD JACKQUIS: Calm yourself, Porpoise! You told me that already! I know that these two must NEVER be betrothed. For the Mafflings and the Cranktops are sworn enemies of old!

STAVIER: But I love Melingerra Maffling. And this Brackle Bush has brought us together. Our mutual love of sweet fruits has tied us to each other for all eternity.

PORPOISE: Eep! Eeep! Eeeeeep!

STAVIER: Take that back, Porpoise! She is not a wonky-eyed peasant with bad breath and a terrible haircut! She is my betrothed. Put up your fins, sir! And prepare to fight!

OLD JACKQUIS: No good shall come of this!

[Stavier and the Porpoise fight. They bump into Melingerra, who falls upon the Brackle Bush. The bush now leans.]

MELINGERRA: Oh! I am cut through by the Brackle Bush! How I wish that its thorns were not filled with poison! But they are. Oh, Stavier! I die!

[She dies]

PORPOISE: Eeeeeeeeeeeeeep!

OLD JACKQUIS: It's too late to be sorry now, Porpoise. If you were joking, you should have said. Now look what you've done.

STAVIER: *(weeping)* My beloved is dead. I do not wish to spend one more day breathing or eating sweet fruits. I shall throw myself upon the Brackle Bush and die too.

[He does. He dies.]

OLD JACKQUIS: Well, this is a mess. I told you not to say anything. I could have handled this. But oh no. You had to put your big blue snout in, didn't you?

PORPOISE: Eeeeeeep!

OLD JACKQUIS: To commemorate this day of sorrow, I hereby divide this island into two. On the Farside shall live everyone who knew the Cranktops and has a bit of money. Their lives shall be rich and filled with ease. And corn crumbles. And the other side shall be the Lowside, to honor the Mafflings, and all who live there shall be poor and live in servitude. And eat sprout tops. I think that's the best way of remembering this. It's what they would have wanted. If you disagree, well, bad luck. I've made my mind up. Would you like to say anything, Porpoise?

PORPOISE: Eeeeeep. Eeeeeep. Eeeeeeeeeep. Eeeeeeeep. Eeep. Eeeeeeep. Eeeeeeep. Eeeeeep. Eeeeeep. Eeeep. Eeeeeep. Eeep. Eeeeeep. Eeeeeeeep. Eeeep. Eeeep. Eeeeeep. Eeeeeep. Eeeep. Eeep. Eeeeeep. Eeeeeep. Eeeep. Eeep. Eeeeeep. Eeeep. Eeeep. Eeep. Eeeeeep. Eeeeeep. Eeeeeeeeeep. Eeeeeeep. Eeep. Eeeeeep. Eeeeeep. Eeeeeep. Eeeeeep. Eeeep. Eeeeeep. Eeep. Eeeeeep. Eeeeeeeep. Eeeep. Eeeep. Eeeeeep. Eeeeeep. Eeeep. Eeep. Eeeeeep. Eeeeeep. Eeeep. Eeep. Eeeeeep. Eeeep. Eeeep. Eeep. Eeeeeep. Eeeeeep. Eeeeeeeeeep. Eeeeeeep. Eeep. Eeeeeep. Eeeeeep. Eeeeeep. Eeeeeep. Eeeep. Eeeeeep. Eeep. Eeeeeep. Eeeeeeeep. Eeeep. Eeeep. Eeeeeep. Eeeeeep. Eeeep. Eeep. Eeeeeep. Eeeeeep. Eeeep. Eeeep. Eeeeeep. Eeeep. Eeeep. Eeep. Eeeeeep. Eeeeeep. Eeeeeeeeeep. Eeeeeeep. Eeep. Eeeeeep. Eeeeeep. Eeeeeep. Eeeeeep.

Eeeeep. Eeeeeeep. Eeep. Eeeeeep. Eeeeeeeep.
Eeeeep. Eeeep. Eeeeeep. Eeeeeep. Eeeep. Eeep.
Eeeeeep. Eeeeeep. Eeeep. Eeep. Eeeeeep. Eeeep.
Eeeep. Eeep. Eeeeeep. Eeeeeep. Eeeeeeeeeep.
Eeeeeeep. Eeep. Eeeeeep. Eeeeeep. Eeeeeep.
Eeeeeep. Eeeep. Eeeeeep. Eeep. Eeeeeep.
Eeeeeeeep. Eeeep. Eeeep. Eeeeeep. Eeeeeep.
Eeeep. Eeep. Eeeeeep. Eeeeeep. Eeeep. Eeep.
Eeeeeep. Eeeeeep. Eeeep. Eeep. Eeeeeep.
Eeeeeep. Eeeep. Eeeeeep. Eeeep. Eeeep. Eeep.

OLD JACKQUIS: *(crying)* Why, Porpoise. That
may be the most beautiful speech ever made by
anyone. Let it be carved into every stone and
learned by all the Cooper children for ever more.

NARRATOR: And so it was that the island was
divided. And the Brackle Bush was revered. And
everyone learned the words of the Porpoise.
Cooper be praised!

BRACKLE BUSH: *(shakes leaves)*

If you missed Wilma's other adventures,
turn the page for a chapter
of the first book in the series . . .

Wilma Tenderfoot

The Case of the Frozen Hearts

Wilma Tenderfoot wasn't quite sure how she'd managed it, but somehow she was hanging upside down from a meat hook in the pantry. In her hand was an empty toilet paper roll, which, although not quite as effective as a proper telescope, concentrated the mind whenever peered through with one eye. As she hung, gently swaying, Wilma was forced to conclude that maybe she didn't have this detective lark pinned down quite yet and made a mental note to remember in the future not to try to climb up a rack of hams in order to investigate a theft of Madam's sausages without first taking the appropriate precautions.

Her hero, Theodore P. Goodman, the island's greatest living detective, wouldn't have got himself into this predicament, thought Wilma, taking a bite out of a particularly delicious joint of beef as she swung toward it. No. He would have done things properly and wouldn't have slipped on a slab of greasy bacon, flown through the air, and ended up suspended from a hook by the back of his pants.

One day, dreamed Wilma as she rocked from side to side, she would be a great detective too and get to solve all manner of mysteries and conundrums, but for now she had an urgent problem to solve: how to get down from the rack of hams without being caught by Madam Skratch. Being an orphan at the Cooper Island Lowside Institute for Woeful Children was bad enough without being found upside down among the cold meats by the meanest matron who had ever lived.

Wilma could hear Madam Skratch's voice barking orders beyond the door. She didn't have a moment to lose. Straightening her dress and unbuttoning her pinafore pocket, Wilma pulled out a tatty heap of squashed and torn bits of paper attached by their corners to a large metal ring. Frantically thumbing through the scraps, Wilma found what she was looking for: an old folded newspaper clipping that had the words *Theodore P. Goodman's Escape from Giant Clock* scrawled on its exterior. Opening it out as fast as she could, she examined the diagram that showed her favorite detective tied to the bottom of a massive pendulum.

"That's it!" she whispered, tapping at the picture. "He used the pendulum to swing himself onto a ledge! If I can swing a bit harder on this ham hook, then maybe I can reach that can of peaches in syrup and then use the syrup to loosen up the hook and then . . ." But before Wilma had reached the end of her brilliant plan, events had taken a turn. The fabric of her pinafore had given way, and with one ripping tear she landed headfirst in a basket of onions. The door to the pantry swung open.

"Wilma Tenderfoot!" yelled Madam Skratch, who looked like a vulture and smelled like cabbage. "My office! Now!"

Wilma looked up and spat a shallot out of her mouth. She was in trouble. Again.

Somewhere between England and France is an island with only one small hill that no one has ever bothered to discover. If you go and look at a map right now, you'll be able to see it. It's just there, above that bit. It should come as no surprise that the small and ordinary-looking Cooper Island has never been discovered. Exploring is, after all, no longer taught in schools, and curiosity, the mainstay of any discoverer, has been discouraged since the unfortunate news that it can kill cats.

Hundreds of years ago the island was almost discovered by an explorer called Marco Polo. You might have heard of him. He had a beard and discovered impressive things like China and First-Class Mail, so an island with one small hill somewhere between England and France was not at the top of his To Do list. It was a Tuesday, and Marco Polo had been hard at it. "I've been discovering nonstop for sixteen years," he said,

4

standing on his poop deck, "and in all that time I haven't had one day off. Not one."

It was at this point that a small man named Angelo Pizza, whose daughter would invent the snack of the same name, shouted down from the ship's crow's nest. "Ahoy!" he called. "I can see an island with one small hill on it!"

Marco Polo had sighed at this news and thought about how his job as a discoverer of new lands and efficient postal systems was interfering with his enjoyment of life. If you know many adults, I expect you've heard them moaning about their jobs. Well, Marco Polo was just the same. Marco Polo didn't want to go to work that day. He wanted to lie in a hammock, eat a fresh, crisp apple, and have his face painted to look like a tiger. "I can't be bothered!" he shouted up to Angelo Pizza. "Do me a favor and just pretend you didn't see it."

"All right!" shouted down Angelo Pizza, who carried on looking out, though he was careful not to look out again in the direction of the island with the one small hill.

5

It might seem strange that no one has tried to discover Cooper Island since. But most discoverers are only interested in impressive things like the tallest mountain or the longest river. So Cooper Island, which didn't have anything that was tallest or longest or deepest, was overlooked and forgotten about, and the people who lived there were left to get on with things and mind their own business. You would think that a place ignored by the world would be a haven of calm and happiness, but you'd be wrong. Even small, insignificant islands can be hotbeds of trouble and bother, and this story is about one trouble so terrible that if you have a nervous disposition I would advise you to put this book down immediately.

Wilma had been packing for five minutes. She had been ordered to do so by Madam Skratch after being dragged from the pantry by one ear and then yelled at for thirty-seven minutes, at the end of which the screaming matron had pulled a crumpled letter from her pocket, waved it under Wilma's nose, and spluttered, "That's it! I give up!

Your tomfoolery and nonsense have tested me for the last time! You're leaving! Today!" Wilma had been surprised but quietly thrilled, an emotion that was to prove woefully misplaced. The letter was from a dried-up misery of a woman named Mrs. Waldock, who had written in requesting a "servant, one not too hungry nor too quarrelsome." The unlucky wretch would go to live on the Farside of the island, where he or she would be expected to do chores like grating the dead skin off the bottom of Mrs. Waldock's feet and climbing down drains to clear blockages. It would not only be Wilma's first job, but it would be the first time in ten years that she had stepped outside the Lowside Institute for Woeful Children's front gates to go anywhere other than the obligatory Tuesday-afternoon school classes, where, as well as the usual reading and writing, Wilma and the other unfortunates learned essential woeful life skills like Scraping and Scrubbing.

Wilma, who was the smallest and scrawniest of the Institute's ten-year-olds, had lived at the orphanage all her life. She didn't know much about where she had come from, only that she had been left in a shabby cardboard box at the Institute's gates during a storm so fierce that the orphanage's only tree had been split clean in two. She had been wrapped in muslin and abandoned with no further clues as to her background other than one small luggage tag tied around her neck that had three words written on it: *because they gone.* She didn't know who had left her there or to whom the luggage tag referred. It was a mystery as deep as the seas. But one day, Wilma had decided long ago, she would find out. She may have been small, but she was very determined.

In the ten years that Wilma had lived at the Institute for Woeful Children she had made few if any friends. She had had a best friend once, when she was four, but it had all ended rather badly when the poor unfortunate had fallen into a furnace and been accidentally melted down and turned into a batch of wrenches. Wilma quickly realized that, if she was to minimize pain and anguish in such a revolting environment, it was probably best not to get to like anyone. Instead she found her comfort in books, secreted out of the Institute's meager library, and magazines, stolen from Madam Skratch's waste-paper basket, both filled with the to-ings and fro-ings of life on the Farside and, in particular, the adventures and triumphs of the island's greatest detective, Theodore P. Goodman. When she was young, it was the pictures of his great adventures that caught her imagination, but as soon as she could read and piece together his methods and advice, Wilma was well and truly hooked. Not only was he the island's greatest detective, he was the finest, most upstanding man that Wilma could ever imagine meeting. His noble deeds and intentions lifted Wilma from the drudgery of her everyday existence. How she longed to be a detective like him!

Every Wednesday at four, when Madam Skratch was eating cake in the turret room, and the rest of the Institute children were playing Lantha, a board game much favored by all Cooperans, Wilma would creep down to the matron's office and quietly pick out that week's discarded copy of

9

Boom! Cooper Island's weekly magazine for ladies of a certain age. Taking great care, Wilma would tear out the pages filled with tales of Detective Goodman's solved cases and read them over and over so that they were practically committed to memory. By learning how Theodore P. Goodman solved the island's crimes, Wilma could learn the theories of detective work and, one day, find the answers to her past. If she was going to be a detective, she decided, she would have to start practicing, and she grabbed every opportunity to do so.

Once, when she was six, a large gristle pie had gone missing from the Institute's kitchen and Madam Skratch had demanded that the culprit be caught. Wilma, leaping at her first chance to have a crack at detecting, quietly decided that the pie thief had been none other than an unpredictable young lad named Thomas. His guilt, she concluded, was confirmed by the presence of flaky pastry trembling on his upper lip. But it turned out that Thomas hadn't been eating flaky pastry at all; he was experiencing a rather unpleasant attack of eczema, and as she stood having this oversight pointed out to her by a sneering Madam Skratch, Wilma discovered that hasty predictions can lead to severe embarrassments. Detection, it would appear, was a subtler art than Wilma was quite ready for.

When she was seven, Wilma, not deterred by her earlier setback, had taken it upon herself to solve another baffling mystery. Socks were vanishing in the orphanage. Not pairs of socks, just the left ones, and Wilma was convinced that a one-legged child named Melody Trimble was the only possible suspect. But it turned out (yet again) that Wilma's suspicions were ill-conceived. Melody Trimble, as Madam Skratch exasperatedly revealed, could not have been the culprit because her one foot was a right foot, not a left. And besides, the sock thief, who had already been caught, turned out to have been a local hand puppeteer who had fallen on hard times and run out of socks. Case closed. It was another failure for the would-be detective, and one that didn't make her terribly popular. All the same, Wilma was still determined.

Then there was the time, at the age of nine, when she had tried to get to the bottom of why she, of all the Institute's Woeful Children, never seemed to get sent to a new home. Children from the Lowside Institute for Woeful Children were, as a rule, farmed out to customers on the Farside of the island from the age of eight. But never Wilma. Being a curious creature, with detective-ish aspirations, she had decided to conduct a small investigation. However, because she was still not fully trained in the art of investigating, her methods were quite basic. So basic in fact that all she did was tug on Madam Skratch's sleeve and ask, "Why am I still here, please?" But Madam Skratch answered her with nothing more illuminating than a sharp pinch of the ear and a truckload of onions to peel, so Wilma, despite her best efforts, was none the wiser. The mystery remained just that.

But here she was, being sent out into the wider world of the island at last. She might even get a chance to do some proper detecting. The thought of it made Wilma as excited as a bottle of bees. But all that would have to wait; for now she was a

Lowsider from the Institute for Woeful Children who had a battleaxe with cracked and crusty feet to meet.

In order to leave the Institute, Wilma had been furnished by the horrible matron with papers allowing her to pass from the island's Lowside to the more desirable Farside. She was allowed to take a bath, in cold water, and was handed a fresh pinafore and top shirt so that she would not "offend the eye" of anyone with the misfortune to catch sight of her. "Lowsiders are not welcome on the Farside of the island, and you will do well to remember it!" Madam Skratch told Wilma repeatedly, with a firm wag of her bony finger. But Wilma didn't need reminding. Every Lowsider knew that most Farsiders despised them. No one knew why. It was just the way things were.

Some children might have felt nervous and jelly-legged at the prospect of leaving the only place they had ever known, but not Wilma. She had spent too many hours staring out through the bars of the orphanage gates, wondering what the rest of Cooper Island was like and longing to visit all the places she had seen in Madam Skratch's magazines. At the age of four, as she was tied to a rope and lowered down the orphanage well to catch frogs for supper, she had daydreamed about the sugar-cane trees that lined the Avenue of the Cooperans. At the age of five, when she was given a large spoon and told to make a statue of Madam Skratch out of chicken fat, she was so busy imagining herself posing in front of the magnificent Poulet Palace that she inadvertently gave the matron three eyes and a wonky nose, and at the age of six and three-quarters, as she was shoved up the Institute's chimneys strapped to the end of a broom to shoo away the bats, her mind flitted off to the extravagant shows put on at the Valiant Vaudeville Theatre. But most of all Wilma thought about Theodore P. Goodman and how one day, if she was very determined, he would help her find out where she had come from. In short, Wilma really couldn't wait to leave.

Given that Wilma didn't have anything much to call her own, she was ready, hat in hand and good to go, in a matter of moments. "Tender-foot!" yelled Madam Skratch, standing in the doorway to the dormitory. "Have you packed your things?"

"Yes, Madam Skratch, I have," replied Wilma with a twinkle.

"Well, hurry yourself! Mrs. Waldock will be waiting. Come here and let me look at you." Wilma trotted toward the doorway and stiffened her back, ready to be inspected. Madam Skratch towered over her and stared, tutting as her eyes darted over her grubby charge. "You will never amount to anything," she said, lifting Wilma's chin with a sharp finger. "Your eyes are too green, your nose is too small, your hair is too pale, and you have a mouth that is nothing but mischief. You have very little to commend you. Do as you are told, Wilma Tenderfoot, and you might have a passable life. Do not do what you are told, and your life will be a fraught and thorny misery. Do you understand?"

"Yes, Madam Skratch," replied Wilma, tucking a wayward lock of hair behind her ear.

"And don't fidget!" snapped the matron, pursing her lipless mouth. "I can't bear a child that wriggles. Just like a maggot! Now pick up your things and go down to the courtyard. The cart will take you to Mrs. Waldock. And take this," she added, handing Wilma a letter from her new employer outlining her instructions.

Wilma ran back to the thin and tiny bed where she had slept every night for the past ten years and picked up her small bundle of clothes. Taking care to keep her back to Madam Skratch, she reached under her mattress and pulled out her two most precious possessions: the luggage label of her birthright and a folded-up, tatty piece of paper that was now so faded it was almost wasted away. Quickly and quietly Wilma tied the label to her wrist and pressed the paper, a list of Detective Goodman's top tips for detecting, inside her bundle. She had no real need of it, of course, as she knew it by heart, and she whispered it to herself as she headed for the dorm door.